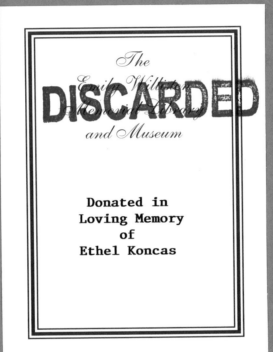

ALL
TOMORROW'S
PARTIES

DISCARDED

ALSO BY WILLIAM GIBSON

Neuromancer

Count Zero

Burning Chrome

Mona Lisa Overdrive

Virtual Light

Idoru

G. P. PUTNAM'S SONS | NEW YORK

ALL TOMORROW'S PARTIES

WILLIAM GIBSON

This is a work of fiction. Names, characters, places, and incidents either are the product of the author's imagination or are used fictitiously, and any resemblance to actual persons, living or dead, business establishments, events, or locales is entirely coincidental.

G. P. PUTNAM'S SONS
Publishers Since 1838
a member of
Penguin Putnam Inc.
375 Hudson Street
New York, NY 10014

Library of Congress Cataloging-in-Publication Data

Gibson, William, date
    All tomorrow's parties / William Gibson.
        p.   cm.
    ISBN 0-399-14579-6
    I. Title.
    PS3557.I2264A79   1999   99-30997 CIP
    813'.54—dc21

Printed in the United States of America

10   9   8   7   6   5   4   3   2   1

THIS BOOK IS PRINTED ON ACID-FREE PAPER. ∞

Book Design by Gretchen Achilles

TO GRAEME
AND THE BADCHAIRS

ALL
TOMORROW'S
PARTIES

1. CARDBOARD CITY

THROUGH this evening's tide of faces unregistered, unrecognized, amid hurrying black shoes, furled umbrellas, the crowd descending like a single organism into the station's airless heart, comes Shinya Yamazaki, his notebook clasped beneath his arm like the egg case of some modest but moderately successful marine species.

Evolved to cope with jostling elbows, oversized Ginza shopping bags, ruthless briefcases, Yamazaki and his small burden of information go down into the neon depths. Toward this tributary of relative quiet, a tiled corridor connecting parallel escalators.

Central columns, sheathed in green ceramic, support a ceiling pocked with dust-furred ventilators, smoke detectors, speakers. Behind the columns, against the far wall, derelict shipping cartons huddle in a ragged train, improvised shelters constructed by the city's homeless. Yamazaki halts, and in that moment all the oceanic clatter of commuting feet washes in, no longer held back by his sense of mission, and he deeply and sincerely wishes he were elsewhere.

He winces, violently, as a fashionable young matron, features swathed in Chanel micropore, rolls over his toes with an expensive three-wheeled stroller. Blurting a convulsive apology, Yamazaki glimpses the infant passenger through flexible curtains of some pink-tinted plastic, the glow of a video display winking as its mother trundles determinedly away.

Yamazaki sighs, unheard, and limps toward the cardboard shelters. He wonders briefly what the passing commuters will think, to see him enter the carton fifth from the left. It is scarcely the height of his chest, longer than the others, vaguely coffin-like, a flap of thumb-smudged white corrugate serving as its door.

Perhaps they will not see him, he thinks. Just as he himself has never seen anyone enter or exit one of these tidy hovels. It is as though their inhabitants are rendered invisible in the transaction that allows such structures to exist in the context of the station. He is a student of existential sociology, and such transactions have been his particular concern.

And now he hesitates, fighting the urge to remove his shoes and place them beside the rather greasy-looking pair of yellow plastic sandals arranged beside the entrance flap on a carefully folded sheet of Parco gift wrap. No, he thinks, imagining himself waylaid within, struggling with faceless enemies in a labyrinth of cardboard. Best he not be shoeless.

Sighing again, he drops to his knees, the notebook clutched in both hands. He kneels for an instant, hearing the hurrying feet of those who pass behind him. Then he places the notebook on the ceramic tile of the station's floor and shoves it forward, beneath the corrugate flap, and follows it on his hands and knees.

He desperately hopes that he has found the right carton.

He freezes there in unexpected light and heat. A single halogen fixture floods the tiny room with the frequency of desert sunlight. Unventilated, it heats the space like a reptile's cage.

"Come in," says the old man, in Japanese. "Don't leave your ass hanging out that way." He is naked except for a sort of breechclout twisted from what may once have been a red T-shirt. He is seated, cross-legged, on a ragged, paint-flecked tatami mat. He holds a brightly colored toy figure in one hand, a slender brush in the other. Yamazaki sees that the thing is a model of some kind, a robot or military exoskeleton. It glitters in the sun-bright light, blue and red and silver. Small tools are spread on the tatami: a razor knife, a sprue cutter, curls of emery paper.

The old man is very thin, clean-shaven but in need of a haircut. Wisps of gray hair hang on either side of his face, and his mouth is set in what looks to be a permanent scowl of disapproval. He wears glasses with heavy black plastic frames and archaically thick lenses. The lenses catch the light.

Yamazaki creeps obediently into the carton, feeling the door flap drop shut behind him. On hands and knees, he resists the urge to try to bow.

"He's waiting," the old man says, his brush tip poised above the figure in his hand. "In there." Moving only his head.

Yamazaki sees that the carton has been reinforced with mailing tubes, a system that echoes the traditional post-and-beam architecture of Japan, the tubes lashed together with lengths of salvaged poly-ribbon. There are too many objects here, in this tiny space. Towels and blankets and cooking pots on cardboard shelves. Books. A small television.

"In there?" Yamazaki indicates what he takes to be another door, like the entrance to a hutch, curtained with a soiled square of melon-yellow, foam-cored blanket, the sort of blanket one finds in a capsule hotel. But the brush tip dips to touch the model, and the old man is lost in the concentration this requires, so Yamazaki shuffles on hands and knees across the absurdly tiny space and draws the section of blanket aside. Darkness.

"Laney-San?"

What seems to be a crumpled sleeping bag. He smells sickness—

"Yeah?" A croak. "In here."

Drawing a deep breath, Yamazaki crawls in, pushing his notebook before him. When the melon-yellow blanket falls across the entrance, brightness glows through the synthetic fabric and the thin foam core, like tropical sunlight seen from deep within some coral grotto.

"Laney?"

The American groans. Seems to turn, or sit up. Yamazaki can't see. Something covers Laney's eyes. Red wink of a diode. Cables. Faint gleam of the interface, reflected in a thin line against Laney's sweat-slick cheekbone.

"I'm deep in, now," Laney says, and coughs.

"Deep in what?"

"They didn't follow you, did they?"

"I don't think so."

"I could tell if they had."

Yamazaki feels sweat run suddenly from both his armpits, coursing down across his ribs. He forces himself to breathe. The air here is foul, thick. He thinks of the seventeen known strains of multi-drug-resistant tuberculosis.

Laney draws a ragged breath. "But they aren't looking for me, are they?"

"No," Yamazaki says, "they are looking for her."

"They won't find her," Laney says. "Not here. Not anywhere. Not now."

"Why did you run away, Laney?"

"The syndrome," Laney says and coughs again, and Yamazaki feels the smooth, deep shudder of an incoming maglev, somewhere deeper in the station, not mechanical vibration but a vast pistoning of displaced air. "It finally kicked in. The 5-SB. The stalker effect." Yamazaki hears feet hurrying by, perhaps an arm's length away, behind the cardboard wall.

"It makes you cough?" Yamazaki blinks, making his new contact lenses swim uncomfortably.

"No," Laney says and coughs into his pale and upraised hand. "Some bug. They all have it, down here."

"I was worried when you vanished. They began to look for you, but when she was gone—"

"The shit really hit the fan."

"Shit?"

Laney reaches up and removes the bulky, old-fashioned eyephones. Yamazaki cannot see what outputs to them, but the shifting light from the display reveals Laney's hollowed eyes. "It's all going to change, Yamazaki. We're coming up on the mother of all nodal points. I can see it, now. It's *all* going to change."

"I don't understand."

"Know what the joke is? It didn't change when they thought it would. Millennium was a Christian holiday. I've been looking at history, Yamazaki. I can see the nodal points in history. Last time we had one like this was 1911."

"What happened in 1911?"

"Everything changed."

"How?"

"It just did. That's how it works. I can see it now."

"Laney," Yamazaki says, "when you told me about the stalker effect, you said that the victims, the test subjects, became obsessed with one particular media figure."

"Yes."

"And you are obsessed with her?"

Laney stares at him, eyes lit by a backwash of data. "No. Not with her. Guy named Harwood. Cody Harwood. They're coming together, though. In San Francisco. And someone else. Leaves a sort of negative trace; you have to infer everything from the way he's not there . . ."

"Why did you ask me here, Laney? This is a terrible place. Do you wish me to help you to escape?" Yamazaki is thinking of the blades of the Swiss Army knife in his pocket. One of them is serrated; he could easily cut his way out through the wall. Yet the psychological space is powerful, very powerful, and overwhelms him. He feels very far from Shinjuku, from Tokyo, from anything. He smells Laney's sweat. "You are not well."

"Rydell," Laney says, replacing the eyephones. "That rent-a-cop from the Chateau. The one you knew. The one who told me about you, back in LA."

"Yes?"

"I need a man on the ground, in San Francisco. I've managed to move some money. I don't think they can trace it. I dicked with DatAmerica's banking sector. Find Rydell and tell him he can have it as a retainer."

"To do what?"

Laney shakes his head. The cables on the eyephones move in the dark like snakes. "He has to be there, is all. Something's coming down. Everything's changing."

"Laney, you are sick. Let me take you—"

"Back to the island? There's nothing there. Never will be, now she's gone."

And Yamazaki knows this is true.

"Where's Rez?" Laney asks.

"He mounted a tour of the Kombinat states, when he decided she was gone."

Laney nods thoughtfully, the eyephones bobbing mantis-like in the dark. "Get Rydell, Yamazaki. I'll tell you how he can get the money."

"But why?"

"Because he's part of it. Part of the node."

LATER Yamazaki stands, staring up at the towers of Shinjuku, the walls of animated light, sign and signifier twisting toward the sky in the unending ritual of commerce, of desire. Vast faces fill the screens, icons of a beauty at once terrible and banal.

Somewhere below his feet, Laney huddles and coughs in his cardboard shelter, all of DatAmerica pressing steadily into his eyes. Laney is his friend, and his friend is unwell. The American's peculiar talents with data are the result of experimental trials, in a federal orphanage in Florida, of a substance known as 5-SB. Yamazaki has seen what Laney can do with data, and what data can do to Laney.

He has no wish to see it again.

As he lowers his eyes from the walls of light, the mediated faces, he feels his contacts move, changing as they monitor his depth of focus. This still unnerves him.

Not far from the station, down a side street bright as day, he finds the sort of kiosk that sells anonymous debit cards. He purchases one. At another kiosk, he uses it to buy a disposable phone good for a total of thirty minutes, Tokyo–LA.

He asks his notebook for Rydell's number.

2. LUCKY DRAGON

"HEROIN," declared Durius Walker, Rydell's colleague in security at the Lucky Dragon on Sunset. "It's the opiate of the masses."

Durius had finished sweeping up. He held the big industrial dustpan carefully, headed for the inbuilt hospital-style sharps container, the one with the barbed biohazard symbol. That was where they put the needles, when they found them.

They averaged five or six a week. Rydell had never actually caught anyone shooting anything up, in the store, although he wouldn't have put it past them. It just seemed like people dropped used needles on the floor, usually back by the cat food. You could find other things, sweeping up in the Lucky Dragon: pills, foreign coins, hospital identification bracelets, crumpled paper money from countries that still used it. Not that you wanted to go poking around in that dustpan. When Rydell swept up, he wore the same Kevlar gloves that Durius was wearing now, and latex underneath that.

He supposed Durius was right though, and it made you wonder: all the new substances around to abuse, but people didn't forget the ones that had been around forever. Make cigarettes illegal, say, and people found a way to keep smoking. The Lucky Dragon wasn't allowed to sell rolling papers, but they did a brisk trade in Mexican hair-curler papers that worked just as well. The most popular brand was called Biggerhair, and Rydell wondered if anyone had ever actually used any to curl their hair. And how did you curl your hair with little rectangles of tissue paper anyway?

"Ten minutes to," Durius said over his shoulder. "You wanna do the curb check?"

At four o'clock, one of them got to take a ten-minute break, out back. If Rydell did the curb check, it meant he got to take his break first, then let Durius take one. The curb check was something that Lucky Dragon's parent corporation, back in Singapore, had instituted on the advice of an in-house team of American cultural anthropologists. Mr.

Park, the night manager, had explained this to Rydell, ticking off points on his notebook. He'd tapped each paragraph on the screen for emphasis, sounding thoroughly bored with the whole thing, but Rydell had supposed it was part of the job, and Mr. Park was a definite stickler. " 'In order to demonstrate Lucky Dragon's concern with neighborhood safety, security personnel will patrol curb in front of location on a nightly basis.' " Rydell had nodded. "You not out of store too long," Mr. Park added, by way of clarification. "Five minute. Just before you take break." Pause. Tap. " 'Lucky Dragon security presence will be high-profile, friendly, sensitive to local culture.' "

"What's that mean?"

"Anybody sleeping, you make them move. Friendly way. Hooker working there, you say hello, tell joke, make her move."

"I'm scared of those old girls," Rydell said, deadpan. "Christmastime, they dress up like Santa's elves."

"No hooker in front of Lucky Dragon."

" 'Sensitive to local culture'?"

"Tell joke. Hooker like joke."

"Maybe in Singapore," Durius had said, when Rydell had recounted Park's instructions.

"He's not from Singapore," Rydell had said. "He's from Korea."

"So basically they want us to show ourselves, clear the sidewalk back a few yards, be friendly and sensitive?"

"And tell joke."

Durius squinted. "You know what kinda people hang in front of a convenience store on Sunset, four in the morning? Kids on dancer, tweaked off their dimes, hallucinating monster movies. Guess who gets to be the monster? Plus there's your more mature sociopaths; older, more complicated, polypharmic . . ."

"Say what?"

"Mix their shit," Durius said. "Get lateral."

"Gotta be done. Man says."

Durius looked at Rydell. "You first." He was from Compton, and the only person Rydell knew who had actually been born in Los Angeles.

"You're bigger."

"Size ain't everything."

"Sure," Rydell had said.

ALL that summer Rydell and Durius had been night security at the Lucky Dragon, a purpose-built module that had been coptered into this former car-rental lot on the Strip. Before that, Rydell had been night security at the Chateau, just up the street, and before that he'd driven a wagon for IntenSecure. Still farther back, briefly and he tried not to think about it too often, he'd been a police officer in Knoxville, Tennessee. Somewhere in there, twice, he'd almost made the cut for *Cops in Trouble,* a show he'd grown up on but now managed never to watch.

Working nights at the Lucky Dragon was more interesting than Rydell would have imagined. Durius said that was because it was the only place around, for a mile or so, that sold anything that anyone actually needed, on a regular basis or otherwise. Microwave noodles, diagnostic kits for most STDs, toothpaste, disposable anything, Net access, gum, bottled water . . . There were Lucky Dragons all over America, all over the world for that matter, and to prove it you had your trademark Lucky Dragon Global Interactive Video Column outside. You had to pass it entering and leaving the store, so you'd see whichever dozen Lucky Dragons the Sunset franchise happened to be linked with at that particular moment: Paris or Houston or Brazzaville, wherever. These were shuffled, every three minutes, for the practical reason that it had been determined that if the maximum viewing time was any more, kids in the world's duller suburbs would try to win bets by having sex on camera. As it was, you got a certain amount of mooning and flashing. Or, still more common, like this shit-faced guy in downtown Prague, as Rydell made his exit to do the curb check, displaying the universal finger.

"Same here," Rydell said to this unknown Czech, hitching up the neon-pink Lucky Dragon fanny pack he was contractually obligated to wear on duty. He didn't mind that though, even if it did look like shit: it was bulletproof, with a pull-up Kevlar baby bib to fasten around your neck if the going got rough. A severely lateral customer with a ceramic switchblade had tried to stab Rydell through the Lucky Dragon logo his second week on the job, and Rydell had sort of bonded with the thing after that.

He had that switchblade up in his room over Mrs. Siekevitz's garage. They'd found it below the peanut butter, after the LAPD had taken the lateral one away. It had a black blade that looked like sandblasted glass. Rydell didn't like it; the ceramic blade gave it a weird balance, and it was so sharp that he'd already cut himself with it twice. He wasn't sure what he should do with it.

Tonight's curb check looked dead simple. There was a Japanese girl standing out there with a seriously amazing amount of legs running down from an even more amazingly small amount of shorts. Well, sort of Japanese. Rydell found it hard to make distinctions like that in LA. Durius said hybrid vigor was the order of the day, and Rydell guessed he was right. This girl with all the legs, she was nearly as tall as Rydell, and he didn't think Japanese people usually were. But then maybe she'd grown up here, and her family before her, and the local food had made them taller. He'd heard about that happening. But, no, he decided, getting closer, the thing was, she wasn't actually a girl. Funny how you got that. Usually it wasn't anything too obvious. It was like he really wanted to buy into everything she was doing to *be* a girl, but some subliminal message he got from her bone structure just wouldn't let him.

"Hey," he said.

"You want me to move?"

"Well," Rydell said, "I'm supposed to."

"I'm supposed to stand out here convincing a jaded clientele to buy blow jobs. What's the difference?"

Rydell thought about it. "You're freelance," he decided, "I'm on salary. You go on down the street for twenty minutes, nobody's going to fire you." He could smell her perfume through the complicated pollution and that ghostly hint of oranges you got out here sometimes. There were orange trees around, had to be, but he'd never found one.

She was frowning at him. "Freelance."

"That's right."

She swayed expertly on her stacked heels, fishing a box of Russian

Marlboros from her pink patent purse. Passing cars were already honking at the sight of the Lucky Dragon security man talking to this six-foot-plus boygirl, and now she was deliberately doing something illegal. She opened the red-and-white box and pointedly offered Rydell a cigarette. There were two in there, factory-made filter tips, but one was shorter than the other and had blue metallic lipstick on it.

"No thanks."

She took out the shorter one, partially smoked, and put it between her lips. "Know what I'd do if I were you?" Her lips, around the tan filter tip, looked like a pair of miniature water beds plastered with glittery blue candy coat.

"What?"

She took a lighter from her purse. Like the ones they sold in those tobacciana shops. They were going to make that illegal too, he'd heard. She snapped it and lit her cigarette. Drew in the smoke, held it, blew it out, away from Rydell. "I'd fuck off into the air."

He looked into the Lucky Dragon and saw Durius say something to Miss Praisegod Satansbane, the checker on this shift. She had a fine sense of humor, Praisegod, and he guessed you had to, with a name like that. Her parents were some particularly virulent stripe of SoCal Neo-Puritan, and had taken the name Satansbane before Praisegod had been born. The thing was, she'd explained to Rydell, nobody much knew what "bane" meant, so if she told people her last name, they mostly figured she was a Satanist anyway. So she often went by the surname Proby, which had been her father's before he'd gotten religion.

Now Durius said something else, and Praisegod threw back her shoulders and laughed. Rydell sighed. He wished it had been Durius' turn to do curb check.

"Look," Rydell said, "I'm not telling you you can't stand out here. The sidewalk's public property. It's just that there's this company policy."

"I'm going to finish this cigarette," she said, "and then I'm calling my lawyer."

"Can't we just keep it simple?"

"Uh-uh." Big metallic-blue, collagen-swollen smile.

Rydell glanced over and saw Durius making hand signals at him.

Pointing to Praisegod, who held a phone. He hoped they hadn't called LAPD. He had a feeling this girl really did have herself a lawyer, and Mr. Park wouldn't like that.

Now Durius came out. "For you," he called. "Say it's Tokyo."

"Excuse me," Rydell said, and turned away.

"Hey," she said.

"Hey what?" He looked back.

"You're cute."

3. DEEP IN

LANEY hears his piss gurgle into the screw-top plastic liter bottle. It's awkward kneeling here, in the dark, and he doesn't like the way the bottle warms in his hand, filling. He caps it by feel and stands it upright in the corner that's farthest from his head when he sleeps. In the morning, he'll carry it under his coat to the Men's and empty it. The old man knows he's too sick now to crawl out, to walk the corridor every time, but they have this agreement. Laney pisses in the bottle and takes it out when he can.

He doesn't know why the old man lets him stay here. He's offered to pay, but the old man just keeps building his models. It takes him a day to complete one, and they're always perfect. And where do they go when he finishes them? And where do the unbuilt kits come from?

Laney has a theory that the old man is a sensei of kit-building, a national treasure, with connoisseurs shipping in kits from around the world, waiting anxiously for the master to complete their vintage Gundams with his unequaled yet weirdly casual precision, his Zen moves, perhaps leaving each one with a single minute and somehow perfect *flaw*, at once his signature and a recognition of the nature of the universe. How nothing is perfect, really. Nothing ever finished. Everything is process, Laney assures himself, zipping up, settling back into his squalid nest of sleeping bags.

But the process is all a lot stranger than he ever bargained for, he reflects, bunching a fold of sleeping bag to pillow his head against the cardboard, through which he can feel the hard tile wall of the corridor.

Still, he thinks, he *needs* to be here. If there's any place in Tokyo Rez's people won't find him, this is it. He's not quite sure how he got here; things got a little fuzzy around the time the syndrome kicked in. Some kind of state change, some global shift in the nature of his perception. Insufficient memory. Things hadn't stuck.

Now he wonders if in fact he did make some deal with the old man. Maybe he's already covered this, the rent, whatever. Maybe that's why the old man gives him food and bottles of flat mineral water and tolerates the smell of piss. He thinks that might be it, but he isn't sure.

It's dark in here, but he sees colors, faint flares and swathes and stipplings, moving. Like the afterimages of the DatAmerica flows are permanent now, retinally ingrained. No light penetrates from the corridor outside—he's blocked every pinhole with black tape—and the old man's halogen is off. He assumes the old man sleeps there, but he's never seen him do it, never heard any sounds that might indicate a transition from model-building to sleep. Maybe the old man sleeps upright on his mat, Gundam in one hand, brush in the other.

Sometimes he can hear music from the adjacent cartons, but it's faint, as though the neighbors use earphones.

He has no idea how many people live here in this corridor. It looks as though there might be room for six, but he's seen more, and it may be that they shelter here in shifts. He's never learned much Japanese, not after eight months, and even if he could understand, he guesses, these people are all crazy, and they'd only talk about the things crazy people talk about.

And of course anyone who could see him here now, with his fever and his sleeping bags, his eyephones and his cellular data port and his bottle of cooling piss, would think he was crazy too.

But he isn't. He knows he isn't, in spite of everything. He has the syndrome now, the thing that came after every test subject from that Gainesville orphanage, but he isn't crazy. Just obsessed. And the obsession has its own shape in his head, its own texture, its own weight. He knows it from himself, can differentiate, so he goes back to it whenever he needs to and checks on it. Monitors it. Makes sure it still isn't him. It reminds him of having a sore tooth, or the way he felt once when he was in love and didn't want to be. How his tongue always found the tooth, or how he'd always find that ache, that absence in the shape of the beloved.

But the syndrome wasn't like that. It was separate from him and had nothing to do with anyone or anything he, Laney, was even interested in. When he'd felt it starting, he'd taken it for granted that it would be about her, about Rei Toei, because there he was, close to her, or as close as you could get to anyone who didn't physically exist. They'd talked almost every day, Laney and the idoru.

And at first, he considered now, maybe it *had* been about her, but then it was as though he'd been following something back through the data flows, doing it without really thinking about it, the way your hand will find a thread on a garment and start pulling at it, unraveling it.

And what had unraveled was the way he'd thought the world worked. And behind that he'd found Harwood, who was famous, but famous in that way of being famous for *being* famous. Harwood who they said had elected the president. Harwood the PR genius, who'd inherited Harwood Levine, the most powerful PR firm in the world, and had taken it somewhere seriously else, into a whole other realm of influence. But who'd managed somehow never to become prey to the mechanism of celebrity itself. Which grinds, Laney so well knew, exceedingly fine. Harwood who, maybe, just maybe, ran it all, but somehow managed never to get his toe caught in it. Who managed, somehow, to be famous without seeming to be important, famous without being central to anything. Really, he'd never even gotten much attention, except when he'd split with Maria Paz, and even then it had been the Padanian star who'd made the top of every sequence, with Cody Harwood smiling from a series of sidebars, embedded hypertext lozenges: the beauty and this gentle-looking, secretive, pointedly uncharismatic billionaire.

"Hello," Laney says, his fingers finding the handle of a mechanical flashlight from Nepal, a crude thing, its tiny generator driven by a mechanism like a pair of spring-loaded pliers. Pumping it to life, he raises it, the faintly fluctuating beam finding the cardboard ceiling. Which is plastered, inch by inch, with dozens of stickers, small and rectangular, produced to order by a vending machine inside the station's west entrance: each one a different shot of the reclusive Harwood.

He can't remember going to the machine, executing a simple image search for Harwood, and paying to have these printed out, but he supposes he must have. Because he knows that that is where they are from. But neither can he remember peeling the adhesive backing from each one and sticking them up on the ceiling. But someone did. "I see you," Laney says and relaxes his hand, letting the dim beam brown and vanish.

4. FORMAL ABSENCES OF PRECIOUS THINGS

IN Market Street, the nameless man who haunts Laney's nodal configuration has just seen a girl.

Drowned down three decades, she steps fresh as creation from the bronze doors of some brokerage. And he remembers, in that instant, that she is dead, and he is not, and that this is another century, and this quite clearly another girl, some newly minted stranger, one with whom he will never speak.

And passing this one now, through a faint chromatic mist of incoming night, he bows his head some subtle increment in honor of that other, that earlier passing.

And sighs within his long coat, and the harness he wears beneath that: a taking in and giving up of one resigned breath, thronged around by the traders descending from their various places of employment. Who continue to emerge into the October street, toward drink or dinner or whatever home, whatever sleep, awaits them.

But now the one with whom he will not speak is gone as well, and he awash in some emotion, not loss exactly but a very particular awareness of his own duration in the world and in its cities, and this one most of all.

Beneath his right arm, reliably concealed, depends a knife that sleeps head down, like a vampire bat, honed to that edge required by surgeons, when surgeons cut with steel.

It is secured there with magnets set within a simple hilt of nickel silver. The blade's angled tip, recalling a wood carver's chisel, inclines toward the dark arterial pulse in the pit of his arm, as if reminding him that he too is only ever inches from that place the drowned girl went, so long ago, that timelessness. That other country, waiting.

He is by trade a keeper of the door to that country.

Drawn, the black blade becomes a key. When he holds it, he holds the wind in his hand.

The door swings gently open.

But he does not draw it now, and the traders see only a gray-haired man, wolfishly professorial, in a coat of grayish green, the color of certain lichens, who blinks behind the fine gold rims of his small round glasses and raises his hand to halt a passing cab. Though somehow they do not, as they easily might, rush to claim it as their own, and the man steps past them, his cheeks seamed vertically in deep parentheses, as though it has been his habit frequently to smile. They do not see him smile.

THE Tao, he reminds himself, mired in traffic on Post Street, is older than God.

He sees a beggar seated beneath a jeweler's windows. In those windows are small empty pedestals, formal absences of precious things, locked away now for the night. The beggar has wrapped his legs and feet in brown paper tape, and the effect is startlingly medieval, as though someone has partially sculpted a knight from office materials. The trim calves, the tapered toes, an elegance calling out for ribbons. Above the tape, the man is a blur, a spastic scribble, his being abraded by concrete and misfortune. He has become the color of pavement, his very race in question.

The cab lurches forward. The man in the loden coat reaches within it to adjust the knife against his ribs. He is left-handed, and he has thought often about such subtle polarities.

The girl who drowned so long ago has settled now, swept down in a swirl of toffee hair and less hurtful memories, to where his youth turns gently, in its accustomed tides, and he is more comfortable that way.

The past is past, the future unformed.

There is only the moment, and that is where he prefers to be.

And now he leans forward, to rap, once, upon the driver's tinted safety shield.

He asks to be taken to the bridge.

THE cab draws up before a rain-stained tumble of concrete tank traps, huge rhomboids streaked with rust, covered with the stylized initials of forgotten lovers.

This spot has a certain place in the local mythology of romance and has been the subject of any number of popular ballads.

"Pardon me, sir," says the cab driver, through several layers of protective plastic and digital translation, "but do you wish me to leave you here? This neighborhood is dangerous. I will be unable to wait for you." The question is rote, required by law against the possibility of litigation.

"Thank you. I will be in no danger." His English as formal as that of the translation program. He hears a musical rattle, his words rendered in some Asian language he doesn't recognize. The driver's brown eyes look back at him, mild and dispassionate, through goggles, shield; multiple layers of reflection.

The driver releases a magnetic lock.

The man opens the door and steps from the cab, straightening his coat. Above him, beyond the tank traps, lift the ragged, swooping terraces, the patchwork superstructure in which the bridge is wrapped. Some aspect of his mood lifts: it is a famous sight, a tourist's postcard, the very image of this city.

He closes the door, and the cab pulls away, leaving behind it the baking-sugar sweetness of exhausted gasohol.

He stands looking up at the bridge, at the silvered plywood of uncounted tiny dwellings. It reminds him of the favelas of Rio, though the scale of the parts is different, somehow. There is a fairy quality to the secondary construction, in contrast to the alternating swoop and verticality of the core structure's poetry of suspension. The individual shelters—if in fact they are shelters—are very small, space being at an absolute premium. He remembers seeing the entrance to the lower roadway flanked with guttering torches, though now, he knows, the residents largely cooperate with the city's air-pollution measures.

"Dancer?"

In concrete shadow she palms the tiny vial. Feral grimace intended to facilitate commerce. This drug causes the user's gums steadily to recede, producing in those few who survive its other rigors a characteristic and terrible smile.

He replies with his eyes, the force of his gaze punching through her intent as if through paper. Briefly in her eyes the light of panic, then she is gone.

Toffee hair swirls in the depths.

He looks down at the toes of his shoes. They are black and very precise, against the random mosaic of impacted litter.

He steps over an empty can of King Cobra and walks between the nearest rhomboids, toward the bridge.

These are not kindly shadows through which he moves, the legs of his narrow trousers like the blades of a deeper darkness. This is a lurking place, where wolves come down to wait for the weaker sheep. He has no fear of wolves, nor of any other predator the city might field, tonight or any other night. He simply observes these things, in the moment.

But now he allows himself to anticipate the sight that awaits him, past the last rhomboid: the bridge's mad maw, the gateway to dream and memory, where sellers of fish spread their wares on beds of dirty ice. A perpetual bustle, a coming and going, that he honors as the city's very pulse.

And steps out, into unexpected light, faux-neon redline glare above a smooth sweep of Singaporean plastic.

Memory is violated.

Someone brushes past him, too close, unseeing, and very nearly dies, the magnets letting go with that faint click that he feels more than hears. But he does not draw the blade fully, and the drunk staggers on, oblivious.

He reseats the hilt and stares bleakly at this latest imposition: LUCKY DRAGON swirling in bland script up a sort of fin or pylon whose base seems comprised of dozens of crawling video screens.

5. MARIACHI STATIC

"SO she left you for this TV producer," the country singer said, slipping what was left of thirteen ounces of vodka back into the waistband of his indigo jeans, so new and taut that they creaked when he walked. The flat bottle's concavity rode there behind an antique buckle that resembled an engraved commemorative plaque, something someone had once won, Rydell supposed, for calf-roping or some similar competitive activity. Rydell powered the side window down, a crack, to let the fumes out.

"Production coordinator," Rydell said, wishing the vodka would put his passenger, whose name was Buell Creedmore, to sleep again. The man had spent the better part of their drive up the coast asleep, snoring lightly, and Rydell hadn't minded that. Creedmore was a friend, or maybe more of an acquaintance, of Durius Walker's. Durius had been a drug dealer before, in South Central, and had gotten addicted to the stuff. Now that he'd gotten his recovery, he spent a lot of time with other people who had drug problems, trying to help them. Rydell assumed Buell Creedmore was one of those, though as far he could see the man was just basically a drunk.

"Bet that one burned your ass," Creedmore said, his eyes slit with spirits. He was a small man, lightly built, but roped with the sort of whipcord muscle that had never seen the inside of a gym. Ditchdigger muscle. What Rydell took to be several layers of artificial tan were wearing off over an inherent pallor. Bleached hair with dark roots was slicked straight back with some product that kept it looking like he'd just stepped out of a shower. He hadn't, though, and he was sweating in spite of the air-conditioning.

"Well," Rydell said, "I figured it's her call."

"What kind of bleeding-ass liberal bullshit is that?" Creedmore asked. He pulled the bottle from his waistband and eyed the remaining liquor narrowly, as though he were a carpenter checking a level. It seemed to fail to meet his standards just then, so he returned it to its place behind the commemorative plaque. "What kind of man are you, anyway?"

Rydell briefly entertained the idea of pulling over on the margin, beating Creedmore senseless, then leaving him there at the side of the Five, to get up to San Francisco as best he could. But he didn't and, in fact, said nothing.

"Pussy-assed attitude like that, that's what's wrong with America today."

Rydell thought about illegal choke holds, brief judicious constriction of the carotid artery. Maybe Creedmore wouldn't even remember if Rydell put one on him. But it wouldn't keep him under, not that long anyway, and they'd taught Rydell in Knoxville that you couldn't count on how a drunk would react to anything.

"Hey, Buell," Rydell asked, "whose car is this anyway?"

Creedmore fell silent. Grew, Rydell felt, restive.

Rydell had wondered from the start if the car might not be stolen. He hadn't wanted to think about it really, because he needed the ride up to NoCal. A plane ticket would've had to come out of his severance from the Lucky Dragon store, and he had to be extra careful with that until he determined whether or not there was anything to this story of Yamazaki's, that there was money for him to earn, up in San Francisco.

Yamazaki was deep, Rydell told himself. He'd never actually figured out what it was that Yamazaki did. Sort of a freelance Japanese anthropologist who studied Americans, as near as Rydell could tell. Maybe the Japanese equivalent of the Americans Lucky Dragon hired to tell them they needed a curb check. Good man, Yamazaki, but not easy to say where he was coming from. The last time he'd heard from Yamazaki, he'd wanted Rydell to find him a netrunner, and Rydell had sent him this guy named Laney, a quantitative researcher who'd just quit Slitscan, and had been moping around the Chateau, running up a big bill. Laney had taken the job, had gone over to Tokyo, and Rydell had subsequently gotten fired for, they called it, fraternizing with the guests. That was basically how Rydell had wound up working night security in a convenience store, because he'd tried to help Yamazaki.

Now he was driving this Hawker-Aichi roadster up the Five, very definitely the designated driver, no idea what was waiting for him up there, and halfway wondering if he weren't about to transport a stolen vehicle across a state line. And all because Yamazaki said that that same Laney, over in Tokyo, wanted to hire him to do some fieldwork. That was what Yamazaki called it, "fieldwork."

And that, after he'd talked with Durius, had been enough for Rydell.

The Lucky Dragon had been starting to get old for Rydell. He hadn't ever gotten along with Mr. Park too well, and when he'd take his break, out back, after the curb check every morning, he'd started to feel really down. The patch of ground the Lucky Dragon had been set down on was sort of scooped out of the foot of the hillside there, and at some point the exposed, nearly vertical cut had been quake-proofed with some kind of weird, gray, rubbery polymer, a perpetual semi-liquid that knit the soil behind it together and trapped whatever was thrown or pressed against it in a grip like summer tar. The polymer was studded with hubcaps, because the place had been a car lot once. Hubcaps and bottles and more nameless junk. In the funk that had started to come over him, out back there on his breaks, he'd collect a handful of rocks and stand there, throwing them, as hard as he could, into the polymer. They didn't make much of a noise when they hit, and in fact they vanished entirely. Just ripped straight into it and then it sealed over behind them, like nothing had happened. And Rydell had started to see that as emblematic of broader things, how he was like those rocks, in his passage through the world, and how the polymer was like life, sealing over behind him, never leaving any trace at all that he'd been there.

And when Durius would come back to take his own break and tell Rydell it was time to get back out front, sometimes he'd find Rydell that way, throwing those rocks.

"Hit you a hubcap, man," Durius would advise, "break you a bottle."

But Rydell hadn't wanted to.

And when Rydell had told Durius about Yamazaki and Laney and some money, maybe, to be made up in San Francisco, Durius had listened carefully, asking a few questions, then advised Rydell to go for it.

"What about job security?" Rydell had asked.

"Job security? Doing *this* shit? Are you crazy?"

"Benefits," Rydell countered.

"You tried to actually use the medical coverage they give you here? Gotta go to Tiajuana to get it."

"Well," Rydell had said, "I don't like to just quit."

"That's 'cause you got fired from every last job you ever had," Durius had explained. "I seen your résumé."

So Rydell had given Mr. Park written notice, and Mr. Park had promptly fired him, citing numerous violations of Lucky Dragon policy on Rydell's part, up to and including offering medical aid to the victim of a one-car collision on Sunset, an act which Mr. Park insisted could have involved Lucky Dragon's parent corporation in costly insurance litigation.

"But she walked in here under her own power," Rydell had protested. "All I did was offer her a bottle of iced tea and call the traffic cops."

"Smart lawyer claim ice tea put her in systemic shock."

"Shock my butt."

But Mr. Park had known that if he fired Rydell, the last paycheck would be smaller than if Rydell quit.

Praisegod, who could get all emotional if someone was leaving, had cried and given him a big hug, and then, as he'd left the store, she'd slipped him a pair of Brazilian GPS sunglasses, with inbuilt phone and AM-FM radio, about the most expensive item Lucky Dragon carried. Rydell hadn't wanted to take them, because he knew they'd turn up missing on the next inventory.

"Fuck the inventory," Praisegod had said.

Back in his room over Mrs. Siekevitz's garage, six blocks away and just below Sunset, Rydell had stretched out on his narrow bed and tried to get the radio in the glasses to work. All he'd been able to get, though, was static, faintly inflected with what might have been mariachi music.

He'd done a little better with the GPS, which had a rocker keypad built into the right temple. The fifteen-channel receiver seemed to have really good lock-on, but the tutorial seemed to have been translated badly, and all Rydell could do was zoom in and out of what he quickly realized was a street map of Rio, not LA. Still, he'd thought, taking the glasses off, he'd get the hang of it. Then the phone in the left temple had beeped, so he'd put the glasses back on.

"Yeah?"

"Rydell, hey."

"Hey, Durius."

"You want a ride up to NoCal tomorrow in a nice new car?"

"Who's going?"

"Name of Creedmore. Knows a guy I know in the program."

Rydell had had an uncle who was a Mason, and this program Durius belonged to reminded him of that. "Yeah? Well, I mean, is he okay?"

"Prob'ly not," Durius had said, cheerfully, "so he needs a driver. This three-week-old 'lectric needs to get ferried up there though, and he says it's fine to drive. You used to be a driver, didn't you?"

"Yeah."

"Well, it's free. This Creedmore, he'll pay for the charge."

Which was how Rydell came to find himself, now, driving a Hawker-Aichi two-seater, one of those low-slung wedges of performance materials that probably weighed, minus its human cargo, about as much as a pair of small motorcycles. There didn't seem to be any metal involved at all, just streamlined foam-core sandwiches reinforced with carbon fiber. The motor was in the back, and the fuel cells were distributed through the foam sandwiches that simultaneously passed for chassis and bodywork. Rydell didn't want to know what happened if you hit something, driving a rig like this.

It was damn near silent though, handled beautifully, and went like a bat once you got it up to speed. Something about it reminded Rydell of a recumbent bicycle he'd once ridden, except you didn't have to pedal.

"You never did tell me whose car this is," Rydell reminded Creedmore, who'd just downed the last two fingers of his vodka.

"This friend of mine," Creedmore said, powering down the window on his side and tossing out the empty bottle.

"Hey," Rydell said, "that's a ten-thousand-dollar fine, they catch you."

"They can kiss our asses good-bye, is what they can do," Creedmore said. "Sons of bitches," he added, then closed his eyes and slept.

Rydell found himself starting to think about Chevette again. Regretting he'd ever let the singer get him on the topic. He knew he didn't want to think about that.

Just drive, he told himself.

On a brown hillside, off to his right, a wind farm's white masts. Late afternoon sunlight.

Just drive.

6. SILENCIO

SILENCIO gets to carry. He's the smallest, looks almost like a kid. He doesn't use, and if the cops grab him, he can't talk. Or anyway about the stuff.

Silencio has been following Raton and Playboy around for a while now, watching them use, watching them get the money they need in order to keep using. Raton gets mean when he's needing to use, and Silencio's learned to keep back from him then, out of range of feet and fists.

Raton has a long, narrow skull and wears contacts with vertical irises, like a snake. Silencio wonders if Raton is supposed to look like a rat who's eaten a snake, and now maybe the snake is looking out through its eyes. Playboy says Raton is a pinche Chupacabra from Watsonville and they all look this way.

Playboy is the biggest, his bulk wrapped in a long, formal topcoat worn over jeans and old work boots. He has a Pancho Villa mustache, yellow aviator glasses, a black fedora. He is kinder to Silencio, buys him burritos from the stalls, water, cans of pop, one time a big smooth drink made from fruit.

Silencio wonders if maybe Playboy is his father. He doesn't know who his father might be. His mother is crazy, back in los projectos. He doesn't think Playboy is his father really, because he remembers how he met Playboy in the market on Bryant Street, and that was just an accident, but sometimes he wonders anyway, when Playboy buys him food.

Silencio sits watching Raton and Playboy use, here behind this empty stall with its smell of apples. Raton has a little flashlight in his mouth so he can see what he is doing. It is the black tonight, and Raton is cutting the little plastic tube with the special knife, its handle longer than its short curved blade. The three of them are sitting on plastic crates.

Raton and Playboy use the black two, maybe three times in a day and a night. Three times with the black, then they must use the white as well. The white is more expensive, but too much black and they start to talk fast and maybe see people who are not there. "Speaking with Jesus," Playboy calls that, but the white he calls "walking with the king." But it is not walking: white brings stillness, silence, sleep. Silencio prefers the white nights.

Silencio knows that they buy the white from a black man, but the black from a white man, and he assumes this is the mystery depicted in the picture Raton wears on the chain around his neck: the black and the white teardrops swirling together to make roundness; in the white teardrop a small round of black, in the black a small round of white.

To get the money they talk to people, usually in dark places, so the people are frightened. Sometimes Raton shows them a different knife, while Playboy holds their arms so they cannot move. The money is in little tabs of plastic printed with pictures that move. Silencio would like to keep these when the money is gone out of them, but this is not allowed. Playboy throws them away, after wiping them carefully. He drops them down the slots beside the street. He does not want his fingers to leave marks on them. Sometimes Raton hurts the people, so that they will tell the charms that make money come from the moving pictures. The charms are names, letters, numbers. Silencio knows every charm that Raton and Playboy have learned, but they do not know this; if he told them, they might be angry.

The three of them sleep in a room in the Mission. Playboy pulls the mattress from the bed and puts it on the floor. Playboy sleeps there, Raton on the other part of the bed. Silencio sleeps on the floor.

Now Raton has cut the tube and puts half of the black on Playboy's finger. Playboy has licked his finger so the black will stick. Playboy puts the finger in his mouth and rubs the black against his gums. Silencio wonders what it tastes like, but he does not ever wish to speak with Jesus. Now Raton is rubbing his own gums with black, the flashlight forgotten in his other hand. Raton and Playboy look foolish doing this, but it does not make Silencio laugh. Soon they will want to use again, and the black gives them energy to get the money they will need. Silencio knows there is now no money, because they have not eaten since yesterday.

Usually they find people in the dark places between the big shapes at the foot of Bryant Street, but now Raton thinks the police are watching those places. Raton has told Silencio that the police can see in the dark. Silencio has looked at the eyes of the police, passing in their cars, and wondered how they can see in the dark.

But tonight Raton has led them out, onto the bridge where people live, and he says they will find money here. Playboy has said he does not like the bridge, because the bridge people are pinche; they do not like outsiders working here. Raton says he feels lucky.

Raton tosses the empty vial into the darkness, and Silencio hears it hit something, a single small click.

Raton's snake-eyes are wide with the black. He runs his hand back through his hair and gestures. Playboy and Silencio follow him.

SILENCIO passes the bodega for the second time, watching the man in his long coat, where he sits at his small white table, drinking coffee.

Raton says it is a fine coat. See the old man's glasses, says Raton: they are made of gold. Silencio supposes Playboy's are made of gold too, but Playboy's have yellow glass. The man's are plain. He has gray hair cut very short and deep lines in his cheeks. He sits alone, looking at the smallest cup of coffee Silencio has ever seen. A doll's cup.

They have followed the old man here. He has walked in the direction of Treasure Island. This part of the bridge is for the tourists, Playboy says. There are bodegas, shops with glass windows, many people walking.

Now they are waiting to see which way the old man goes when he finishes his little coffee. If he walks back, toward Bryant, it will be difficult. If he goes on, toward Treasure, Raton and Playboy will be happy.

It is Silencio's job to tell them when the man leaves.

Silencio feels the man's eyes on him as he passes, but the man is only watching the crowd.

SILENCIO watches Raton and Playboy follow the man toward Treasure Island.

They are in the bridge's lower level now, and Silencio keeps looking up to see the bottom of the upper deck, its paint peeling. It reminds him of a wall in los projectos. There are only a few bridge people here. Only a few lights. The man walks easily. He does not hurry. Silencio feels the man is only walking; he has nowhere to go. Silencio feels the man needs nothing: he is not looking for money, to eat or to use. This must be because he already has the money he needs to eat or to use, and this is why Raton and Playboy have chosen him, because they see he has the money they need.

Raton and Playboy keep pace with the man, but they hang back. They do not walk together. Playboy has his hands in the pockets of his big coat. He has taken off his yellow glasses and his eyes are dark-circled with the look of those who have used the black. He looks sad when he is going to get the money to use. He looks like he is paying very close attention.

Silencio follows them, looking back sometimes. Now it is his job to tell them if someone comes.

The man stops, looking into the window of a shop. Silencio steps behind a cart piled with rolls of plastic, as he sees Raton and Playboy step behind other things, in case the man looks back. The man doesn't, but Silencio wonders if the man is watching the street in the glass. Silencio has done this himself.

The man does not look back. He stands with his hands in the pockets of his long coat, looking into the glass.

Silencio unbuttons his jeans and quietly waters the rolls of plastic, careful that it makes no sound. As he buttons his jeans, he sees the man step away from the window, still moving toward Treasure, where Playboy says there are people who live like animals. Silencio, who knows only dogs and pigeons and gulls, has a picture in his head of dog-toothed men with wings. When Silencio has a picture in his head, the picture doesn't go away.

Stepping from behind the cart, as Raton and Playboy step out to follow the man, Silencio sees the man turn right. Gone. The man is gone. Silencio blinks, rubs his knuckles against his eyes, looks again. Raton and Playboy are walking faster now. They are not trying to hide. Silencio walks faster too, not to be lost, and arrives at the place where the man turned. Raton's narrow back goes around that corner, after Playboy, and is gone.

Silencio stops. Feels his heart beating. Steps forward and looks around the corner.

It is a space where a shop is meant to be, but there is no shop. Sheets of plastic hang down from above. Pieces of wood, more rolls of plastic. He sees the man.

The man stands at the back of the space and looks from Playboy to Raton to Silencio. Looks through the round pieces of glass. Silencio feels how still the man is.

Playboy is walking toward the man, his boots stepping over the wood, the plastic. Playboy says nothing. His hands are still in the pockets of his coat. Raton is not moving but is ready to, and then he takes the knife from where he keeps it and opens it, flicking his wrist that way he practices, letting the man see it.

The man's face does not change when he sees it, and Silencio remembers other faces, how they changed when they saw Raton's knife.

Now Playboy steps down from the last of the wood, his hands coming out to take the man by the arms and spin him. That is how it is done.

Silencio sees the man move but only, it seems, a little.

Everything stops.

Silencio knows that he has seen the man's left hand reach into the long coat, which was buttoned before but now is not. But somehow he has not seen that hand return, and still it has. The man stands with his fist against Playboy's chest, just at the center. Pressing the thumb of his closed fist against Playboy's coat. And Playboy is not moving. His hands have stopped, almost touching the man, fingers spread, but he is not moving.

And then Silencio sees Playboy's fingers close, on nothing, and open. And the man's right hand comes up to push Playboy back, and the thin black thing is pulled out of Playboy's chest, and Silencio wonders how long it could have been hidden there, and Playboy falls back over the wood and the rolls of plastic.

Silencio hears someone say pinche madre and this is Raton. When Raton uses the black and fights, he is very fast and you do not know what he will do; he hurts people and then shakes, laughing, sucking air through his mouth. Now he comes over the rolls of plastic like he is flying, with his knife shining in his hand, and Silencio sees the picture of a man with dog teeth and wings, and Raton's teeth are like that, his snake eyes wide.

And the black thing, like a long wet thumb, goes through Raton's neck. And everything stops again.

Then Raton tries to speak, and blood comes on his lips. He swings his knife at the man, but the knife cuts only air, and Raton's fingers can no longer hold it.

The man pulls the black thing from Raton's throat. Raton sways on loose knees, and Silencio thinks of how it is when Raton uses too much white, then tries to walk. Raton puts his hands up to cover his throat on both sides. His mouth moves, but no words come out. One of Raton's snake eyes falls out. The eye behind it is round and brown.

Raton falls down on his knees, with his hands still on his throat. His snake eye and his brown eye look up at the man, and Silencio feels they look from different distances, seeing different things.

Then Raton makes a small, soft sound in his throat and falls over backward, still on his knees, so that he lies on his back with his knees spread wide and his legs twisted back, and Silencio watches Raton's gray pants go dark between his legs.

Silencio looks at the man. Who is looking at him.

Silencio looks at the black knife, how it rests in the man's hand. He feels that the knife holds the man. That the knife may decide to move.

Then the man moves the knife. Its point is almost square, like the real point has been snapped off. It only moves a little. Silencio understands this means he must move.

He steps sideways, so the man can see him.

The point moves again. Silencio understands.

Closer.

7. SHAREHOUSE

LEAVE a house empty in Malibu, Tessa told Chevette, and you get the kind of people come down from the hills and barbecue dogs in your fireplace.

Hard to get rid of, those kind of people, and locks wouldn't keep them out. That was why the people who used to live here, before the Spill, were willing to rent them out to students.

Tessa was Australian, a media sciences student at USC and the reason Chevette was out here now, couching it.

Well, that and the fact that she, Chevette, didn't have a job or any money, now she'd split with Carson.

Tessa said Carson was a piece of work.

And look where it had all gotten her, Chevette thought, pumping her way up the trainer's illusion of a Swiss mountain road and trying to ignore the reek of moldy laundry from the other side of the drywall partition. Someone had left a wet load in the machine, probably last Tuesday, before the fire, and now it was rotting in there.

Which was too bad, because that made it hard to get into riding the trainer. You could configure it for a dozen different bikes, and as many terrains, and Chevette liked this one, an old-fashioned steel-frame ten-speed you could take up this mountain road, wildflowers blurring in your peripheral vision. Her other favorite was a balloon-tired cruiser you rode along a beach, which was good for Malibu because you couldn't ride along the beach, not unless you wanted to climb over rusty razor wire and ignore the biohazard warnings every hundred feet.

But that gym-sock mildew reek kept catching in the back of her sinuses, nothing alpine meadow about it at all, telling her she was broke and out of work and staying in a sharehouse in Malibu.

The house was right on the beach, with the wire about thirty feet out from the deck. Nobody knew exactly what it was that had spilled, because the government wasn't telling. Something off a freighter, some people said, and some said it was a bulklifter that had come down in a storm. The government was using nanobots to clean it up though; everybody agreed on that, and that was why they said you shouldn't walk out there.

Chevette had found the trainer her second day here, and she'd ride two or three times a day or, like now, late at night. Nobody else seemed to be interested in it or ever to come into this little room off the garage, next to the laundry room, and that was fine with her. Living on the bridge, she'd been used to people being around, but everybody had always had something to do up there. The sharehouse was full of USC media sciences students, and they got on her nerves. They sat around accessing media all day and talking about it, and nothing ever seemed to get done.

She felt sweat run between the headband of the interface visor and her forehead, then down the side of her nose. She was getting a good burn on now; she could feel groups of muscles working in her back, ones that didn't usually get it.

The trainer did a better job on the bike's chartreuse lacquer than on the shift levers, she noticed. They were sort of cartoony, with road surface blurring past beneath them in generic texture map. The clouds would be generic too, if she looked up; just basic fractal stuff.

She was definitely not too happy with being here, or with her life in general at this point. She'd been talking with Tessa about that after dinner. Well, arguing about it.

Tessa wanted to make this documentary. Chevette knew what a documentary was because Carson had worked for a channel, Real One, that only just ran those, and Chevette had had to watch about a thousand of them. As a result, she thought, she now knew a whole lot about nothing in particular, and nothing in particular about whatever it was she was actually supposed to know. Like what to do now that her life had gotten her to this place.

Tessa wanted to take her back up to San Francisco, but Chevette had mixed feelings. The documentary Tessa wanted to make was about interstitial communities, and Tessa said Chevette had lived in one, because Chevette had lived on the bridge. Interstitial meant in between things, and Chevette figured that that made a kind of sense, anyway.

And she did miss it up there, miss the people, but she didn't like thinking about it. Because of how things had gone since she'd come down here, and because she hadn't kept in touch.

Just pump, she told herself, cresting the illusion of a rise. Shift again. Pump harder. The road surface started to look glassy in places, because she was overtaking the simulator's refresh rate.

"Zoom in." Tessa's voice, in miniature.

"Shit," Chevette said. Flipping up the visor.

The camera platform, like a helium-filled cushion of silver Mylar, at eye level in the open doorway. Kid's toy with little caged propellers, controlled from Tessa's bedroom. Ring of light reflected in the lens housing as it extruded, zooming.

The propellers blurred to gray, brought it forward through the door, stopped; blurred to gray again, reversing. Rocked there, till it steadied on the ballast of the underslung camera. God's Little Toy, Tessa called her silver balloon. Disembodied eye. She sent it on slow cruises through the house, mining for image fragments. Everyone who lived here was constantly taping everyone else, except Iain, and Iain wore a motion-capture suit, even slept in it, and was recording every move he ever made.

The trainer, performance machine that it was, sensed Chevette's loss of focus and sighed, slowing, complex hydraulics beginning to deconfigure. The narrow wedge of seat between her thighs widened, spreading to support her butt in beach-bike mode. The handlebars unfolded, upward, raising her hands. She kept on pedaling, but the trainer was winding her down now.

"Sorry." Tessa's voice from the tiny speaker. But Chevette knew she wasn't.

"Me too," Chevette said, as the pedals made a final arc, locking for dismount. She swung the bars up and stepped down, batting at the platform, spoiling Tessa's shot.

"Une petite problemette. Concerns you, I think."

"What?"

"Come into the kitchen and I'll show you." Tessa reversed one set of props, turning the platform on its axis. Then two forward and it sailed back through the doorway, into the garage. Chevette followed it, pulling a towel from a nail driven into the doorjamb. Closing the door behind her. Should've had it closed when she was riding, but she'd forgotten. God's Little Toy couldn't open doors.

The towel needed washing. A little stiff but it didn't smell bad. She used it to wipe sweat from her pits and chest. She overtook the balloon, ducked under it, entered the kitchen.

Sensed roaches scurrying for cover. Every flat surface, except the floor, was solid with unwashed dishes, empties, pieces of recording equipment. They'd had a party, the day before the fire, and nobody had cleaned up yet.

No light here now but a couple of telltales and the methodical flicker as the security system flipped from one external night-vision camera to the next. 4:32 A.M. showing in the corner of the screen. They kept maybe half the security shut down because people were in and out all day, and there was always someone there.

Whir of the platform as Tessa brought it up behind her.

"What is it?" Chevette asked.

"Watch the driveway."

Chevette moved closer to the screen.

The deck, slung out over the sand . . .

The space between the house and the next one . . .

The driveway. With Carson's car sitting there.

"Shit," Chevette said, as the Lexus was replaced with the between-houses view on the other side, then a view from a camera under the deck.

"Been there since 3:24."

The deck . . .

"How'd he find me?"

Between houses . . .

"Web search, probably. Image matching. Someone was uploading pictures from the party. You were in some of them."

The Lexus in the driveway. Nobody in it.

"Where is he?"

Between the houses . . .

Under the deck . . .

"No idea," Tessa said.

"Where are you?"

Deck again. Watch this and you start to see things that aren't there. She looked down at the mess on the counter and saw a foot-long butcher knife lying in what was left of a chocolate cake, the blade clotted with darkness.

"Upstairs," Tessa said. "Best you come up."

Chevette felt suddenly cold in her bike shorts and T-shirt. Shivered. Left the kitchen for the living room. Pre-dawn gray through walls of glass. English Iain stretched, snoring lightly, on a long leather couch, a red LED on his motion-capture suit winking over his sternum. The lower half of Iain's face never seemed to be in focus to Chevette; teeth uneven, different colors, like he was lightly pixilated. Mad, Tessa said. And never changed the suit he slept in now; kept it laced corset-tight.

Muttered in his sleep, turning his back to her as she passed.

She stood with her face a few inches from the glass, feeling the chill that radiated from it. Nothing on the deck but a ghostly white chair, empty beer cans. Where was he?

The stair to the second floor was a spiral, wedge-shaped sections of very thick wood spun out from an iron shaft. She took that now, the carbon-fiber pedal clips set into the soles of her shoes clicking with each step.

Tessa waited at the top, slim blonde shadow bulked in a puffy coat Chevette knew was burnt-orange in daylight. "The van's parked next door," she said. "Let's go."

"Where?"

"Up the coast. My grant came through. I was up talking to Mum, telling her that, when the boyfriend arrived."

"Maybe he just wants to talk," Chevette said. She'd told Tessa about him hitting her that time. Now she half regretted it.

"I don't think that's a chance you want to take. We're away, right? See? I'm packed." Bumping her hip against the bulging rectangle of a gear bag slung from her shoulder.

"I'm not," Chevette said.

"You never *unpacked*, remember?" Which was true. "We'll go out over the deck, go 'round past Barbara's, get in the van: we're gone."

"No," Chevette said, "let's wake everybody up, turn on the outside lights. What can he do?"

"I don't know what he can do. But he can always come back. He knows you're here now. You can't stay."

"I don't know for sure he'd try to hurt me, Tessa."

"Want to be with him?"

"No."

"Did you invite him here?"

"No."

"Want to see him?"

Hesitation. "No."

"Then get your bag." Tessa pushed past, leading with the gear bag. "Now," she said, over her shoulder, descending.

Chevette opened her mouth to say something, then closed it. Turned, felt her way along the corridor, to the door to her room. A closet, this had been, though bigger inside than some houses on the bridge. A frosted dome came on in the ceiling when you opened the door. Someone had cut a thick slab of foam so that it fit the floor down half the length of the narrow, windowless space, between an elaborate shoe rack of some pale tropical hardwood and a baseboard of the same stuff. Chevette had never seen anything made of wood that was put together that well. The whole house was like that, under the sharehouse dirt, and she'd wondered who'd lived in it before, and how they'd felt about having to leave. Whoever it was, to judge by the rack, had had more shoes than Chevette had owned in her life.

Her knapsack sat at the end of the narrow foam bed. Like Tessa had said, still packed. Open, though. The mesh bag with her toilet stuff and makeup beside it. Skinner's old biker jacket hung above it, shoulders set broad and confident on a fancy wooden hanger. Black once, its horsehide had gone mostly gray with wear and time. Older than she was, he'd said. A pair of new black jeans were draped over the rod beside it. She pulled these down and worked her feet out of the riding shoes. Got the jeans on over her shorts. A black sweatshirt from the open mouth of the knapsack. Smell of clean cotton as she pulled it over her head; she'd washed everything, at Carson's, when she'd decided she was leaving. She crouched at the foot of the foam, lacing up lug-soled high-tops, no socks. Stood and took Skinner's jacket from the hanger. It was heavy, as if it retained the weight of horses. She felt safer in it. Remembering how she'd always ridden with it in San Francisco, in spite of the weight. Like armor.

"Come on." Tessa, calling softly from the living room.

Tessa had come over to Carson's with another girl, South African, the day they'd first met, to interview him about his work at Real One. Something had clicked; Chevette smiling back at the skinny blonde whose features were all a little too big for her face; who looked great anyway and laughed and was so smart.

Too smart, Chevette thought, stuffing the mesh bag into the knapsack, because now she was on her way to San Francisco with her, and she wasn't sure that was such a good idea.

"Come *on*."

Bent to stuff the mesh bag into the knapsack, buckle it. Put that over her shoulder. Saw the riding shoes. No time now. Stepped out and closed the closet door.

Found Tessa in the living room, making sure the alarms on the sliding glass doors were deactivated.

Iain grunted, thrashing out at something in a dream.

Tessa tugged one of the doors open, just wide enough to get out, its frame scraping in the corroded track. Chevette felt cold sea air. Tessa stepped out, reached back through to pull her gear bag out.

Chevette stepped through, knapsack rattling against the frame. Something brushed her hair, Tessa reaching out to capture God's Little Toy there. She handed the inflated platform to Chevette, who took it by one of the propeller cages; it felt weightless and awkward and too easy to break. Then she and Tessa both grabbed the door handle one-handed, and together they pulled it shut against the friction of the track.

She straightened, turned, looked out at the lightening gray that was all she could see of the ocean now, past the black coils of razor wire, and felt a kind of vertigo, as though for just a second she stood at the very edge of the turning world. She'd felt that before, on the bridge, up on the roof of Skinner's place, high up over everything; just standing there in a fog that socketed the bay, throwing every sound back at you from a new and different distance.

Tessa took the four steps down to the beach, and Chevette heard the sand squeak under her shoes. It was that quiet. She shivered. Tessa crouched, checking under the deck. Where was he?

And they never saw him, not there and not then, as they trudged through the sand, past old Barbara's deck, where the wide windows were all blanked with quilted foil and sun-faded cardboard. Barbara was an owner from before the Spill, and not often seen. Tessa had tried to cultivate her, wanted her in her documentary, an interstitial community of one, become a hermit in her house, holed up amid sharehouses. Chevette wondered if Barbara was watching them go, past her house and around between it and the next, back to where Tessa's van waited, almost cubical, its paintwork scoured with windblown sand.

All this more dreamlike somehow with each step she took, and now Tessa was unlocking the van, after checking through the window with a flashlight to see he wasn't waiting there, and when Chevette climbed up the passenger side and settled in the creaking seat, blanket laced over ripped plastic with bungee cord, she knew that she was going. Somewhere.

And that was okay with her.

8. THE HOLE

DRIFT.

Laney is in drift.

That is how he does it. It is a matter, he knows, of letting go. He admits the random.

The danger of admitting the random is that the random may admit the Hole.

The Hole is that which Laney's being is constructed around. The Hole is absence at the fundamental core. The Hole is that into which he has always stuffed things: drugs, career, women, information.

Mainly—lately—information.

Information. This flow. This . . . corrosion.

Drift.

ONCE, before he'd come to Tokyo, Laney woke in the bedroom of his suite in the Chateau.

It was dark, only a shush of tires up from Sunset; muffled drumming of a helicopter, hunting the hills behind.

And the Hole right there, beside him in the lonely queen-size expanse of his bed.

The Hole, up close and personal.

9. SWEEP SECOND

BRIGHT pyramids of fruit, beneath buzzing neon.

He watches as the boy drains a second liter of the pulped drink. Swallowing the entire contents of the tall plastic cup in an unbroken stream, with no apparent effort.

"You should not drink cold things so quickly."

The boy looks at him. There is nothing between the boy's gaze and his being: no mask. No personality. He is not, apparently, deaf, because he has understood the suggestion of the cold drink. But there is no evidence, as yet, that he is capable of speech.

"Do you speak Spanish?" This in the language of Madrid, unspoken for many years.

The boy places the empty cup beside the first one and looks at the man. There is no fear in him.

"The men who attacked me, they were your friends?" Raising an eyebrow.

Nothing at all.

"How old are you?"

Older, the man guesses, than his emotional age. Touches of razored stubble at the corners of his upper lip. Brown eyes clear and placid.

The boy looks at the two empty plastic cups on the worn steel counter. He looks up at the man.

"Another? You wish to drink another?"

The boy nods.

The man signals to the Italian behind the counter. He turns back to the boy.

"Do you have a name?"

Nothing. Nothing moves in the brown eyes. The boy regards him as calmly as might some placid dog.

The silver pulping machine chugs briefly, amid the stacked fruit. Shaved ice whirs into the pulp. The Italian transfers the drink to a plastic cup and places it before the boy. The boy looks at it.

The man shifts on the creaking metal stool, his long coat draped like resting wings. Beneath his arm, carefully cleaned now, the knife in its magnetic sheath swings free, sleeping.

The boy raises the cup, opens his mouth, and pours the thick sludge of ice and fruit pulp down his throat.

Defective, the man thinks. Syndromes of the city's tragic womb. The signal of life distorted by chemicals, by starvation, by blows of fortune. Yet he, like everyone else, like the man himself, is exactly where, exactly what, exactly when he is meant to be. It is the Tao: darkness within darkness.

The boy places the empty cup beside the other two.

The man straightens his legs, stands, buttoning his coat.

The boy reaches out. Two fingers touch the watch the man wears on his left wrist. He opens his mouth as if to speak.

"The time?"

Something moves in the affectless brown depths of the boy's eyes.

The watch is very old, purchased from a specialist dealer in a fortified arcade in Singapore. It is military ordnance. It speaks to the man of battles fought in another day. It reminds him that every battle will one day be as obscure, and that only the moment matters, matters absolutely.

The enlightened warrior rides into battle as if to a loved one's funeral, and how could it be otherwise?

The boy leans forward now, the thing behind his eyes seeing only the watch.

The man thinks of the two he leaves tonight on the bridge. Hunters of sorts, now they will hunt no more. And this one, following them. To pick up scraps.

"You like this?"

Nothing registers. Nothing breaks the concentration, the link between that which has surfaced behind the boy's eyes and the austere black face of the watch.

The Tao moves.

The man unfastens the steel buckle that secures the strap. He hands the watch to the boy. He does this without thought. He does this with the same unthinking certainty with which, earlier, he killed. He does this because it fits, is fitting; because his life is alignment with the Tao.

There is no need to say good-bye.

He leaves the boy lost in contemplation of the black face, the hands.

He leaves now. The moment in balance.

10. AMERICAN ACROPOLIS

RYDELL managed to get part of the San Francisco grid on the Brazilian glasses coming in, but he still needed Creedmore to tell him how to get to the garage where they were leaving the Hawker-Aichi. Creedmore, when Rydell woke him for that, seemed uncertain as to who Rydell was, but did a fairly good job of covering it up. He did know, after consulting a folded business card he took from the watch pocket of his jeans, exactly where they should go.

It was an old building, in the kind of area where buildings like that were usually converted to residential, but the frequency of razor wire suggested that this was not yet gentrified territory. There were a couple of Universal square badges controlling entry, a firm that mostly did low-level industrial security. They were set up in an office by the gate, watching Real One on a flatscreen propped up on a big steel desk that looked like someone had gone over every square inch of it with a ball peen hammer. Cups of take-out coffee and white foam food containers. It all felt kind of homey to Rydell, who figured they'd be going off shift soon, seven in the morning. Wouldn't be a bad job, as bad jobs went.

"Delivering a drive-away," Rydell told them.

There was a deer on the flatscreen. Behind it the familiar shapes of the derelict skyscrapers of downtown Detroit. The Real One logo in the lower right corner gave him the context: one of those nature shows.

They gave him a pad to punch in the reservation number on Creedmore's paper, and it came up paid. Had him sign on the pad, there. Told him to put it in slot twenty-three, level six. He left the office, got back into the Hawker, swung up the ramp, wet tires squealing on concrete.

Creedmore was conducting a grooming operation in the illuminated mirror behind the passenger-side sun visor. This consisted of running his fingers repeatedly back through his hair, wiping them on his jeans, then rubbing his eyes. He considered the results. "Time for a drink," he said to the reflection of his bloodshot eyes.

"Seven in the morning," Rydell said.

"What I said," Creedmore said, flipping the visor back up.

Rydell found the number twenty-three painted on the concrete, between two vehicles shrouded in white dustcovers. He edged the Hawker carefully in and started shutting it down. He was able to do this without having to go to the help menu.

Creedmore got out and went over to urinate on somebody's tire.

Rydell checked the interior to see they hadn't left anything, undid the harness, leaned over to pull the passenger-side door shut, popped the trunk, opened the driver-side door, checked that he had the keys, got out, closed the door.

"Hey, Buell. Your friend's gonna pick this up, right?" Rydell was pulling his duffel out of the Hawker-Aichi's weirdly narrow trunk, a space suggestive of the interior of a child's coffin. There was nothing else in there, so he assumed Creedmore was traveling without luggage.

"No," Creedmore said, "they gonna leave it up here get all dusty." He was buttoning his fly.

"So I give the keys to those Universal boys dowstairs?"

"No," Creedmore said, "you give 'em to me."

"I signed," Rydell said.

"Give 'em to me."

"Buell, this vehicle is my responsibility now. I've signed it in here." He closed the trunk, activated the security systems.

"Please step back," said the Hawker-Aichi. "Respect my boundaries as I respect yours." It had a beautiful, strangely genderless voice, gentle but firm.

Rydell took a step back, another.

"That's my friend's car and my friend's keys, and I'm supposed to give 'em to him." Creedmore rested his hand on the big roper's buckle like it was the wheel of his personal ship of state, but he looked uncertain, as though his hangover were leaning on him.

"Just tell him the keys'll be here. That's how you do it. Safer all 'round, that way." Rydell shouldered his bag and started down the ramp, glad to be stretching his legs. He looked back at Creedmore. "See you 'round, Buell."

"Son of a bitch," Creedmore said, though Rydell took it to be more a reference to the universe that had created Rydell than to Rydell himself. Creedmore looked lost and disconnected, squinting under the greenish-white strip lighting.

Rydell kept walking, down the battered concrete spiral of the parking garage, five more levels, till he came abreast of the office at the entrance. The Universal guards were drinking coffee, watching the end of their nature show. Now the deer moved through snow, snow that blew sideways, frosting the perfectly upright walls of Detroit's dead and monumental heart, vast black tines of brick reaching up to vanish in the white sky.

They made a lot of nature shows there.

He went out into the street, looking for a cab or a place that made breakfast. Smelling how San Francisco was a different place than Los Angeles, and feeling that was fine by him. He'd get something to eat, use the Brazilian glasses to phone Tokyo.

Find out about that money.

11. OTHER GUY

CHEVETTE had never driven a standard, so it fell to Tessa to drive them up to San Francisco. Tessa didn't seem to mind. She had her head full of the docu they were going to make, and she could work it out as she drove, telling Chevette about the different communities she wanted to cover and how she was going to cut it all together. All Chevette had to do was listen, or look like she was listening, and finally just fall asleep. She fell asleep as Tessa was telling her about a place called the Walled City, how there'd actually been this place, by Hong Kong, but it had been torn down before Hong Kong went back to being part of China. And then these crazy net people had built their own version of it, like a big communal website, and they'd turned it inside out, vanished in there. It wasn't making much sense when Chevette nodded out, but it left pictures in her head. Dreams.

"What about the other guy?" Tessa was asking, when Chevette woke from those dreams.

Chevette blinked out at the Five, the white line that seemed to reel up beneath the van. "What other guy?"

"The cop. The one you went to Los Angeles with."

"Rydell," Chevette said.

"So why didn't that work?" Tessa asked.

Chevette didn't really have an answer. "It just didn't."

"So you had to hook up with Carson?"

"No," Chevette said, "I didn't have to." What were those white things, so many of them, off in a field there? Wind things: they made electricity. "It just seemed like the thing to do."

"I've done a few of those myself," Tessa said.

12. EL PRIMERO

FONTAINE'S first glimpse of the boy comes as he starts to lay out the morning's stock in his narrow display window: rough dark hair above a forehead pressed against the armored glass.

Fontaine leaves nothing of value in the window at night, but he dislikes the idea of an entirely empty display.

He doesn't like to think of someone passing and glimpsing that vacancy. It makes him think of death. So each night he leaves out a few items of relatively little value, ostensibly to indicate the nature of the shop's stock, but really as a private act of propitiatory magic.

This morning the window contains three inferior Swiss mechanicals, their dials flecked with age, an IXL double penknife with jigged bone handles and shield, fair condition, and an East German military field telephone that looks as though it has been designed not only to survive a nuclear explosion but to function during one.

Fontaine, still on the morning's first coffee, stares down, through the glass, at the matted, spiky hair. Thinking this at first a corpse, and not the first he's discovered this way, but never propped thus, kneeling, as in attitude of prayer. But no, this one lives: breath fogs Fontaine's window.

In Fontaine's left hand: a 1947 Cortebert triple-date moon phase, manual wind, gold-filled case, in very nearly the condition in which it left the factory. In his right, a warped red plastic cup of black Cuban coffee. The shop is filled with the smell of Fontaine's coffee, as burnt and acrid as he likes it.

Condensation slowly pulses on the cold glass: gray aureoles outline the kneeler's nostrils.

Fontaine puts the Cortebert back in the tray with the rest of his better stock, narrow divisions of faded green velour holding a dozen watches. He sets the tray aside, on the counter behind which he stands when he does business, transfers the red plastic cup to his left hand, and with his right reassures himself of the Smith & Wesson .32-.22 Kit

Gun in the right side pocket of the threadbare trench coat that serves him as a dressing gown.

The little gun is there, older than some of his better watches, its worn walnut grip comforting and familiar. Probably intended to be kept in a freshwater fisherman's tackle box, against the dispatching of water snakes or the decapitation of empty beer bottles, the Kit Gun is Fontaine's considered choice: a six-shot rimfire revolver with a four-inch barrel. He doesn't want to kill anyone, Fontaine, though if truth be known, he has, and very probably could again. He dislikes recoil, in a handgun, and excessive report, and distrusts semi-automatic weapons. He is an anachronist, a historian: he knows that the Smith & Wesson's frame evolved for a .32-caliber center-fire round, long extinct, that was once the standard for American pocket pistols. Rechambered for the homely .22, it survived, in this model, well into the middle of the twentieth century. A handy thing and, like most of his stock, a rarity.

He finishes the coffee, places the empty cup on the counter beside the tray of watches.

He is a good shot, Fontaine. At twelve paces, employing an archaic one-handed duelist's stance, he has been known to pick the pips from a playing card.

He hesitates before unlocking the shop's front door, a complicated process. Perhaps the kneeler is not alone. Fontaine has few enemies on the bridge proper, but who is to say what might have drifted in from either end, San Franciso or Oakland? And the wilds of Treasure Island traditionally offer a more feral sort of crazy.

But still.

He throws the last hasp and draws the pistol.

Sunlight falls through the bridge's wrapping of scrap wood and plastic like some strange benison. Fontaine scents the salt air, a source of corrosion.

"You," he says, "mister." The gun in his hand, hidden by the folds of the trench coat.

Under the trench coat, which is beltless, open, Fontaine wears faded plaid flannel pajama bottoms and a long-sleeved white thermal undershirt rendered ecru by the vagaries of the laundry process. Black shoes, sockless and unlaced, their gloss gone matte in the deeper creases.

Dark eyes look up at him, from a face that somehow refuses to come into focus.

"What you doing there?"

The boy cocks his head, as if listening to something Fontaine cannot hear.

"Get away from my window."

With a weird and utter lack of grace that strikes Fontaine as amounting to a species of grace in itself, this person gets to his feet. The brown eyes stare at Fontaine but somehow do not see him, or do not recognize him, perhaps, as another being.

Fontaine displays the Smith & Wesson, his finger on the trigger, but he does not quite point it at the boy. He never points a gun at anyone he is not yet entirely willing to shoot, a lesson learned long ago from his father.

This kneeler, this breather on his glass, is not of the bridge. It would be difficult for Fontaine to explain how he knows this, but he does. It is a function of having lived here a long time. He doesn't know everyone on the bridge, nor would he want to, but he nonetheless distinguishes bridge dwellers from others, and with absolute certainty.

This one, now, has something missing. Something wrong; not a state bespeaking drugs, but some more permanent mode of not-being-there. And while the population of the bridge possesses its share of these, they are somehow worked into the fabric of the place and not inclined to appear thus, so randomly, as to disturb mercantile ritual.

Somewhere high above, the bay wind whips a loose flap of plastic, a frenzied beating, like the idiot wing of some vast wounded bird.

Fontaine, looking into brown eyes in the face that still refuses to come into focus (because, he thinks now, it is incapable), regrets having unlocked his door. Salt air even now gnaws at the bright metal vitals of his stock. He gestures with the barrel of his pistol: go.

The boy extends his hand. A watch.

"What? You want to sell that?"

The brown eyes register no language.

Fontaine, motivated by something he recognizes as compulsion, takes a step forward, his finger tightening on the pistol's double-action trigger. The chamber beneath the firing pin is empty, for safety's sake, but a quick, long pull will do the trick.

Looks like stainless. Black dial.

Fontaine takes in the filthy black jeans, the frayed running shoes, the faded red T-shirt hiked above a paunch that betrays the characteristic bloat of malnutrition.

"You want to show that to me?"

The boy looks down at the watch in his hand, then points to the three in the window.

"Sure," Fontaine says, "we got watches. All kinds. You want to see?"

Still pointing, the boy looks at him.

"Come on," Fontaine says, "come on in. Cold out here." Still holding the gun, though his finger has relaxed, he steps back into the shop. "You coming?"

After a pause, the boy follows, holding the watch with the black dial as though it were a small animal.

Be nothing, Fontaine thinks. Army Waltham with the guts rusted out. Bullshit. Bullshit he's let this freak in here.

The boy stands, staring, in the center of the shop's tiny floor space. Fontaine closes the door, locks it once only, and retreats behind his counter. All this done without lowering the gun, getting within grabbing distance, or taking his eyes off his visitor.

The boy's eyes widen as he sees the tray of watches. "First things first," Fontaine says, whisking the tray out of sight with his free hand. "Let's see." Pointing at the watch in the boy's hand. "Here," Fontaine commands, tapping the faded gilt Rolex logo on a padded round of dark green leatherette.

The boy seems to understand. He places the watch on the pad. Fontaine sees the black beneath the ragged nails as the hand withdraws.

"Shit," Fontaine says. Eyes acting up. "Back up, there, a minute," he says, gently indicating direction with the barrel of the Smith & Wesson. The boy takes a step back.

Still watching the boy, he digs in the left side pocket of the trench coat and comes up with a black loupe, which he screws into his left eye. "Don't you move now, okay? Don't want this gun to go off . . ."

Fontaine picks up the watch, affords himself a quick squint through the loupe. Whistles in spite of himself. "Jaeger LeCoultre." He unsquints, checking; the boy hasn't moved. Squints again, this time at the ordnance markings on the caseback. "Royal Australian Air Force, 1953," he translates. "Where'd you steal this?"

Nothing.

"This is near mint." Fontaine feels, all at once, profoundly and unexpectedly lost. "This a redial?"

Nothing.

Fontaine squints through the loupe. "All original?"

Fontaine wants this watch.

He puts it down on the green pad, atop the worn symbol of a golden crown, noting that the black calf band is custom-made, handsewn around bars permanently fixed between the lugs. This work itself, which he takes to be either Italian or Austrian, may have cost more than some of the watches in his tray. The boy immediately picks it up.

Fontaine produces the tray. "Look here. You want to trade? Gruen Curvex here. Tudor 'London,' 1948; nice original dial. Vulcain Cricket here, gold head, very clean."

But already he knows that his conscience will never allow him to divest this lost soul of this watch, and the knowledge hurts him. Fontaine has been trying all his life to cultivate dishonesty, what his father called "sharp practices," and he invariably fails.

The boy is leaning forward over the tray, Fontaine forgotten.

"Here," Fontaine says, sliding the tray aside and replacing it with his battered notebook. He opens it to the pages where he shops for watches. "Just push this, then push this, it'll tell you what you're looking at." He demonstrates. A Jaeger with a silver face.

Fontaine presses the second key. "1945 Jaeger chronometer, stainless steel, original dial, engraving on case back," says the notebook.

"Case," the boys says. "Back."

"This," Fontaine shows the boy the stainless back of a gold-filled

Tissot tank. "But with writing on, like 'Joe Blow, twenty-five years with Blowcorp, congratulations.'"

The boy looks blank. Presses a key. Another watch appears on the screen. He presses the second key. "A 1960 Vulcain jump-hour, chrome, brassing at lugs, dial very good."

" 'Very good,' " Fontaine advises. "Not good enough. See these spots here?" Indicating certain darker flecks scattered across the scan. "If it were 'very fine,' sure."

"Fine," says the boy, looking up at Fontaine. He presses the key that produces the image of another watch.

"Let me see that watch, okay?" Fontaine points at the watch in the boy's hand. "It's okay. I'll give it back."

The boy looks from the watch to Fontaine. Fontaine puts the Smith & Wesson away in its pocket. Shows the boy his empty hands.

"I'll give it back."

The boy extends his hand. Fontaine takes the watch.

"You gonna tell me where you got this?"

Blank.

"You want a cup of coffee?"

Fontaine gestures back, toward the simmering pot on the hotplate. Smells its bitter brew, thickening.

The boy understands.

He shakes his head.

Fontaine screws the loupe into his eye and settles into contemplation.

Damn. He wants this watch.

LATER in the day, when the bento boy brings Fontaine his lunch, the Jaeger LeCoultre military is in the pocket of Fontaine's gray tweed slacks, high-waisted and extravagantly pleated, but Fontaine knows that the watch is not his. The boy has been put in the back of the shop, in that cluttered little zone that divides Fontaine's business from his private life, and Fontaine has become aware of the fact that he can, yes, smell his visitor; under the morning's coffee smell a definite and insistent reek of old sweat and unwashed clothes.

As the bento boy exits to his box-stacked bicycle, Fontaine undoes the clips on his own box. Tempura today, not his favorite for bento, because it cools, but still he's hungry. Steam wafts from the bowl of miso as he unsnaps its plastic lid. He pauses.

"Hey," he says, back into the space behind the shop, "you want some miso?" No reply. "Soup, you hear me?"

Fontaine sighs, climbs off his wooden stool, and carries the steaming soup into the back of the shop.

The boy is seated cross-legged on the floor, the notebook open on his lap. Fontaine sees the image of a large, very complicated chronometer floating there on the screen. Something from the eighties, by the look of it.

"You want some miso?"

"Zenith," says the boy. "El Primero. Stainless case. Thirty-one jewels, 3019PHC movement. Heavy stainless bracelet with flip lock. Original screwdown crown. Crown dial and movement signed."

Fontaine stares at him.

13. SECONDHAND DAYLIGHT

YAMAZAKI returns with antibiotics, packaged foods, coffee in self-heating tins. He wears a black nylon flight jacket and carries these things, along with his notebook, in a blue mesh bag.

He descends into the station through a crowd of only ordinary density, well before the evening rush hour. He has found it difficult to sleep, his dreams haunted by the perfect face of Rei Toei, who is in a sense his employer, and who in another sense does not exist.

She is a voice, a face, familiar to millions. She is a sea of code, the ultimate expression of entertainment software. Her audience knows that she does not walk among them; that she is media, purely. And that is a large part of her appeal.

If not for Rei Toei, Yamazaki considers, Laney would not be here now. It was the attempt to understand her, to second-guess her motivation, that had originally brought Laney to Tokyo. In the employ of Rez's management team, the singer Rez having declared his intention to marry her. And how, they asked, was that to be? How could any human, even one so thoroughly mediated, marry a construct, a congeries of software, a dream?

And Rez, the Chinese-Irish singer, the pop star, had tried. Yamazaki knows this. He knows as much about this as any living human, including Rez, because Rei Toei has discussed it with him. He understands that Rez exists as thoroughly, in the realm of the digital, as it is possible for a living human to exist. If Rez-the-man were to die, today, Rez-the-icon would certainly live on. But Rez's yearning was to go there, literally to go where Rei Toei is. Or was, she having now effectively vanished.

The singer had sought to join her in some realm of the digital or in some not-yet-imagined borderland, some intermediate state. And had failed.

But has she gone there now? And why had Laney fled as well?

Rez tours the Kombinat states now. Insists on traveling by rail.

Station to station, Moscow his goal, rumors of madness flickering in the band's wake.

It is a dark business, Yamazaki thinks and wonders, taking the stairs to the cardboard city, what exactly Laney is about here. Speaking of nodal points in history, of some emerging pattern in the texture of things. Of everything changing.

Laney is a sport, a mutant, the accidental product of covert clinical trials of a drug that induced something oddly akin to psychic abilities in a small percentage of test subjects. But Laney isn't psychic in any non-rational sense; rather he is able, through the organic changes wrought long ago by 5-SB, this drug, to somehow perceive change emerging from vast flows of data.

And now Rei Toei is gone, her management claims, and how can that be? Yamazaki suspects that Laney may know why, or where, and that is a factor in Yamazaki's having decided to return here and find him. He has been extremely careful to avoid being followed, but he also knows that that can mean next to nothing.

The smell of the Tokyo subway, familiar as the smell of his mother's apartment, comforts him now. It is a smell at once utterly distinctive and impossible to describe. It is the smell of Japanese humanity, of which he very much feels himself a part, as manifested in this singular environment, this world of tubes, of white corridors, of whispering silver trains.

He finds the passageway between the two escalators, the tiled columns. He half suspects that the shelters will be gone.

But they are here, and when he dons a white micropore mask and enters the model-builder's brightly lit hutch, nothing has changed except the kit the old man concentrates on now: a multi-headed dinosaur with robotic hind limbs in navy and silver. The brush tip works in the eye of one reptilian head. The old man does not look up.

"Laney?"

Nothing from behind the square of melon-yellow blanket.

Yamazaki nods to the old man and crawls past on hands and knees, pushing his mesh bag of supplies before him.

"Laney?"

"Hush," Laney says, from the narrow fetid dark. "He's talking."

"Who is talking?" Pushing the bag past the limp, foam-filled fabric, its touch on his face reminding him of nursery school.

As Yamazaki enters, Laney activates a projector in the clumsy eye-phones: the images he sees splay across Yamazaki, blinding him. Yamazaki twists to avoid the beam. Sees figures framed in secondhand daylight. "—'magine he does this on a regular basis?" Hand-held but digitally stabilized. "Something to do with phases of the moon?"

Zooms in on one of the figures, lean and male, as all are. Mouth obscured by a dark scarf. Stiff black hair above a high white forehead. "No evidence of that. Opportunistic. He waits for them to come to him. Then he takes them. These," and the camera swings smoothly to frame the face and bare chest of a dead man, eyes staring, "are jackers. This one had dancer in his pocket." There is a dark comma on the dead man's pale chest, just below the sternum. "The other one was stabbed through the throat, but somehow he managed to miss the arteries."

"He would," says the unseen man.

"We have profiles," the man with the scarf says, off-camera, the face of the corpse thrown across Laney's cardboard wall, the melon blanket. "We have a full forensic psych run-up. But you ignore them."

"Of course I do."

"You're in denial." Two pairs of hands, in latex gloves, grasp the dead man, flip him over. There is a second, smaller wound visible, beneath one shoulder blade; blood has pooled within the body, darkened. "He poses as real a danger to you as to anyone else."

"But he's interesting, isn't he?"

The wound, in close-up, is a small unsmiling mouth. The blood reads black. "Not to me."

"But you aren't interesting, are you?"

"No," and the camera pans up, light catching a sharp cheekbone above the black scarf, "and you don't want me to be, do you?"

There is a faint chime as the transmission is terminated. Laney throws back his head, the image of the man with the scarf in freeze-frame across the ceiling of the carton, too bright, distorted, and Yamazaki sees that the cardboard there is shingled with tiny, self-adhesive printouts, dozens of different images of a bland-looking man, oddly familiar. Yamazaki blinks, his contacts shifting, and misses his glasses. He feels incomplete without them. "Who was that man, Laney?"

"The help," Laney says.

" 'Help'?"

"Hard to get good help these days." Laney kills the projector and removes the massive eyephones. In the sudden gloom, his face is reduced to a child's drawing, smudged black eyeholes against a pallid smear. "The man who was taking that call—"

"The one who spoke?"

"He owns the world. Near as anyone does."

Yamazaki frowns. "I have brought medicine—"

"That was from the bridge, Yamazaki."

"San Francisco?"

"They followed my other man there. They followed him, last night, but they lost him. They always do. This morning they found those bodies."

"Followed who?"

"The man who isn't there. The one I'm having to infer."

"These are pictures of Harwood? Of Harwood Levine?" Yamazaki has recognized the face replicated on the stickers.

"Spooks are his. Best money can buy, probably, but they can't get close to the man who isn't there."

"What man?"

"I think he's someone Harwood . . . collected. Collects people. Interesting people. I think he might've worked for Harwood, taken commissions. He doesn't leave a trace, none at all. When he crosses someone's path, they're just gone. Then he erases himself."

Yamazaki fumbles the antibiotics from his bag. "Will you take these, Laney? Your cough—"

"Where's Rydell, Yamazaki? He's supposed to be up there now. It's all coming together."

"What is?"

"I don't know," Laney says, leaning forward to dig through the contents of the bag. He finds a coffee and activates it, tossing it from hand to hand as it heats. Yamazaki hears the pop, the vacuum hiss, as Laney opens it. Smell of coffee. Laney sips from the steaming can.

"Something's happening," Laney says and coughs into his hand, slopping hot creamed coffee on Yamazaki's wrist. Yamazaki flinches. "Everything's changing. Or it's not, really. How I *see it* is changing. But since I've been able to see it the new way, something else has started. There's something building up. Big. Bigger than big. It'll happen soon, then there'll be a cascade effect . . ."

"What will happen?"

"I don't know." Another fit of coughing requires that he set aside the coffee. Yamazaki has opened the antibiotics and tries to offer them. Laney waves them aside. "Have you been back to the island? Do they have any idea where she is?"

Yamazaki blinks. "No. She is simply not present."

Laney smiles, faint gleam of teeth against the darkness of his mouth. "That's good. She's in it too, Yamazaki." He reaches for the coffee. "She's in it too."

14. BREAKFAST, COOKING

RYDELL found a place in one of those buildings that had clearly been a bank, when banks had needed to have buildings. Thick walls. Someone had turned it into an all-day breakfast-special place, and that was what Rydell was after. Actually it looked like it had been some kind of discount store before that, and who knew what else before, but it had that eggs-and-grease smell, and he was hungry.

There were a couple of size-large construction types, covered with white drywall dust, waiting for a table, but Rydell saw that the counter was empty, so he went over there and took a stool. The waitress was a distracted-looking woman of indeterminate ancestry, acne scars sprinkled across her cheekbones, and she poured his coffee and took his order without actually indicating she understood English. Like the whole operation could be basically phonetic, he thought, and she'd have learned the sound of "two eggs over easy" and the rest. Hear it, translate it into whatever she wrote in, then give it to the cook.

Rydell got the Brazilian glasses out, put them on, and scrolled for the number Yamazaki had given him in Tokyo. Someone picked up on the third ring, but the glasses didn't map a location for the answering phone. Probably meant another mobile.

Silence on the line, but it had a texture.

"Hey," Rydell said, "Yamazaki?"

"Rydell? Laney—" Cut off by a burst of coughing and then dead silence as someone hit mute.

When Laney came back on, he sounded strangled. "Sorry. Where are you?"

"San Francisco," Rydell said.

"I know that," Laney said.

"In a diner on, on . . ." Rydell was scrolling the GPS menu, trying to get in, but he kept getting what looked like Rio transit maps.

"Never mind," Laney said. Sounded tired. What time would it be in

Tokyo? That would be in the phone menu, if he could find it. "What matters is you're there."

"Yamazaki said you had something for me to do up here."

"I do," said Laney, and Rydell remembered his cousin's wedding, Clarence having sounded just about as happy, saying that.

"You want to tell me what it is?"

"No," said Laney, "but I want to put you on retainer. Money up front for as long as you're up there."

"Is it legal, Laney, what you want done?"

There was a pause. "I don't know," Laney said. "Some of it hasn't ever been done before probably, so it's hard to say."

"Well, I think I need to know a little more than that before I can take it on," Rydell said, wondering how the hell he'd ever get back down to Los Angeles if this didn't pan out. Or indeed if there was any point in his going back.

"You could say it's a missing person," Laney said after another pause.

"Name?"

"Doesn't have one. Probably has a few thousand, more like it. Listen, you like cop stuff, right?"

"What's that supposed to mean?"

"No offense; you told me cop stories when I met you, remember? Okay: so this person I'm looking for is very, very good at not leaving traces. Nothing ever turns up, not in the deepest quantitative analysis." Laney meant netsearch stuff; that was what he did. "He's just a physical presence."

"How do you know he's a physical presence if he doesn't leave traces?"

"Because people die," Laney said.

And just then there were people taking seats on either side of him and a sharp reek of vodka—

"Get back to you," Rydell said, thumbing the pad and pulling the glasses off.

Creedmore grinning on his left. "Howdy," said Creedmore. "This here's Marjane."

"Maryalice." On the stool to Rydell's right, a big old blonde with most of the top of her strapped up into something black and shiny, the unstrapped part forming a cleavage where Creedmore could easily have wedged one of those pint bottles. Rydell caught something deep in her tired eyes, some combination of fear, resignation, and a kind of blind and automatic hope: she was not having a good morning, year, or life probably, but there was something there that wanted him to like her. Whatever it was, it stopped Rydell from getting up with his bag and walking out, which was really what he knew he should be doing.

"Ain't you gonna say hi?" Creedmore's breath was toxic.

"Hey, Maryalice," Rydell said. "Name's Rydell. Pleased to meet you."

Maryalice smiled, about a decade's wear lifting, just for a second, from her eyes. "Buell here tells me you're from Los Angeles, Mr. Rydell."

"Does he?" Rydell looked at Creedmore.

"Are you in the media down there, Mr. Rydell?" she asked.

"No," Rydell said, fixing Creedmore with the hardest look he could muster, "retail."

"I'm in the music business myself," Maryalice said. "My ex and I operated one of the most successful country music venues in Tokyo. But I felt the need to get back to my roots. To God's country, Mr. Rydell."

"You talk too much," said Creedmore, across Rydell, as the waitress brought Rydell's breakfast.

"Buell," Rydell said, with something approximating a tone of even good cheer, "shut the fuck up." Rydell started cutting the hardened edges off his eggs.

"Beer me," Buell said.

"Oh, Buell," Maryalice said. She hauled a big plastic zip bag up off the floor, some kind of advertising giveaway, and rummaged inside. Came up with a tall sweaty can of something she passed to Creedmore over Rydell's lap, under the counter. Creedmore popped it, held it to his ear, as if admiring the hiss of carbonation.

"Sound of breakfast cooking," he said, then drank.

Rydell sat there, chewing his leathery eggs.

"SO you go to this site," Laney was saying, "give them my name, 'Colin-space-Laney,' cap C, cap L, first four digits of this phone number, and 'Berry.' That's your nickname, right?"

"Actually it's my name," Rydell said. "Family name on my mother's side." He was seated in a capacious but none too clean cubicle in the former bank's restroom. He'd gone there to get away from Creedmore and company, and so he could ring Laney back. "So I give them that. What'll they give me?" Rydell looked up at his bag, where he'd hung it on the sturdy chrome hook on the cubicle door. He hadn't wanted to leave it out in the restaurant.

"They'll give you another number. You take that to any banking machine, show it picture ID, key the number. It'll issue you a credit chip. Should be enough to hold you for a few days, but if it's not, phone me."

Something about being in there made Rydell feel like he was in one of those old-fashioned submarine movies, the part where they shut off the engines and wait, really quiet, for the depth charges they know are on the way. It was that quiet in here, probably because the bank was so solidly built; the only sound was the running of the toilet tank, which he thought added to the illusion.

"Okay," Rydell said, "assuming all that works, who is it you're look-ing for, and what was that you said about people dying?"

"European male, mid to late fifties, probably has a military back-ground but that was a long time ago."

"That narrows it to maybe a million probables, up here in NoCal alone."

"How this is going to work, Rydell, is he'll find you. I'll tell you where to go and what to ask for, and one thing and another will bring you to his attention."

"Sounds too easy."

"Coming to his attention will be easy. Staying alive once you do will not be."

Rydell considered. "So what am I supposed to do for you when he finds me?"

"Ask him a question."

"What question?"

"I don't know yet," Laney said. "I'm working on it."

"Laney," Rydell said, "what's this all about?"

"If I knew that," Laney said, and suddenly he sounded very tired, "I wouldn't have to be here." He fell silent. Clicked off.

"Laney?"

Rydell sat listening to the toilet run. Eventually he got up, took his bag down from the hook, and exited the cubicle. He washed his hands in a trickle of cold water that ran into a black imitation marble sink crusted with yellowish industrial soap and made his way back along a corridor made narrow by cartons of what he took to be janitorial supplies.

He hoped that Creedmore and the country music mamma would've forgotten about him, gone away.

Not so. The woman was working on her own plate of eggs, while Creedmore, his beer clipped between his denim thighs, was staring balefully at the two enormous, gypsum-dusted construction workers.

"Hey," Creedmore said, as Rydell walked past, carrying his bag.

"Hey, Buell," Rydell said, heading for the door to the street.

"Hey, where you going?"

"To work," Rydell said.

"Work," he heard Creedmore say and "shit," but the door swung shut behind him, and he was on the street.

15. BACK UP HERE

CHEVETTE stood beside the van, watching Tessa release God's Little Toy. The camera platform, like a Mylar muffin or an inflated coin, caught the day's watery light as it rose, wobbling, then leveled out, swaying, at fifteen feet or so.

Chevette felt very strange, being here, seeing this: the concrete tank traps, beyond them the impossible shape of the bridge itself. Where she had lived, though it now seemed a dream, or someone else's life, atop the nearest cable tower. Way up in a cube of plywood there, sleeping while the wind's great hands shoved and twisted and clawed, and she'd heard the tendons of the bridge groan all in secret, a sound carried up the twisted strands for only her to hear, Chevette with her ear pressed against the graceful dolphin back of cable that rose through the oval hole sliced for it through Skinner's plywood floor.

Now Skinner was dead, she knew. He'd gone while she was in Los Angeles, trying to become whoever it was she'd thought she wanted to be. She hadn't come up. The bridge people weren't big on funerals, and possession, here, was most points of the law. She wasn't Skinner's daughter, and even if she had been, and had wanted to hold his place atop the cable tower, it would've been a matter of staying there for as long as she intended it to be hers. She hadn't wanted that.

But she'd had no way to grieve him in Los Angeles, and now it all came up, came back, the time she'd lived with him. How he had found her, too sick to walk, and taken her home, feeding her soups he bought from the Korean vendors until she was well. Then he'd left her alone, asking nothing, accepting her there the way you'd accept a bird on a windowsill, until she'd learned to ride a bicycle in the city and become a messenger. And soon the roles had reversed: the old man failing, needing help, and she the one to go for soup, bring water, see that coffee was made. And that was how it had been, until she'd gotten herself into the trouble that had resulted in her first having met Rydell.

"Wind'll catch that," she cautioned Tessa, who had put on the glasses that let her watch the feed from the floating camera.

"I've got three more in the car," Tessa said, pulling a sleazy-looking black control glove over her right hand. She experimented with the touch pads, revving the platform's miniature props and swinging it through a twenty-foot circle.

"We've got to hire someone to watch the van," Chevette said, "if you want to see it again."

"Hire someone? Who?"

Chevette pointed at a thin black child with dusty dreadlocks to his waist. "You. What's your name?"

"What's it to you?"

"Pay you watch this van. We come back, chip you fifty. Fair?"

The boy regarded her evenly. "Name Boomzilla," he said.

"Boomzilla," Chevette said, "you take care of this van?"

"Deal," he said.

"Deal," Chevette said to Tessa.

"Lady," Boomzilla said, pointing up at God's Little Toy, "I want that."

"Stick around," Tessa said. "We'll need a grip."

Tessa touching fingers to black-padded palm. The camera platform executing a second turn and gliding out of sight, above the tank traps. Tessa smiling, seeing what it saw. "Come on," she said to Chevette and stepped between the nearest traps.

"Not that way," Chevette said. "Over here." There was a path you followed if you were just walking through. To take another route indicated either ignorance or the desire to do business.

She showed Tessa the way. It stank of urine between the concrete slabs. Chevette walked more quickly, Tessa behind her.

And emerged again into that wet light, but here it ran not across the stalls and vendors of memory, but across the red-and-white front of a modular convenience store, chunked down front and center across the entrance to the bridge's two levels, LUCKY DRAGON and the shudder of video up the trademark tower of screens.

"Fucking hell," said Tessa, "how interstitial is that?"

Chevette stopped, stunned. "How could they do that?"

"It's what they do," Tessa said. "Prime location."

"But it's like . . . like Nissan County or something."

" 'Gated attraction.' The community's a tourist draw, right?"

"Lots of people won't go where there's no police."

"Autonomous zones are their own draw," Tessa said. "This one's been here long enough to become the city's number-one postcard."

"God-awful," Chevette said. "It . . . ruins it."

"Who do you think Lucky Dragon Corp is paying rent to?" Tessa asked, swinging the platform around for a pan across the store.

"No idea," Chevette said. "It's right in the middle of what used to be the street."

"Never mind," Tessa said, moving on, into the pedestrian traffic flowing to and from the bridge. "We're just in time. We're going to document the life before it's theme-parked."

Chevette followed, not knowing what it was exactly that she felt.

THEY ate lunch in a Mexican place called Dirty Is God.

Chevette didn't remember it from before, but places changed names on the bridge. They changed size and shape too. You'd get these strange mergers, a hair place and an oyster bar deciding to become a bigger place that cut hair and sold oysters. Sometimes it worked: one of the longest-running places on the San Francisco end was an old-style, manual tattoo parlor that served breakfast. You could sit there over a plate of eggs and bacon and watch somebody get needled with some kind of hand-drawn flash.

But Dirty Is God was just Mexican food and Japanese music, a pretty straightforward proposition. Tessa got the huevos rancheros and Chevette got a chicken quesadilla. They both had a Corona, and Tessa parked the camera platform up near the tented plastic ceiling. Nobody noticed it up there apparently, so Tessa could do documentary while she ate.

Tessa ate a lot. She said it was her metabolism: one of those people who never gains any weight regardless of how much she ate, but she needed to do it to keep her energy up. Tessa put away her huevos before Chevette was halfway through her quesadilla. She drained her glass bottle of Corona and started fiddling with the wedge of lime, squeezing it, working it into the neck.

"Carson," Tessa said. "You worried about him?"

"What about him?"

"He's an abusive ex, is what about him. That was his car back in Malibu, wasn't it?"

"I think so," Chevette said.

"You think so? You aren't sure?"

"Look," Chevette said, "it was early in the morning. It was all pretty strange. It wasn't my idea to come up here, you know? It was your idea. You want to make your movie."

The lime popped down into the empty Corona bottle, and Tessa looked at it as though she'd just lost a private wager. "You know what I like about you? I mean one of the things I like about you?"

"What?" Chevette asked.

"You aren't middle class. You just aren't. You move in with this guy, he starts hitting you, what do you do?"

"Move out."

"That's right. You move out. You don't take a meeting with your lawyers."

"I don't have any lawyers," Chevette said.

"I know. That's what I mean."

"I don't like lawyers," Chevette said.

"Of course you don't. And you don't have any reflex to litigation."

"Litigation?"

"He beat you up. He's got eight hundred square feet of strata-title loft. He's got a job. He beats you up, you don't automatically order a surgical strike; you're not middle class."

"I just don't want anything to do with him."

"That's what I mean. You're from Oregon, right?"

"More or less," Chevette said.

"You ever think of acting?" Tessa inverted the bottle. The squashed lime wedge fell down into the neck. A few drops of beer fell on the scratched black plastic of the table. Tessa inserted the little finger of her right hand and tried to snag the lime wedge.

"No."

"Camera loves you. You've got a body makes boys chew carpet."

"Get off," Chevette said.

"Why do you think they were putting those party shots of you up on the website back in Malibu?"

"Because they were drunk," Chevette said. "Because they don't have anything better to do. Because they're media students."

Tessa hooked the lime wedge, what was left of it, out of the bottle. "Right on all three," she said, "but the main reason's your looks."

Behind Tessa, on one of Dirty Is God's recycled wall screens, a very beautiful Japanese girl had appeared. "Look at her," Chevette said. "That's looks, right?"

Tessa looked over her shoulder. "That's Rei Toei," she said.

"So she's beautiful. *She* is."

"Chevette," Tessa said, "she doesn't exist. There's no live girl there at all. She's code. Software."

"No way," Chevette said.

"You didn't know that?"

"But she's based on somebody, right? Some kind of motion-capture deal."

"Nobody," Tessa said. "Nothing. She's the real deal. Hundred-percent unreal."

"Then that's what people want," Chevette said, watching Rei Toei swan through some kind of retro Asian nightclub, "not ex bicycle messengers from San Francisco."

"No," Tessa said, "you've got it exactly backwards. People don't know what they want, not before they see it. Every object of desire is a *found* object. Traditionally, anyway."

Chevette looked at Tessa across the two empty Corona bottles. "What are you getting at, Tessa?"

"The documentary. It has to be about *you*."

"Forget it."

"No. I've got vision thing working big-time on this. I need you for the focus. I need narrative traction. I *need* Chevette Washington."

Chevette was actually starting to feel a little scared. It made her angry. "Don't you have a grant to do this one particular project you've been talking about? These innersitual things—"

"Look," Tessa said, "if that's a problem, and I'm not saying it is, it's *my* problem. And it's not a problem, it's an opportunity. It's a *shot*. *My* shot."

"Tessa, there is no way you are going to get me to act in your movie. None. You understand?"

" 'Acting' isn't in it, Chevette. All you have to do is be yourself. And that will involve finding out who you really are. I am going to make a film about you finding out who you really are."

"You are not," said Chevette, getting up and actually bumping into the camera platform, which must have descended to level with her head while they were talking. "Stop that!" Swatting at God's Little Toy.

The other four customers in Dirty Is God just looking at them.

16. SUB-ROUTINES

THAT Hole at the core of Laney's being, that underlying absence, he begins to suspect, is not so much an absence in the self as *of* the self.

Something has happened to him since his descent into the cardboard city. He has started to see that previously he had, in some unthinkably literal way, no self.

But what was there, he wonders, before?

Sub-routines: maladaptive survival behaviors desperately conspiring to approximate a presence that would be, and never quite be, Laney. And he has never known this before, although he knows that he has always, somehow, been aware of something having been desperately and utterly wrong.

Something tells him this. Something in the core and totality, it seems, of DatAmerica. How can that be?

But now he lies, propped in sleeping bags, in darkness, as if at the earth's core, and beyond cardboard walls are walls of concrete, sheathed in ceramic tile, and beyond them the footing of this country, Japan, with the shudder of the trains a reminder of tectonic forces, the shifting of continent-wide plates.

Somewhere within Laney, something else is shifting. There is movement, and potential for greater movement still, and he wonders why he is no longer afraid.

And all of this is somehow a gift of the sickness. Not of the cough, the fever, but of that underlying dis-ease that he takes to be the product of the 5-SB he ingested so long ago in the orphanage in Gainesville.

We were all volunteers, he thinks, as he clutches the eyephones and follows his point of view over the edge of a cliff of data, plunging down the wall of this code mesa, its face compounded of fractally differentiated fields of information he has come to suspect of hiding some power or intelligence beyond his comprehension.

Something at once noun and verb.

While Laney, plunging, eyes wide against the pressure of information, knows himself to be merely adjectival: a Laney-colored smear, meaningless without context. A microscopic cog in some catastrophic plan. But positioned, he senses, centrally.

Crucially.

And that is why sleep is no longer an option.

17. ZODIAC

THEY take Silencio, naked, the black man with the long face and the fat white man with the red beard, into a room with wet wooden walls. Leave him. Hot rain falls from holes in the black plastic pipes above. Falls harder, stings.

They have taken his clothes and shoes away in a plastic bag, and now the fat man returns, gives him soap. He knows soap. He remembers the warm rain falling from a pipe in los projectos but this is better, and he is alone in the tall wooden room.

Silencio with his belly full, soaping himself repeatedly, because that is what they want. He rubs the soap into his hair.

He closes his eyes against the burning of the soap and sees the watches arrayed beneath greenish, randomly abraded glass, like fish from some warmer season frozen hard in lake ice. Bright highlights off steel and gold.

He has been colonized by an order uncomprehended: the multifold fact of these potent objects, their endless differentiation, their individual specificities. Infinite variety arising from the expression of dial, hands, numerals, hour markers . . . He likes the warm rain but he needs desperately to return, to see more, to hear the words.

He has become the words, what they mean.

Breguette hands. Tapestry dial. Bombay lugs. Original stem. Signed.

The rain slows, stops. The fat man, who wears plastic sandals, brings Silencio a thick dry cloth.

The fat man peers at him. "Watches, you say he likes?" the fat man asks the black man. "Yes," the black man says, "he seems to like watches."

The bearded man drapes the towel around Silencio's shoulders. "Does he know how to tell time?"

"I don't know," says the black man.

"Well," says the fat man, stepping back, "he doesn't know how to use a towel."

Silencio feels confused, ashamed. He looks down.

"Leave him alone, Andy," the black man says. "Get me those clothes I brought."

THE black man's name: Fontaine. Like a word in the language of los projectos, a meaning about water. The warm rain in the wooden room.

Now Fontaine leads him through the upper level, where some people call out, selling fruit, past others selling old things spread on blankets, to where a thin dark man stands waiting beside a plastic crate. The crate is upturned, its bottom padded with foam and ragged silver tape, and this man wears a striped cloth thing with pockets down his front, and in the pockets are scissors, and things like the thing Raton liked to run endlessly through his hair, when he had balanced the black perfectly with the white.

Silencio is wearing the clothes Fontaine has given him: they are large, loose, not his own, but they smell good. Fontaine has given him shoes made of white cloth. Too white. They hurt his eyes.

The soap and the warm rain have made Silencio's hair strange as well, and now Fontaine tells Silencio to sit upon the crate, this man will cut his hair.

Silencio sits, trembling, as the thin dark man flicks at his hair with one of the Raton-things from his pockets, making small noises behind his teeth.

Silencio looks at Fontaine.

"It's okay," Fontaine says, unwrapping a small sharp stick of wood and inserting it into the corner of his mouth, "you won't feel a thing."

Silencio wonders if the stick is like the black or the white, but Fontaine does not change. He stands there with the stick in his mouth, watching the thin dark man snip away Silencio's hair with the scissors. Silencio watches Fontaine, listens to the sound of the scissors, and to the new language in his head.

Zodiac Sea Wolf. Case very clean. Screw-down crown. Original bezel.

"Zodiac Sea Wolf," Silencio says.

"Man," says the thin dark man, "you deep."

18. SELWYN TONG

RYDELL had a theory about virtual real estate. The smaller and cheaper the physical site of a given operation, the bigger and cheesier the website. According to this theory, Selwyn F.X. Tong, notary public, of Kowloon, was probably operating out of a rolled-up newspaper.

Rydell couldn't figure out a way to skip the approach segment, which was monolithic, vaguely Egyptian, and reminded him of what his buddy Sublett, a film buff, had called "corridor metaphysics." This was one long-ass corridor, and if it had been physical, you could've driven a very large truck down it. There were baroque sconce lights, virtual scarlet wall-to-wall, and weird tacky texture mapping that tended to gold-flecked marble.

Where had Laney found this guy?

Eventually Rydell did manage to kill the music, something vaguely classical and swelling, but it still seemed to take him three minutes to get to Selwyn F.X. Tong's doors. Which were tall, very tall, and mapped to resemble some generic idea of tropical hardwood.

"Teak my ass," said Rydell.

"Welcome," said a breathless, hyper-feminine voice, "to the offices of Selwyn F.X. Tong, notary public!"

The doors swung open. Rydell figured that if he hadn't killed the music, it would be peaking about now.

Virtually, the notary's office was about the size of an Olympic pool but scarce on detail. Rydell used the rocker-pad on his glasses to scoot his POV right up to the desk, which was about the size of a pool table, and mapped in that same ramped-down wood look. There were a couple of nondescript, metallic-looking objects on it and a few pieces of virtual paper.

"What's the 'F.X.' stand for?" Rydell asked.

"Francis Xavier," said Tong, who presented as a sort of deadpan cartoon of a small Chinese man in a white shirt, black tie, black suit. His black hair and the black suit were mapped in the same texture, a weird effect and one Rydell took to be unintentional.

"I thought you might be in video," Rydell said, "like it's a nickname: FX, 'effects,' right?"

"I am Catholic," Tong said, his tone neutral.

"No offense," Rydell said.

"None taken," said Tong, his plastic-looking face as shiny as his plastic-looking eyes.

You always forgot, Rydell reflected, just how bad this stuff could look if it hadn't been handled right.

"What can I do for you, Mr. Rydell?"

"Laney didn't tell you?"

"Laney?"

"Colin," Rydell said. "Space. Laney."

"And . . . ?"

"Six," Rydell said. "Zero. Four. Two."

Tong's plastic-looking eyes narrowed.

"Berry."

Tong pursed his lips. Behind him, through a broad window, at a different rate of resolution, Rydell could see the skyline of Hong Kong.

"Berry," Rydell repeated.

"Thank you, Mr. Rydell," the notary said. "My client has authorized me to give you this seven-digit identification number." A gold fountain pen appeared in Tong's right hand, like a continuity error in a student film. It was a very large pen, elaborately mapped with swirling dragons, their scales in higher resolution than anything else in the site. Probably a gift, Rydell decided. Tong wrote the seven digits on one of the sheets of virtual paper, then reversed it on the desktop so that Rydell could read it. The pen had vanished, as unnaturally as it had appeared. "Please don't repeat this number aloud," Tong said.

"Why not?"

"Issues of encryption," Tong said obscurely. "You have as long as you like to memorize the number."

Rydell looked at the seven digits and began to work out a mnemonic. He finally arrived at one based on his birthday, the number of states when he was born, his father's age when he'd died, and a mental image of two cans of 7-Up. When he was certain that he'd be able to recall the number, he looked up at Tong. "Where do I go to get the credit chip?"

"Any automated teller. You have photo identification?"

"Yes," Rydell said.

"Then we are finished."

"One thing," Rydell said.

"What is that?"

"Tell me how I get out of here without having to go back down that corridor of yours. I just want a straight exit, right?"

Tong regarded him blandly. "Click on my face."

Rydell did, using the rocker-pad to summon a cursor shaped like a neon green cartoon hand, pointing. "Thanks," he said, as Tong's office folded.

He was in the corridor, facing back the way he had come.

"Damn," Rydell said.

The music began. He worked the rocker-pad, trying to remember how he'd killed it before. He wanted to get a GPS fix on the nearest ATM, though, so he didn't unplug the glasses.

He clicked for the end of the corridor.

The click seemed to trigger a metastatic surge of bit rot, every bland texture map rewritten in some weirder hand: the red carpet went gray-green, its knap grown strange and unevenly furry, like something at the bottom of a month-old cup of coffee, while the walls went from whore-house marble to a moist fish-belly pallor, the sconce lights glowing dim as drowned corpse candles. Tong's fake-classical theme cracked and hollowed, weird bass notes rumbling in just above the threshold of the subsonic.

It all took about a second to happen, and it took Rydell maybe another second to get the idea that someone wanted his undivided attention.

"Rydell." It was one of those voices that they fake up from found audio: speech cobbled from wind down skyscraper canyons, the creaking of Great Lakes ice, tree frogs clanging in the Southern night. Rydell had heard them before. They grated on the nerves, as they were meant to, and conveniently disguised the voice of the speaker. Assuming the speaker had a voice in the first place.

"Hey," Rydell said, "I was just trying to click out."

A virtual screen appeared in front of him, a round-cornered rectangle whose dimensions were meant to invoke the cultural paradigm of twentieth-century video screens. On it, an oddly angled, monochromatic view of some vast shadowy space, dimly lit from above. Nothing there. Impression of decay, great age.

"I have important information for you." The vowel in *you* suggested a siren dopplering past, then gone.

"Well," said Rydell, "if your middle name is 'F. X.,' you're sure going to some trouble."

There was a pause, Rydell staring at the dead, blank space depicted or recorded on the screen. He was waiting for something to move there; probably that was the point of it, that nothing did.

"You'd better take this information very seriously, Mr. Rydell."

"I'm serious as cancer," Rydell said. "Shoot."

"Use the ATM at the Lucky Dragon, near the entrance to the bridge. Then present your identification at the GlobEx franchise at the rear of the store."

"Why?"

"They're holding something for you."

"Tong," Rydell said, "is that you?"

But there was no answer. The screen vanished, and the corridor was as it had been.

Rydell reached up and disconnected the rented cable from the Brazilian glasses.

Blinked.

A coffee place near Union Square, the kind that had potted plants and hotdesks. An early office crowd was starting to line up for sandwiches.

He got up, folded the glasses, tucked them into the inside pocket of his jacket, and picked up his bag.

19. INTERSTITIAL

CHEVETTE moves past the colorless flame of a chestnut vendor's charcoal fire, powdery gray burning itself down in the inverted, V-nosed hood of some ancient car.

She sees another fire, in memory: coke glow of a smith's forge, driven by the exhaust of a vacuum cleaner. Beside her the old man held the drive chain of some extinct motorcycle, folded neatly into a compact mass and fastened with a twist of rusty wire. To be taken in the smith's tongs and placed within the forge. To be beaten, finally, incandescent, into a billet of their strangely grained Damascus, ghosts of those links emerging as the blade is forged, quenched, shaped, and polished on the wheel.

Where did that knife go? she wonders.

She'd watched the maker craft and braise a hilt of brass, rivet slabs of laminated circuit board and shape them on a belt grinder. The rigid, brittle-looking board, layers of fabric trapped in green phenolic resin, was everywhere on the bridge, a common currency of landfills. Each sheet mapped with dull metallic patterns suggesting cities, streets. When they came from the scavengers they were studded with components, easily stripped with a torch, melting the gray solder. The components fell away, leaving the singed green boards with their inlaid foil maps of imaginary cities, residue of the second age of electronics. And Skinner would tell her that these boards were immortal, inert as stone, proof against moisture and ultraviolet and every form of decay; that they were destined to litter the planet, hence it was good to reuse them, work them when possible into the fabric of things, a resource when something needed to be durable.

She knows she needs to be alone now, so she's left Tessa on the lower level, collecting visual texture with God's Little Toy. Chevette can't hear any more about how Tessa's film has to be more personal, about her, Chevette, and Tessa hasn't been able to shut up about that, or take no for an answer. Chevette remembers Bunny Malatesta, her dispatcher when she rode here, how he'd say "and what part of 'no' is it that you don't understand?" But Bunny could deliver lines like that as though he were a force of nature, and Chevette knows she can't, that she lacks Bunny's gravity, the sheer crunch required to get it across.

So she's taken an escalator, one she doesn't remember, to the upper level, and is making her way, without really thinking about it, to the foot of their tower, the wet light having turned to a thin and gusting rain, blowing through the bridge's tattered secondhand superstructure. People are hauling their laundry in, where they've hung it, draped on lines, and there's a general pre-storm bustle that she knows will fade if the weather changes.

And so far, she thinks, she's not seen a single face she knows from before, and no one has greeted her, and she finds herself imagining the bridge's entire population replaced in her absence. No, there went the bookstall woman, the one with the ivory chopsticks thrust into her dyed black bun, and she recognizes the Korean boy with the bad leg, rumbling his father's soup wagon along as though it should have brakes.

The tower she'd ascended each day to Skinner's plywood shack is bundled in subsidiary construction, its iron buried at the core of an organic complex of spaces appropriated for specific activities. Behind taut, wind-shivered sheets of milky plastic, the unearthly light of a hydroponics operation casts outsize leaf shadows. She hears the snarl of an electric saw from the tiny workshop of a furniture-maker, whose assistant sits patiently, rubbing wax into a small bench collaged from paint-flecked oak scavenged from the shells of older houses. Someone else is making jam, the big copper kettle heated by a propane ring.

Perfect for Tessa, she thinks: the bridge people maintaining their interstices. Doing their little things. But Chevette has seen them drunk. Has seen the drugged and the mad dive to their deaths in the gray and unforgiving chop. Has seen men fight to the death with knives. Has seen a mother, dumbstruck, walking with a strangled child in her arms, at dawn. The bridge is no tourist's fantasy. The bridge is real, and to live here exacts its own price.

It is a world within the world, and, if there be such places between the things of the world, places built in the gaps, then surely there are things there, and places between them, and things in those places too. And Tessa doesn't know this, and it is not Chevette's place to tell her.

She ducks past a loose flap of plastic, into moist warmth and the spectrum of grow lamps. A reek of chemicals. Black water pumped amid pale roots. These are medicinal plants, she supposes, but probably not drugs in the street sense. Those are grown nearer Oakland, in a sector somehow allotted for that, and on warm days there the fug of resin hangs narcotic in the air, bringing an almost perceptible buzz, faint alteration of perception and the will.

"Hey. Anybody here?"

Gurgle of liquid through transparent tubing. A silt-slimed pair of battered yellow waders dangle nearby, but no sign of who hung them there. She moves quickly, her feet remembering, to where corroded aluminum rungs protrude from fist-sized blobs of super-epoxy.

The ball-chain zip pulls on Skinner's old jacket jingle as she climbs. These rungs are a back way, an emergency exit if needed.

Climbing past the sickly greenish sun of a grow lamp, housed in a corroded industrial fixture, she pulls herself up the last aluminum rung and through a narrow triangular opening.

It is dark here, shaded by walls of rain-swollen composite. Shadowed where she remembers light, and she sees that the bulb, above, in this enclosed space, is missing. This is the lower end of Skinner's "funicular," the little junkyard elevator trolley, built for him by a black man named Fontaine, and it was here that she'd lock her bike in her messengering days, after shouldering it up another, less covert ladder.

She studies the cog-toothed track of the funicular, where the grease shows dull with accumulated dust. The gondola, a yellow municipal recycling bin, deep enough to stand in and grasp the rim, waits where it should. But if it is here, it likely means that the current resident of the cable tower is not. Unless the car has been sent in expectation of a visitor, which Chevette doubts. It is better to be up there with the car up. She knows that feeling.

Now she climbs wooden rungs, a cruder ladder of two-by-fours, until her head clears the ply and she winces in wind and silvery light. Sees a gull hang almost stationary in the air, not twenty feet away, the towers of the city as backdrop.

The wind tugs at her hair, longer now than when she lived here, and a feeling that she can't name comes like something she has always known, and she has no interest in climbing farther, because she knows now that the home she remembers is no longer there. Only its shell, humming in the wind, where once she lay wrapped in blankets, smelling machinist's grease and coffee and fresh-cut wood.

Where, it comes to her, she was sometimes happy, in the sense of being somehow complete, and ready for what another day might bring.

And knows she is no longer that, and that while she was, she scarcely knew it.

She hunches her shoulders, drawing her neck down into the carapace of Skinner's jacket, and imagines herself crying, though she knows she won't, and climbs back down.

20. BOOMZILLA

BOOMZILLA sitting on the curb, beside the truck these two bitches say they pay him to watch. They don't come back, he'll get some help and strip it. Wants that robot balloon the blonde bitch had. That's fine. Fly that shit around.

Other bitch kind of biker-looking, big old coat looked like she got it off a dumpster. That one kick your ass, looked like.

Where they gone? Hungry now, wind blowing grit in his face, splashes of rain.

"Have you seen this girl?" Movie-looking white man, face painted dark like they do down the coast. How they dress when they had time to think about coming here, everything worn out just right. Leather jacket like he's left his old airplane around the corner. Blue jeans. Black T.

Boomzilla, he'd puke, anybody try to put him in that shit. Boomzilla know how he going to dress, time he get his shit together.

Boomzilla looking at the printout the man holds out. Sees the biker-looking bitch, but dressed better.

Boomzilla looks up at the tinted face. See how pale the blue eyes look against it. Something say: cold. Something say: don't fuck with me.

Boomzilla thinks: he don't know it's they truck.

"She's lost," the man says.

You ass is, Boomzilla thinks. "Never seen her."

Eyes lean in a little closer. "Missing, understand? Trying to help her. A lost child."

Thinks: child my ass; bitch my momma's age.

Boomzilla shakes his head. How he does it serious, just a little, side to side. Means: no.

The blue eyes swing away, looking for somebody else to show the picture to; swing right past the truck. No click.

Man moving off, toward a clutch of people by a coffee stand, holding the picture.

Boomzilla watches him go.

A lost child himself, he has every intention of staying that way.

21. PARAGON ASIA

SAN Francisco and Los Angeles seemed more like different planets than different cities. It wasn't the NoCal-SoCal thing, but something that went down to the roots. Rydell remembered sitting with a beer somewhere, years ago, watching the partition ceremonies on CNN, and it hadn't impressed him much even then. But the difference, that was something.

A stiff gust of wind threw rain into his face, as he was coming down Stockton toward Market. Office girls held their skirts down and laughed, and Rydell felt like laughing too, though that had passed before he'd crossed Market and started down 4th.

This was where he'd met Chevette, where she'd lived.

She and Rydell had had their adventure up here, had met in the course of it, and the end of it had taken them to LA.

She hadn't liked LA, he always told himself, but he knew that really wasn't why it had gone the way it had.

They had moved down there, the two of them, while Rydell pursued the mediation of what they'd just gone through together. *Cops in Trouble* was interested, and *Cops in Trouble* had been interested in Rydell once before, back in Knoxville.

Fresh out of the academy, back then, he'd used deadly force on a stimulant abuser who was trying to kill his, the abuser's, girlfriend's children. The girlfriend had subsequently been looking to sue the department, the city, and Rydell, so *Cops in Trouble* had decided Rydell might warrant a segment. So they'd flown him out to SoCal, where they were based. He'd gotten an agent and everything, but the deal had fallen apart, so he'd taken a job driving armed response for IntenSecure. When he'd managed to get himself fired from that, he wound up going up to NoCal to do temp work, off the record, for the local IntenSecure operation there. That was what had gotten him into the trouble that introduced him to Chevette Washington.

So when Rydell turned up back in LA with a story to tell, and Chevette on his arm, *Cops in Trouble* had perked right up. They were moving into a phase where they tried to spin individual segments off into series for niche markets, and the demographics people liked it that Rydell was male, not too young, not too educated, and from the South. They also liked it that he wasn't racist, and they really liked it that he was with this really cute alt-dot kind of girl, one who looked like she could crush walnuts between her thighs.

Cops in Trouble had installed them in a small stealth hotel below Sunset, and they had been so happy, the first few weeks, that Rydell could barely stand to remember it.

Whenever they went to bed, it had seemed more like making history than love. The suite was like a little apartment, with its own kitchen and a gas fire, and they'd roll around at night on a blanket on the floor, in front of the fire, with the windows open and the lights out, blue flame flickering low and LAPD gunships drumming overhead, and every time he'd crawl into her arms, or she'd put her face down next to his, he'd known it was good history, the best, and that everything was going to be just fine.

But it hadn't been.

Rydell had never thought about his looks much. He looked, he'd thought, okay. Women had seemed to like him well enough, and it had been pointed out to him that he resembled the younger Tommy Lee Jones, Tommy Lee Jones being a twentieth-century movie star. And because they'd told him that, he'd watched a few of the guy's movies and liked them, though the resemblance people saw puzzled him.

He guessed he'd started to worry though, when *Cops in Trouble* had assigned a skinny blonde intern named Tara-May Allenby to follow him around, grabbing footage with a shoulder-mounted steadicam.

Tara-May had chewed gum and fiddled with filters and had generally put Rydell's teeth on edge. He'd known she was feeding live to *Cops in Trouble,* and he'd started to get the idea they weren't too happy with what was coming through. Tara-May hadn't helped, explaining to Rydell that the camera added an apparent twenty pounds to anybody's looks, but that, hey, *she* liked him just the way he was, all beefy and solid. But she'd kept suggesting he try working out more. Why not go with that girlfriend of yours, she'd say, she's so buff, it hurts.

But Chevette had never seen the inside of a gym in her life; she owed her buffness to her genes and a few years she'd spent pounding up and down San Francisco hills on a competition-grade mountain bike, its frame rolled from epoxy and Japanese construction paper.

So now Rydell sighed, coming up on the corner of 4th and Bryant, and on Bryant turning toward the bridge. The bag on his shoulder was starting to demonstrate its weight, its collusion with gravity. Rydell stopped, sighed again, readjusted the bag. Put thoughts of the past out of his mind.

Just walk.

NO trouble at all finding that branch of Lucky Dragon.

Couldn't miss it, smack in what had been the middle of Bryant, dead center as you approached the entrance to the bridge. He hadn't been able to see it, coming along Bryant, because it was behind the jumble of old concrete tank traps they'd dropped there after the quake, but once you got past those, there it was.

He could see, walking up to it, that it was a newer model than the one he'd worked in on Sunset. It had fewer corners, so there was less to chip off or need repair. He supposed that designing a Lucky Dragon module was about designing something that would hold up under millions of uncaring and even hostile hands. Ultimately, he thought, you'd wind up with something like a seashell, hard and smooth.

The store on Sunset had had a finish that ate graffiti. The gang kids would come and tag it; twenty minutes later these flat, dark, vaguely crab-like patches of dark blue would come gliding around the corner. Rydell had never understood how they worked, and Durius said they'd been developed in Singapore. They seemed to be embedded, a few millimeters down into the surface, which was a sort of non-glossy gel-coat affair, but able to move around under there. Smart material, he'd heard that called. And they'd glide up to the tag, whatever artfully abstract scrawl had been sprayed there to declare fealty or mark territory or swear revenge (Durius had been able to read these things and construct a narrative out of them) and start eating it. You couldn't actually see the crablegs move. They just sort of nuzzled in and gradually the tag started to unravel, de-rez, molecules of paint sucked down into the blue of the Lucky Dragon graffiti-eaters.

And once someone had come with a smart tag, a sort of decal they'd somehow adhered to the wall, although neither Rydell nor Durius had been able to figure how they'd done it without being seen. Maybe, Durius said, they'd shot it from a distance. It was the tag of a gang called the Chupacabras, a fearsome spiky thing, all black and red, insectoid and menacing and, Rydell thought, kind of good-looking, exciting-looking. He'd seen it worn as a tattoo, in the store. The kids who wore it favored those contacts, the kind gave you pupils like a snake's. When the graffiti-eaters came out after it though, it had moved.

They'd edge up to it, and it would sense them and move away. Almost too slow to see it happening, but it moved. Then the graffiti-eaters would move again. Durius and Rydell watched it, the first night, get all the way around to the back of the store. It was starting to work its way back around toward the front when they went off shift.

Next shift it was still there, and a couple of standard spray-bomb tags as well. The graffiti-eaters were locked on the smart tag and not taking care of business. Durius showed it to Mr. Park, who didn't like it that they hadn't told him before. Rydell showed him where they'd logged it in the shift record when they clocked off, which had just pissed Mr. Park off more.

About an hour later, two men in white Tyvek coveralls showed up in an unmarked, surgically clean white van and went to work. Rydell would've liked to watch them get the smart tag off, but there was a run of shoplifters that night and he didn't get to see what they did to it. They didn't use scrapers or solvents, he knew that. They used a notebook and a couple of adhesive probes. Basically, he guessed, they reprogrammed it, messed with its code, and after they left, the graffiti-eaters were back out there, slurping down the latest Chupacabra iconography.

This Lucky Dragon by the bridge was smooth and white as a new china plate, Rydell observed, as he came up to it. It looked like a piece of some different dream, fallen here. The entrance to the bridge had a weird unplanned drama to it, and Rydell wondered if there'd been a lot of meetings, back in Singapore, about whether or not to put this unit here. Lucky Dragon had some units on prime tourist real estate, and Rydell knew that from watching the Global Interactive Video Column back in LA; there was one in the mall under Red Square, that fancy K-Dam branch in Berlin, the big-ass one in Piccadilly, London, but putting one here struck him as a strange, or strangely deliberate, move.

The bridge was a dodgy place, safe enough but not "tourist safe."

There was a walk-on tourist contingent, sure, and a big one, particularly on this end of the bridge, but no tours, no guides. If you went, you went on your own. Chevette had told him how they repelled evangelicals, and the Salvation Army and any other organized entity, in no uncertain terms. Rydell figured that in fact that was part of the draw of the place, that it was unregulated.

Autonomous zone, Durius called that. He'd told Rydell that Sunset Strip had started out as one of those, a place between police jurisdictions, and somehow that had set the DNA of the street, which was why, say, you still got hookers in elf hats there, come Christmas.

But maybe Lucky Dragon knew something people didn't, he thought. Things could change. His father, for instance, used to swear that Times Square had been a really dangerous place.

Rydell made his way through the crowd flowing on and off the bridge and past the Global Interactive Video Column, daydreaming as he did that he'd look up and see the Sunset branch there, with Praisegod beaming sunnily at him from out in front.

What he got was some skater kid in Seoul shaking his nuts at the camera.

He went in, to be immediately stopped by a very large man with a very broad forehead and pale, almost invisible eyebrows. "Your bag," said the security man, who was wearing a pink Lucky Dragon fanny pack exactly like the one Rydell had worn in LA. As a matter of fact, Rydell's was in the very duffel the guy was demanding.

"Please," Rydell said, handing the bag over. Lucky Dragon security were supposed to say that: please. It was on Mr. Park's notebook, and anyway when you asked somebody for their bag, you were admitting you thought they might shoplift, so you might as well be polite about it.

The security man narrowed his eyes. He put the bag in a numbered cubicle behind his station and handed Rydell a Lucky Dragon logo tag that looked like an oversized drink coaster with the number five on the back. It was the size it was, Rydell knew, because it had been determined that this size made the tags just that much too big to fit into most pockets, thereby preventing people from pocketing, forgetting, and wandering away with them. Kept costs down. Everything about Lucky Dragon was worked out that way. You sort of had to admire them.

"You're welcome," Rydell said. He headed for the ATM in the back, Lucky Dragon International Bank. He knew it was watching him as he walked up to it, pulling his wallet from his back pocket.

"I'm here to get a chip issued," he said.

"Identify yourself, please." Lucky Dragon ATMs all had this same voice, a weird, uptight, strangled little castrato voice, and he wondered why that was. But you could be sure they'd worked it out: probably it kept people from standing around, bullshitting with the machine. But Rydell knew that you didn't want to do that anyway, because the suckers would pepper-spray you. They were plastered with notices to that effect too, although he doubted anyone ever actually read them. What the notices didn't say, and Lucky Dragon wasn't telling, was that if you tried seriously to dick with one, drive a crowbar into the money slot, say, the thing would mist you and itself down with water and then electrify itself.

"Berry Rydell," he said, taking his Tennessee driver's license from his wallet and inserting the business end into the ATM's reader.

"Palm contact."

Rydell pressed his hand within the outline of a hand. He hated the way that felt. Bad cootie factor with those palm-scan things. Hand grease.

He wiped his palm on his trousers.

"Please enter your personal identification code."

Rydell did, working through his mnemonic to the two cans of 7-Up.

"Processing credit request," the thing said, sounding as if someone were squeezing its balls.

Rydell looked around and saw that he was pretty much the only customer, aside from a woman with gray hair and black leather pants, who was giving the checker a hard time in what sounded to Rydell like German.

"Transaction completed," the ATM said. Rydell turned back in time to see a Lucky Dragon credit chip emerge from the chip slot. He shoved it partway back in, to see the available come up on the screen. Not bad. Not bad at all. He pocketed the chip, put his wallet away, and turned toward the GlobEx concession, which also doubled as the local USPO. Like the ATM, this was another purpose-built node or swelling in the same plastic wall. They hadn't had one of these on Sunset, and Praisegod had had to double as GlobEx clerk and/or USPO employee, the latter causing her occasionally to frown, as her parents' sect identified all things federal as aspects of Satan.

He who hesitates, Rydell's father had taught him, is safe, and Rydell had tried hard, in the course of his life, to practice that sort of benign procrastination. Just about everything that had ever landed him in deep shit, he knew, had been the result of not hesitating. There was in him, he didn't know why, that which simply went for it, and somehow at the worst possible time.

Look before you leap. Consider consequences. Think about it.

He thought about it. Someone had taken advantage of his brief but unwilling sojourn in Selwyn Tong's VR corridor to convey the suggestion that he should pick up his credit chip from this particular ATM, and then check GlobEx. This could most easily have been Tong himself, speaking as it were through a back channel, or it might have been someone, anyone, else, hacking into what Rydell supposed was scarcely a world-class secure site. The look of the change that had been wrought for Rydell's benefit, though, had had hacker written all over it. In Rydell's experience, hackers just couldn't resist showing off, and they tended to get all arty. And, he knew, they could get your ass in trouble and usually did.

He looked at the GlobEx bulge there.

Went for it.

It took him less time than it had to get the credit chip, to show his license and get the hatch open. It was a bigger package than he'd expected, and it was heavy for its size. Really heavy. Expensive-looking foam-core stuff, very precisely sealed with gray plastic tape, and covered with animated GlobEx Maximum Express holograms, customs stickers. He studied the waybill. It had come from Tokyo, looked like, but the billing was to Paragon-Asia Dataflow, which was on Lygon Street, Melbourne, Australia. Rydell didn't know anybody in Australia, but he did know that it was supposed to be impossible, and definitely was illegal, to ship anything internationally to one of these GlobEx pickups. They needed an address, private or business. These pickup points were only for domestic deliveries.

Damn. Thing was heavy. He got it under his arm, maybe two feet long and six inches on a side, and went back to get his bag.

Which he saw now was open, on the little counter there, and the guard with the pale eyebrows was holding Rydell's pink Lucky Dragon fanny pack.

"What are you doing with my bag?"

The guard looked up. "This is Lucky Dragon property."

"You aren't supposed to open people's bags," Rydell said, "says so on the notebook."

"I have to treat this as theft. You have Lucky Dragon property here."

Rydell remembered that he'd put the ceramic switchblade in the fanny pack, because he hadn't been able to think what else to do with it. He tried to remember whether or not that was illegal up here. It was in SoCal, he knew, but not in Oregon.

"That's my property," Rydell said, "and you're going to give it to me right now."

"Sorry," the man said deliberately.

"Hey, Rydell," said a familiar voice, as the door was opened so forcefully that Rydell distinctly heard something snap in the closing mechanism. "Son of a bitch, how they hangin'?"

Rydell was instantly engulfed in a fog of vodka and errant testosterone. He turned and saw Creedmore grinning fiercely, quite visibly free of the human condition. Behind him loomed a larger man, pale and fleshy, his dark eyes set close together.

"You're drunk," snapped the security guard. "Get out."

"Drunk?" Creedmore winced grotesquely, miming some crippling emotional pain. "Says I'm *drunk . . .*" Creedmore turned to the man behind him. "Randy, this *motherfucker* says I'm drunk."

The corners of the large man's mouth, which was small and strangely delicate in such a heavy, stubbled face, turned instantly down, as if he were genuinely and very, very deeply saddened to learn that it was possible for one human being to treat another in so unkind a way. "So whump his faggot ass, then," the large man suggested softly, as if the prospect held at least some wistful possibility, however distant, of cheer after great disappointment.

"*Drunk?*" Creedmore was facing the security man again. He leaned across the counter, his chin level with the top of Rydell's bag. "What kinda shit you tryin' to lay off on my buddy here?"

Creedmore was radiating an amphetamine-reptile menace now, his anger gone right off the mammalian scale. Rydell saw a little muscle pulsing in Creedmore's cheek, steady and involuntary as some tiny extra heart. Seeing that Creedmore had the guard's undivided attention, Rydell grabbed his bag with one hand, the pink fanny pack with the other.

The guard tried to snatch them back. Which was definitely a mistake, as the attempt occupied both his hands.

"Suck my *dick!*" Creedmore shrieked, striking with far more speed and force than Rydell would've credited him with, and sank his fist wrist-deep into the guard's stomach, just below the sternum. Taken by surprise, the guard doubled forward. Rydell, as Creedmore was winding back to slug the man in the face, managed to tangle Creedmore's wrist in the straps of the fanny pack, almost dropping the bulky parcel in the process.

"Come *on,* Buell," Rydell said, spinning Creedmore back out the door. Rydell knew someone would've hit a foot button by now.

"Motherfucker says I'm drunk," Creedmore protested.

"Well, you are, Buell," said the heavy man, ponderously, behind them.

Creedmore giggled.

"Let's get out of here," Rydell said, starting for the bridge. As he walked, he was trying to stuff the fanny pack back into his duffel and trying not to lose his precarious underarm grip on the GlobEx package. A twisting gust of wind blew grit into his eyes, and, blinking down to clear them, he noticed for the first time that the waybill was addressed not to him but to "Colin Laney."

Colin space Laney. So why had they let Rydell pick it up?

Then they were in the thick of the crowd, headed up the ramp of the lower level.

"What is this shit?" Creedmore asked, peering up.

"San Francisco-Oakland Bay," Rydell said.

"Shit," Creedmore said, squinting at the crowd, "smells like a fuckin' baitbox. Bet you you could get you some weird-ass pussy, out here."

"I need a drink," the heavy man with the delicate mouth said softly.

"I think I do too," said Rydell.

22. VEXED

FONTAINE has two wives.

Not, he will tell you, a condition to aspire to.

They live, these two wives, in uneasy truce, in a single establishment, nearer the Oakland side. Fontaine has for some time now been opting to sleep here, in his shop.

The younger wife (at forty-eight, by some five years) is a Jamaican originally from Brixton, tall and light-skinned, whom Fontaine has come to regard as punishment for all his former sins.

Her name is Clarisse. Incensed, she reverts to the dialect of her childhood: "You tek de prize, Fonten."

Fontaine has been taking the prize for some years now, and he is taking it again today, Clarisse standing angrily before him with a shopping bag full of what appear to be catatonic Japanese babies.

These are in fact life-sized dolls, manufactured in the closing years of the previous century for the solace of distant grandparents, each one made to resemble photographs of an actual infant. Produced by a firm in Meguro called Another One, they are increasingly collectible, each example being to some degree unique.

"I don't want them," Fontaine allows.

"Listen up," Clarisse tells him, folding her dialect smoothly away, "there is no way you are not taking these. You are taking them, you are moving them, you are getting top dollar, and you are giving it to me. Because there is no way, otherwise, that I am staying where you left me, cheek by jowl with that mad bitch you married."

Who I was married to when you married me, thinks Fontaine, and no secret about it. The reference being to Tourmaline Fontaine, aka Wife One, whom Fontaine thinks of as being only adequately described by the epithet "mad bitch."

Tourmaline is an utter terror; only her vast girth and abiding torpor prevent her coming here.

"Clarisse," he protests, "if they were 'mint in box'—"

"These never mint in box, idiot! They always played with!"

"Then you know the market better than I do, Clarisse. You sell 'em."

"You want to talk child support?"

Fontaine looks down at the Japanese dolls. "Man, those things ugly. Look dead, you know?"

"'Cause you gotta turn 'em on, fool." Clarisse sets the bag on the floor and snatches up a naked baby boy. She stabs a long emerald-green fingernail into the back of the doll's neck. She is attempting to demonstrate the thing's other, uniquely individual feature, digitally recorded infant sounds, or possibly even first words, but what they hear instead is heavy, labored breathing, followed by a childish giggle and a ragged chorus of equally childish fuck-you's. Clarisse frowns. "Somebody been messing with it."

Fontaine sighs. "I'll do what I can. You leave 'em here. I'm not promising anything."

"You better believe I leave 'em here," Clarisse says, tossing the baby headfirst into the bag.

Fontaine glances into the rear of the shop, where the boy is seated cross-legged on the floor, barefoot, his head close-cropped, the notebook open on his lap, lost in concentration.

"Who the hell's that?" Clarisse inquires, noticing the boy for the first time as she steps closer to the counter.

Which somewhat stumps Fontaine. He tugs at one of his locks. "He likes watches," he says.

"Huh," Clarisse says, "he likes watches. How come you don't have your own kids over here?" Her eyes narrow, deepening the wrinkles at their outer corners, which Fontaine desires suddenly to kiss. "How come you got some 'spanic fatboy likes watches instead?"

"Clarisse—"

"Clarisse my butt." Her green eyes widen in furious emphasis, a green pale as drift glass, DNA-echo of some British soldier, Fontaine has often surmised, on some close Kingston night, these several generations distant. "You move these dolls or you be vexed, understand?"

She spins smartly on her heel, not easily done in the black galoshes she wears, and marches from his shop, proud and erect, in a man's long tweed overcoat Fontaine recalls purchasing fifteen years earlier in Chicago.

Fontaine sighs. Something weighs heavy on him now, evening coming on. "Legal, here, be married to two women," Fontaine says to the empty, coffee-scented air. "Fucking *crazy,* but legal." He shuffles over in his unlaced shoes and closes the front door, locks it behind her. "You still think I'm a bigamist or something, baby, but this is the State of Northern California."

He goes back and has another look at the boy, who seems to have discovered the Christie's auction.

The boy looks up at him. "Platinum tonneau minute repeating wristwatch," he says. "Patek Philippe, Geneve, number 187145."

"I don't think so," Fontaine says. "Kind of out of our bracket."

"A gold hunter-cased quarter repeating watch—"

"Forget it."

"—with concealed erotic automaton."

"Can't afford that either," Fontaine says. "Look," he says, "tell you what: that notebook's the slow way to look. I'll show you a fast way."

"Fast. Way."

Fontaine goes rummaging through the drawers of a paint-scabbed steel filing cabinet, until eventually he comes up with an old pair of military eyephones. The rubbery lip around the binocular video display is cracked and peeling. It takes another few minutes to find the correct battery pack and to determine that it is charged. The boy ignores him, lost in the Christie's catalog. Fontaine plugs the battery pack into the eyephones and returns. "Here. See? You put this on your head . . ."

23. RUSSIAN HILL

THE apartment is large and has nothing in it that is not of practical use.

Consequently, the dark hardwood floors are bare and quite meticulously swept.

Seated in an expensive, semi-intelligent Swedish workstation chair, he is sharpening the knife.

This is a task (he thinks of it as a function) requiring emptiness.

He sits facing a nineteenth-century reproduction of a seventeenth-century refectory table. Six inches in from its nearest edge, two triangular sockets have been laser-cut into the walnut at precise angles. Into these, he has inserted a pair of nine-inch-long rods of graphite-gray ceramic, triangular in cross section, forming an acute angle. These hones fit the deep, laser-cut recesses perfectly, allowing for no movement whatever.

The knife lies before him on the table, its blade between the ceramic rods.

When it is time, he takes it in his left hand and places the base of the blade against the left hone. He draws it down, a single, smooth, sure stroke, pulling it toward him as he does. He is listening for any indication of imperfection, although this would only be likely if he had struck bone, and it has been many years since the knife struck bone.

Nothing.

He exhales, inhales, places the blade against the right hone.

The telephone rings.

He exhales. Places the knife on the table again, its blade between the hones. "Yes?"

The voice, emerging from several concealed speakers, is a voice he knows well, although it has been nearly a decade since he has shared physical space with the speaker. He knows that the words he hears come in from a tiny, grotesquely expensive piece of dedicated real estate somewhere in the planet's swarm of satellites. It is a direct transmission, and nothing to do with the amorphous cloud of ordinary human communication. "I saw what you did on the bridge last night," the voice says.

The man says nothing. He is wearing a shirt cut from very fine gray cotton flannel, its collar buttoned but tieless, French cuffs secured with plain round links of sandblasted platinum. He places his hands on his thighs and waits.

"They think you're mad," says the voice.

"Who do you employ to tell you these things?"

"Children," the voice says. "Hard and bright. The best I can find."

"Why do you bother?"

"I like to know."

"You like to know," the man says, adjusting the crease along the top of his left trouser leg, "but why?"

"Because you interest me."

"Do you fear me?" the man asks.

"No," the voice says, "I don't believe I do."

The man is silent.

"Why did you kill them?" the voice asks.

"They died," the man says.

"But why were you there?"

"I wished to see the bridge."

"They think you went there knowing you'd attract someone, someone who'd attack you. Someone to kill."

"No," says the man, a note of disappointment in his voice, "they died."

"But you were the agent."

The man shrugs. His lips purse. Then: "Things happen."

" 'Shit happens,' we used to say. Is that it?"

"I am unfamiliar with that expression," the man says.

"It's been a long time since I've asked for your help."

"That is the result of maturation, I would think," the man says. "You are less inclined now to move counter to the momentum of things."

Now the voice falls silent. The silence lengthens. "You taught me that," it says finally.

When he is positive that the conversation has ended, the man picks up the knife and places the base of its blade against the top of the right hone.

He draws it, smoothly, down and back.

24. TWO LIGHTS ON BEHIND

THEY found a dark place that felt as though it hung out beyond where the bridge's handrails would've been. Not a very deep space, but long, the bar along the bridge side and the opposite all mismatched windows, looking south, past the piers, to China Basin. The panes were filthy, patched into their mullions with yellowing translucent gobs of silicone.

Creedmore in the meantime had become startlingly lucid, really positively cordial, introducing his companion, the fleshy man, as Randall James Branch Cabell Shoats, from Mobile, Alabama. Shoats was a session guitarist, Creedmore said, in Nashville and elsewhere.

"Pleased to meet you," said Rydell. Shoats' grip was cool and dry and very soft but studded with concise, rock-hard calluses, so that his hand felt to Rydell like a kid glove set with rough garnets.

"Any friend of Buell's," Shoats said, with no apparent irony.

Rydell looked at Creedmore and wondered what trough or plateau of brain chemistry the man was currently traversing and how long it would be until he decided to alter it.

"I have to thank you for what you did back there, Buell," Rydell said, because it was true. It was also true that Rydell wasn't sure you could say Creedmore had done it so much as been it, but the way things had worked out, it looked as though Creedmore and Shoats had happened along at exactly the right time, although Rydell's own Lucky Dragon experience suggested to him that it was far from over.

"Sons of bitches," Creedmore said, as if commenting generally on the texture of things.

Rydell ordered a round of beer. "Listen, Buell," Rydell said, "it's possible they'll come looking for us, 'cause of what happened."

"Why the fuck? We're here, them sons of bitches back there."

"Well, Buell," Rydell said, pretending to himself he was having to explain this to a stubborn and willfully obtuse six-year-old, "I'd just picked up this package here, before we had us our little argument, and then you poked the security man in the gut. He won't be too happy about it, and chances are he'll recall that I was carrying this package. Big GlobEx logo here, see? So he can look in the GlobEx records and get video of me, voiceprint, whatever, and give it to the police."

"The police? Sumbitch wants to make trouble, we give it to 'im, right?"

"No," said Rydell, "that won't help."

"Well, then," said Creedmore, resting his hand on Rydell's shoulder, "we'll come see you till you're out."

"Well, no, Buell," Rydell said, shrugging off the hand. "I don't think he'll bother much about the police. More he'll want to find out who we work for and if he could sue us and win."

"Sue you?"

" 'Us.' "

"Huh," said Creedmore, absorbing this. "You in an ugly place."

"Maybe not," said Rydell. "Matter of witnesses."

"I hear you," said Randy Shoats, "but I'd have to talk to my label, see what the lawyers say."

"Your label," said Rydell.

"That's right."

Their beer arrived, brown long necks. Rydell took a sip of his. "Is Creedmore on your label?"

"No," said Randy Shoats.

Creedmore looked from Shoats to Rydell, back to Shoats. "All I did was poke him one, Randy. I didn't know it had anything to do with our deal."

"It doesn't," said Shoats, "long as you're able to go into the studio and record."

"Goddamn, Rydell," said Creedmore, "I don't need you comin' in here and fucking things up this way."

Rydell, who was fumbling under the table with his duffel, getting the fanny pack out and opening it, looked at Creedmore but didn't say anything. He felt the Kraton grips of the ceramic switchblade. "You boys excuse me," Rydell said, "I've gotta find the can." He stood up, with the GlobEx box under his arm and the knife in his pocket and went to ask the waitress where the Men's was.

For the second time that day, he found himself seated in but not using a toilet stall, this one considerably more odorous than the last. The plumbing out here was as makeshift as any he'd seen, with bundles of scummy-looking transparent tubing snaking everywhere, and NoCal NOT POTABLE stickers peeling off above the sink taps.

He took the knife out of his pocket and pressed the button, watching the black blade swing out and lock. Then he pressed it again, unlocking the blade, closed it, and opened it again. What was it about switchblades, he wondered, that made you do that? He figured that that was a big part of what made people want them in the first place, something psychological but dumb, monkey-brained. Actually they were kind of pointless, he thought, except in terms of simple convenience. Kids liked them because they looked dramatic, but if somebody saw you open one, then they knew you had a knife, and they'd either run or kick your ass or shoot you, depending on how they felt about it and how they happened to be armed. He supposed there could be very specific situations in which you could just click one open and stick somebody with it, but he didn't think they'd be too frequent.

He had the GlobEx box across his lap. Gingerly, remembering how he'd cut himself back in LA, he used the tip of the blade to slit the gray tape. It went through the stuff like a wire through butter. When he got it to the point where he thought he'd be able to open it, he cautiously folded the knife and put it away. Then he lifted the lid.

At first he thought he was looking at a thermos bottle, one of those expensive brushed-stainless numbers, but as he lifted it out, the heft of it and the general fineness of manufacture told him it was something else.

He turned the thing over, finding an inset rectangular section with a cluster of micro-sockets, but nothing else except a slightly scuffed blue sticker that said FAMOUS ASPECT. He shook it. It neither sloshed nor rattled. Felt solid, and there was no visible lid or other way to open it. He wondered about something like that going through customs, how the GlobEx brokers could explain what it was, whatever that was, and not something full of some kind of contraband. He could think of a dozen kinds of contraband you could stick in something this size and do pretty well if you got it here from Tokyo.

Maybe it did contain drugs, he thought, or something else, and he was being set up. Maybe they'd kick the stall's door in any second and handcuff him for trafficking in proscribed fetal tissue or something.

He sat there. Nothing happened.

He lay the thing across his lap and searched through the fitted foam packing for any message, any clue, something that might explain what this was. But there was nothing, so he put the thing back in its box, exited the stall, washed his hands in non-potable bridge water, and left, intending to leave the bar, and Creedmore and Shoats in it, when he'd picked up his bag, which he'd left them minding.

Now he saw that the woman, that Maryalice, the one from break-fast, had joined them, and that Shoats had found a guitar somewhere, a scuffed old thing with what looked like masking tape patching a long crack down the front. Shoats had pushed his chair back from the table to allow himself room for the guitar, between the table edge and his belly, and was tuning it. He wore that hearing-secret-harmonies expres-sion people wore when they tuned guitars.

Creedmore was hunched forward, watching, his wet-look streaked-blonde hair gleaming in the bar gloom, and Rydell saw a look there, an exposed hunger, that made him feel funny, like he was seeing Creedmore want something through the wall of shit he kept up around himself. It made Creedmore seem suddenly very human, and that some-how made him even less attractive.

Now Shoats, absently, produced what looked like the top of an old-fashioned tube of lipstick from his shirt pocket and began to play, using the gold metal tube as a slide. The sounds he coaxed from the guitar caught Rydell in the pit of his stomach, as surely as Creedmore had sucker-punched that security man: they sounded the way rosin feels on your fingers in a poolroom and made Rydell think of tricks with glass rods and the skins of cats. Somewhere inside the fat looping slack of that sound, something gorgeously, nastily tight was being figured out.

The bar, not crowded at this time of day but far from empty, had gone absolutely silent under the scraping, looping expressions of Shoats' guitar, and then Creedmore began to sing, something high and quavering and dirge-like.

And Creedmore sang about a train pulling out of a station, about the two lights on the back of it: how the blue light was his baby.

How the red light was his mind.

25. SUIT

HAVING abandoned sleep, Laney, neither a smoker nor a drinker, has taken to tossing back the contents of very small brown glass bottles of a patent specific for hangover, an archaic but still-popular Japanese remedy that consists of alcohol, caffeine, aspirin, and liquid nicotine. He knows somehow (somehow now he knows those things he needs to know) that this, along with periodic belts of a blue hypnotic cough syrup, is the combination he needs to continue.

Heart pounding, eyes wide to incoming data, hands cold and distant, he plunges resolutely on.

He no longer leaves the carton, relying both on Yamazaki (who brings medicines he refuses) and on a neighbor in the cardboard city, a meticulously groomed madman whom he takes to be an acquaintance of the old man, the builder of models, from whom Laney has leased, or otherwise obtained, this space.

Laney doesn't remember the advent of this mad one, whom he thinks of as the Suit, but that is not something he needs to know.

The Suit is, evidently, a former salaryman. The Suit wears a suit, the one suit, always. It is black, this suit, and was once a very good suit indeed, and it is evident from its condition that the Suit, in whichever carton he dwells, has a steam iron, lint rollers, surely a needle and thread, and the skill to use them. It is unthinkable, for instance, that this suit's buttons would be anything less than firmly and symmetrically attached, or that the Suit's white shirt, luminous in the halogen of the master model-builder's carton, would be anything less than perfectly white.

But it is also obvious that the Suit has seen better days, as indeed must be true of any inhabitant of this place. It is obvious, for instance, that the Suit's shirt is white because he paints it daily, Laney surmises (though he doesn't need to know) with a white product intended for the renovation of athletic shoes. The heavy black frames of his glasses are held together with worryingly precise ligatures of black electrical tape,

tape cut to narrow custom widths with one of the old man's X-Acto knives and a miniature steel T-square and then applied with lapidary skill.

The Suit is as tidy, as perfectly squared away, as a man can be. But it has been a very long time, months or perhaps years, since the Suit has bathed. Every inch of visible flesh, of course, is scrubbed and spotless, but when the Suit moves, he exudes an odor quite indescribable, a high thin reek, it seems, of madness and despair. He carries, always, three identical, plastic-wrapped copies of a book about himself. Laney, who cannot read Japanese, has seen that the three copies bear the same smiling photograph of the Suit himself, no doubt in better days, and holding, for some reason, a hockey stick. Laney knows (without knowing how he knows) that this was one of those self-advertising, smugly inspirational autobiographies that certain executives pay to have ghostwritten. But the rest of the Suit's story is occluded, to Laney, and very probably to the Suit as well.

Laney has other things on his mind, but it does occur to him that if it is the Suit he sends out to the drugstore as his more presentable representative, then he, Laney, is in bad shape indeed.

And he is, of course, but that seems, against the flood of data flowing Nile-wide and constantly through him, from inner horizon to inner horizon, scarcely a concern.

Laney is aware now of gifts without name. Of modes of perception that may never have previously existed.

He has, for instance, a directly *spatial* sense of something very near the totality of the infosphere.

He feels it as a single indescribable shape, something brailled out for him against a ground or backdrop of he knows not what, and it hurts him, in the poet's phrase, like the world hurts God. Within this, he palps nodes of potentiality, strung along lines that are histories of the happened becoming the not-yet. He is very near, he thinks, to a vision in which past and future are one and the same; his present, when he is forced to reinhabit it, seems increasingly arbitrary, its placement upon the time line that is Colin Laney more a matter of convenience than of any absolute now.

All his life Laney has heard talk of the death of history, but confronted with the literal shape of all human knowledge, all human memory, he begins to see the way in which there never really has been any such thing.

No history. Only the shape, and it comprised of lesser shapes, in squirming fractal descent, on down into the infinitely finest of resolutions.

But there is will. "Future" is inherently plural.

And thus he chooses not to sleep and sends the Suit for more Regain, and he notices, as the Suit crawls out beneath the melon-tinted blanket, that the man's ankles are painted, in imitation of black socks, with something resembling asphalt.

26. BAD SECTOR

CHEVETTE bought two chicken sandwiches off a cart on the upper level and went back to find Tessa.

The wind had shifted, then died down, and with it that pre-storm tension, that weird elation.

Storms were serious business on the bridge, and even a gusty day would up the probability of someone getting hurt. In a rising wind the bridge could feel like a ship, anchored rock solid to the bottom of the bay, but straining. The bridge itself never really moved, no matter what (although she supposed it must have, in the quake, which was why it was no longer used for what it had been built for), but everything that had been added subsequently, all of that, with the wrong kind of luck, could move, and did sometimes with disastrous results. So that was what sent people running, when a wind got up, to check turnbuckles, lengths of aircraft cable, dubious webworks of two-by-four fir . . .

Skinner had taught her all that, more in passing than as formal lessons, though he'd had his way of giving formal lessons. One of those had been about how it had felt to be out here the night the bridge was first occupied by the homeless. What it had felt like to climb and topple the chainlink barriers, erected after the quake caused enough structural damage to suspend traffic.

Not that long ago, as years were measured, but some kind of lifetime in terms of concept of place. Skinner had shown her pictures, what the bridge looked like before, but she simply can't imagine that people wouldn't have lived here. He'd also shown her drawings of older bridges too, bridges with shops and houses on them, and it just made sense to her. How could you have a bridge and not live on it?

She loves it here, admits it now in her heart, but there is also something in her, watching, that feels not a part of. A self-consciousness, as though she herself is making the sort of docu Tessa wanted to make, some inner version of all the products Carson coordinated for Real One.

Like she's back, but she isn't. Like she's become something else in the meantime, without noticing, and now she's watching herself being here.

She found Tessa squatting in front of a narrow shopfront, BAD SEC-TOR spray-bombed across a plywood facade that looks as though it's been painted silver with a broom.

Tessa had God's Little Toy, semi-deflated, on her lap and is fiddling with something near the part that holds the camera. "Ballast," Tessa said, looking up, "always goes first."

"Here," Chevette said, holding out a sandwich, "while it's still warm."

Tessa tucked the Mylar balloon between her knees and accepts the greasy paper packet.

"Got any idea where you want to sleep tonight?" Chevette asked, unwrapping her own sandwich.

"In the van," Tessa said, around a mouthful. "Got bags, foam."

"Not where it is," Chevette told her. "Kinda cannibal, around there."

"Where then?"

"If it's still got wheels, there's a place over by one of the piers, foot of Folsom, where people park and sleep. Cops know about it, but they go easy; easier for them if people all park in one place, to camp. But it can be hard to get a place."

"This is good," Tessa said to her sandwich, wiping grease from her lips with the back of her hand.

"Bridge chickens. Raise 'em over by Oakland, feed 'em scraps and stuff." She bit into her sandwich. The bread was a square bun of sourdough white, dusted with flour. She chewed, staring into the window of this Bad Sector place.

Flat square tabs or sheets of plastic, different sizes and colors, baffled her, but then she got it: these were data disks, old magnetic media. And those big, round, flat black plastic things were analogue audio media, a mechanical system. You stuck a needle in a spiral scratch and spun the thing. Biting off more sandwich, she stepped past Tessa for a better look. There were reels of fine steel wire, ragged pink cylinders of wax with faded paper labels, yellowing transparent plastic reels of quarter-inch brown tape . . .

Looking past the display, she could see a lot of old hardware side by side on shelves, most of it in that grubby beige plastic. Why had people, for the first twenty years of computing, cased everything in that? Anything digital, from that century, it was pretty much guaranteed to be that sad-ass institutional beige, unless they'd wanted it to look more dramatic, more cutting edge, in which case they'd opted for black. But mostly this old stuff was molded in nameless shades of next-to-nothing, nondescript sort-of-tan.

"This is buggered," sighed Tessa, who'd finished her sandwich and gone back to poking at God's Little Toy with the driver. She stuck out her hand, offering Chevette the driver. "Give it back to him, okay?"

"Who?"

"The sumo guy inside."

Chevette took the little micro-torque tool and went into Bad Sector.

There was a Chinese kid behind the counter who looked like he might weigh in somewhere over two hundred pounds. He had that big pumpkin head the sumo guys had too, but his was recently shaven and he had a soul patch. He had a short-sleeve print shirt on, big tropical flowers, and a conical spike of blue Lucite through the lobe of his left ear. He was standing, behind a counter, in front of a wall covered with dog-eared posters advertising extinct game platforms.

"This your driver, right?"

"She have any luck with it?" He made no move to take it.

"I don't think so," Chevette said, "but I think she pinpointed the problem." She heard a faint, rapid clicking. Looked down to see a six-inch robot marching briskly across the countertop on big cartoony feet. It had that man-in-armor look, segmented glossy white shells over shiny steel armatures. She'd seen these before: it was a fully remote peripheral, controlled by a program that would take up most of a standard notebook. It came to a halt, put its hands together, executed a perfect miniature bow, straightened, held up its little clip hands for the driver. She let it take the driver, the pull of the little arms somehow scary. It straightened up, putting the driver over its shoulder like a miniature rifle, and gave her a military salute.

Sumo boy was waiting for a reaction, but Chevette wasn't having any. She pointed at the beige hardware. "How come this old shit is always that same color?"

His forehead creased. "There are two theories. One is that it was to help people in the workplace be more comfortable with radically new technologies that would eventually result in the mutation or extinction of the workplace. Hence the almost universal choice, by the manufac- turers, of a shade of plastic most often encountered in downscale con- doms." He smirked at Chevette.

"Yeah? What's two?"

"That the people who were designing the stuff were unconsciously terrified of their own product, and in order not to scare themselves, kept it looking as unexciting as possible. Literally 'plain vanilla,' you follow me?"

Chevette brought her finger close to the microbot; it did a funny lit- tle fall-back-and-shuffle to avoid being touched. "So who's into this old stuff? Collectors?"

"You'd think so, wouldn't you?"

"Well?"

"Programmers."

"I don't get it," Chevette said.

"Consider," he said, holding out his hand to let the little 'bot offer him the driver, "that when this stuff was new, when they were writing multi-million-line software, the unspoken assumption was that in twenty years that software would have been completely replaced by some better, more evolved version." He took the driver and gestured with it toward the hardware on the shelves. "But the manufacturers were surprised to discover that there was this perverse but powerful resistance to spending tens of millions of dollars to replace existing soft- ware, let alone hardware, plus retraining possibly thousands of employ- ees. Follow me?" He raised the driver, sighting down its shaft at her.

"Okay," Chevette said.

"So when you need the stuff to do new things, or to do old things better, do you write new stuff, from the ground up, or do you patch the old stuff?"

"Patch the old?"

"You got it. Overlay new routines. As the machines got faster, it didn't matter if a routine went through three hundred steps when it could actually be done in three steps. It all happens in a fraction of a second anyway, so who cares?"

"Okay," Chevette said, "so who does care?"

"Smart cookies," he said and scratched his soul patch with the tip of the driver. "Because they understand that all that really happens, these days, is that ancient software is continually encrusted with overlays, to the point where it's literally impossible for any one programmer to fully understand how any given solution is arrived at."

"I still don't see why this stuff would be any help."

"Well, actually," he said, "you're right." He winked at her. "You got it, girl. But the fact remains that there are some very smart people who like to have this stuff around, maybe just to remind themselves where it all comes from and how, really, all any of us do, these days, is just fixes. Nothing new under the sun, you know?"

"Thanks for the screwdriver," Chevette said. "I gotta go see a little black boy now."

"Really? What about?"

"A van," Chevette said.

"Girl," he said, raising his eyebrows, "you deep."

27. BED-AND-BREAKFAST

RYDELL sees it's dark, down here on the lower level, the narrow thoroughfare crowded and busy, greenish light of scavenged fluorescents seen through swooping bundles of that transparent plumbing, pushcarts rattling past to take up the day's positions. He took a flight of clanging steel stairs, up through a hole cut unevenly in the roadbed above, to the upper level.

Where more light fell, diffused through plastic, shadowed by the jackstraw country suspended above, shacks that were no more than boxes, catwalks in between, sails of wet laundry that had gone back up with the dying of the earlier wind.

Young girl, brown eyes big as the eyes in those old Japanese animations, handing out slips of yellow paper, "BED & BREAKFAST." He studied the map on the back.

He started walking, bag over his shoulder and the GlobEx box under his arm, and in fifteen minutes he'd come upon something announced in pink neon as the Ghetto Chef Beef Bowl. He knew the name from the back of the yellow flier, where the map gave it as a landmark to find the bed-and-breakfast.

Line up outside Ghetto Chef, a place with steamed-up windows, prices painted in what looked like nail polish on a sheet of cardboard.

He'd only ever been out here once before, and that had been at night in the rain. Seeing it this way, it reminded him of some gated attraction, Nissan County or Skywalker Park, and he wondered how you could have a place like this and not have security or even a basic police presence.

He remembered how Chevette had told him that the bridge people and the police had an understanding: the bridge people stayed on the bridge, mostly, and the police stayed off it, mostly.

He spotted a sheaf of the yellow fliers, thumbtacked to a plywood door, in a wall set back a few feet from the front of Ghetto Chef. It wasn't locked, and opened on a sort of hallway, narrow, walled with taut white plastic stapled over a framework of lumber. Somebody had drawn murals on either wall, it looked like, with a heavy black industrial marker, but the walls were too close together to see what the overall design was about. Stars, fish, circles with Xs through them . . . He had to hold his bag behind him and the GlobEx box in front, to go down the hallway, and when he got to the end he turned a corner and found himself in somebody's windowless kitchen, very small.

The walls, each covered in a different pattern of striped wallpaper, seemed to vibrate. Woman there, stirring something on a little propane cooker. Not that old, but her hair was gray and parted in the middle. Same big eyes as the girl, but hers were gray.

"Bed-and-breakfast?" he asked her.

"Got a reservation?" She wore a man's tweed sports coat, sleeves worn through at the elbows, over a denim jean jacket and a collarless flannel baseball shirt. No makeup. Looked windburned. Big hawk nose.

"I need a reservation?"

"We book through an agency in the city," the woman said, taking the wooden spoon out of whatever was coming to boil there.

"I got this from a girl," Rydell said, showing her the flier he still held, clutched against his bag.

"You mean she's actually handing them out?"

"Handed me this one," he said.

"You have money?"

"A credit chip," Rydell said.

"Any contagious diseases?"

"No."

"Are you a drug abuser?"

"No," Rydell said.

"A drug dealer?"

"No."

"Smoke anything? Cigarettes, a pipe?"

"No."

"Are you a violent person?"

Rydell hesitated. "No."

"More to the point, have you accepted the Lord Jesus Christ as your personal savior?"

"No," Rydell said, "I haven't."

"That's good," she said, turning down the propane ring. "That's one thing I can't tolerate. Raised by 'em."

"Well," Rydell said, "do I need a reservation to stay here or not?" He was looking around the kitchen, wondering where "here" might be; it was about seven feet on a side, and the doorway he stood in was the only apparent entrance. The wallpaper, which had buckled slightly from cooking steam, made the space look like an amateur stage set or something they'd build for children in a makeshift day care.

"No," she said, "you don't. You've got a handbill."

"You have space?"

"Of course." She took the pot off the cooker, placed it on a round metal tray on the small, white-painted table, and covered it with a clean-looking dish towel. "Go back out the way you came. Go on. I'll follow you."

He did as she said and waited in the open door for her to catch up with him. He saw that the Ghetto Chef line had gotten longer, if anything.

"No," she said, behind him, "up here." He turned and saw her hauling on a length of orange nylon rope, which brought down a counterweighted aluminum ladder. "Go on up," she said. "I'll send your bags."

Rydell put down his duffel and the GlobEx box and stepped up onto the ladder.

"Go on," she said.

Rydell climbed the ladder to discover an incredibly tiny space he was clearly expected to sleep in. His first thought was that someone had decided to build one of those Japanese coffin hotels out of offcuts from all the cheapest stuff at a discount building supply. The walls were some kind of light-colored wood-look sheathing that imitated bad imitations of some other product that had probably imitated some now-forgotten original. The tiny square of floor nearest him, the only part that wasn't taken up by wall-to-wall bed, was carpeted with some kind of ultra-low-pile utility stuff in a weird pale green with orange highlights. There was daylight coming in from the far end, by what he supposed was the head of the bed, but he'd have had to kneel down to make out how that was possible.

"Do you want to take it?" the woman called up.

"Sure do," Rydell said.

"Then pull up your bags."

He looked over and saw her loading his duffel and the GlobEx box into a rusty wire hamper she'd hung on the ladder.

"Breakfast at nine, sharp," she said, without looking up, and then she was gone.

Rydell hauled the ladder, with his luggage, up on its orange rope. When he got his stuff out, the ladder stayed up, held by its hidden counterweight.

He got down on his hands and knees and crawled into his bedroom, over the foam slab made up with one of those micro-furry foam-core blankets, to where some sort of multi-paned, semi-hemispherical plastic bubble, probably part of an airplane, had been epoxied into the outer wall. It was thick with salt, outside, looked like; a crust of dried spray. It let light in, but just a featureless gray brightness. It looked as though you slept with your head right up in there. Okay by him. It smelled funny but not bad. He should've asked her what she charged, but he could do that later.

He sat down on the foot of the bed and took off his shoes. There were holes in the toes of both his black socks. Have to buy more.

He pulled the glasses out of his jacket, put them on, and speed-dialed Laney. He listened to a phone ringing somewhere in Tokyo and imagined the room it was ringing in, some expensive hotel, or maybe it was ringing on a desk the size of Tong's, but real. Laney answered, nine rings in.

"Bad Sector," Laney said.

"What?"

"The cable. They have it."

"What cable?"

"The one you need for the projector."

Rydell was looking at the GlobEx box. "What projector?"

"The one you picked up from GlobEx today."

"Wait a minute," Rydell said, "how do you know about that?"

There was a pause. "It's what I *do,* Rydell."

"Listen," Rydell said, "there was trouble, a fight. Not me, another guy, but I was there, involved. They'll check the GlobEx security recordings and they'll know I signed for you, and they'll have footage of me."

"They don't," Laney said.

"Of course they do," protested Rydell, "I was there."

"No," Laney said, "they've got footage of *me.*"

"What are you talking about, Laney?"

"The infinite plasticity of the digital."

"But I signed for it. My name, not yours."

"On a screen, right?"

"Oh." Rydell thought about it. "Who can get into GlobEx and alter that stuff?"

"Not me," said Laney. "But I can see it's been altered."

"So who did it?"

"That's academic at this point."

"What's that mean?" Rydell asked.

"It means don't ask. Where are you?"

"In a bed-and-breakfast on the bridge. Your cough sounds better."

"This blue stuff," Laney said. Rydell had no idea what he meant. "Where's the projector?"

"Like a thermos? Right here."

"Don't take it with you. Find a shop there called Bad Sector and tell them you need the cable."

"What kind of cable?"

"They'll be expecting you," Laney said and hung up.

Rydell sat there on the end of the bed, with the sunglasses on, thoroughly pissed off at Laney. Felt like bagging the whole deal. Get a job back at that parking garage. Sit around and watch nature in downtown Detroit.

Then his work ethic caught up with him. He took off the glasses, put them in his jacket, and started putting his shoes back on.

28. FOLSOM STREET

FOOT of Folsom in the rain, all these soot-streaked RVs, spavined campers, gut-sprung vehicles of any description, provided that description included old; things that ran, if they ran at all, on gasoline.

"Look at that," Tessa said, as she edged the van past an old Hummer, ex-military, every square inch covered with epoxied micro-junk, a million tiny fragments of the manufactured world glittering in Tessa's headlights and the rain.

"Think there's a spot there," Chevette said, peering through the bad wiper wash. Tessa's van had Malibu-style wiper blades; old and hadn't been wet for quite a while. They'd had to creep this last block along the Embarcadero, when the rain had really started.

It was drumming steadily on the van's flat steel roof now, but Chevette's sense of San Francisco weather told her it wouldn't last all that long.

The black kid with the dreads had earned his fifty. They'd found him crouching there like a gargoyle on the curb, his face somehow already as old as it would ever need to be, smoking Russian cigarettes from a red-and-white pack he kept tucked into the rolled-up sleeve of an old army shirt, three sizes too big. The van still had its wheels on and the tires were intact.

"What do you think he meant," Tessa said, maneuvering between a moss-stained school bus of truly ancient vintage and a delaminating catamaran up on a trailer whose tires had almost entirely rotted away, "when he said somebody was looking for you?"

"I don't know," Chevette said. She'd asked him who, but he'd just shrugged and walked off. This after determinedly trying to hustle Tessa for God's Little Toy. "Maybe if you'd given him the camera platform, he'd've told me."

"No fear," Tessa said, killing the engine. "That's half my share of the Malibu house."

Chevette saw that there were lights on in the tiny cabin of the catboat, through little slit-like windows, and somebody moving in there. She started cranking down the window beside her, but it stuck after two turns, so she opened the door instead.

"That's Buddy's space there," said a girl, straightening up from the catamaran's hatch, her voice raised above the rain, hoarse and a little frightened. She hunched there, under some old poncho or piece of tarp, and Chevette couldn't make out her face.

"S'cuse us," Chevette said, "but we need to stop for the night, or anyway till this rain lets up."

"Buddy parks there."

"Do you know when he'll be back?"

"Why?"

"We'll be out of here dawn tomorrow," Chevette said. "We're just two women. You okay with that?"

The girl raised the tarp a fraction, and Chevette caught a glimpse of her eyes. "Just two of you?"

"Let us stay," Chevette said, "then you won't have to worry who else might come along."

"Well," the girl said. And was gone, ducking back down. Chevette heard the hatch dragged shut.

"Bugger leaks," Tessa said, examining the roof of the van with a small black flashlight.

"I don't think it'll keep up long," Chevette said.

"But we can park here?"

"Unless Buddy comes back," Chevette said.

Tessa turned the light back into the rear of the van. Where rain was already pooling.

"I'll get the foam and the bags up here," Chevette said. "Keep 'em dry till later, anyway."

She climbed back between the seats.

29. VICIOUS CYCLE

RYDELL found a map of the bridge in his sunglasses, a shopping and restaurant guide for tourists. It was in Portuguese, but you could toggle to an English version.

It took him a while; a wrong move on the rocker-pad and he'd wind up back in those Metro Rio maps, but finally he'd managed to pull it up. Not a GPS map, just drawings of both levels, set side by side, and he had no way of knowing how up-to-date it was.

His bed-and-breakfast wasn't on it, but Ghetto Chef Beef Bowl was (three and a half stars) and Bad Sector was too.

The lozenge that popped up when he clicked on Bad Sector described it as a source for "retro hard and soft, with an idiosyncratic twentieth-century bent." He wasn't sure about that last part, but he could at least see where the place was: lower level, not far from that bar he'd gone in with Creedmore and the guitar player.

There was a cabinet to put stuff in, behind the triple-faux paneling, so he did: his duffel and the GlobEx box with the thermos thing. He put the switchblade, after some thought, under the foam slab. He considered tossing it into the bay, but he wasn't sure exactly where you could find a clear shot to do that out here. He didn't want to carry it, and anyway he could always toss it later.

It was raining when he came out beside Ghetto Chef Beef Bowl, and he'd seen it rain on the bridge before, when he'd first been here. What happened was that rain fell on the weird jumble of shanty boxes people had built up there and shortly came sluicing down through all of that in big random gouts, like someone was emptying bathtubs. There was no real drainage here, things having been built in the most random way possible, so that the upper level, while sheltered, was no way dry.

This seemed to have thinned the line for the Ghetto Chef, so that he briefly considered eating, but then he thought of how Laney had him on retainer and wanted him to get right over to this Bad Sector and get that cable. So instead he headed down to the lower level.

The rain had concentrated the action down here, because it was relatively dry. It felt like easing your way through a very long, very homemade rush-hour subway car, except over half the other people were doing that too, in either direction, and the others were standing still, blocking the way and trying hard to sell you things. Rydell eased his wallet out of his right rear pocket and into his right front.

Crowds made Rydell nervous. Well, not crowds so much as crowding. Too close, people up against you. (Someone brushed his back pocket, feeling for the wallet that wasn't there.) Someone shoving those long skinny Mexican fried-dough things at him, repeating a price in Spanish. He felt his shoulders start to bunch.

The smell down here was starting to get to him: sweat and perfume, wet clothing, fried food. He wished he was back in Ghetto Chef Beef Bowl, finding out what those three and a half stars were for.

He couldn't take much more of this, he decided, and looked over the heads of the crowd for another stairway to the upper level. He'd rather get soaked.

But suddenly it opened out into a wider section, the crowd eddying away to either side, where there were food stalls, cafés, and stores, and there was Bad Sector, right there, done up in what looked to him like old-fashioned aluminum furnace paint.

He tried to shrug the crowd-induced knots out of his shoulders. He was sweating; his heart was pounding. He made himself take a few deep breaths to calm down. Whatever it was he was supposed to be doing here, for Laney, he wanted to do it right. Get all jangled, this way, you never knew what could happen. Calm down. Nobody was losing it here.

He lost it almost immediately.

There was a very large Chinese kid behind the counter, shaved almost bald, with one of those little lip beards that always got on Rydell's nerves. *Very* large kid, with that weirdly smooth-looking mass that indicated a lot of muscle supporting the weight. Hawaiian shirt with big mauvy-pink orchids on it. Antique gold-framed Ray-Ban aviators and a shit-eating grin. Really it was that grin that did it.

"I need a cable," Rydell said, and his voice sounded breathless, and somehow it was not liking to hear himself sound that way that took him the rest of the way over.

"I know what you need," the kid said, making sure Rydell heard the boredom in his voice.

"Then you know what *kind* of cable I need, right?" Rydell was closer to the counter now. Ragged old posters tacked up behind it, for things with names like Heavy Gear II and T'ai Fu.

"You need two." The grin was gone now, kid trying his best to look hard. "One's power: jack to any DC source or wall juice with the inbuilt transformer. Think you can manage that?"

"Maybe," Rydell said, getting right up against the front of the counter and bracing his feet, "but tell me about this other one. Like it cables what to what *exactly*?"

"I'm not paid to tell you that, am I?"

There was a skinny black tool lying on the counter. Some kind of specialist driver. "No," Rydell said, picking up the driver and examining its tip, "but you're going to." He grabbed the kid's left ear with his other hand, pinched off an inch of the driver's shaft between thumb and forefinger, and inserted that into the kid's right nostril. It was easy hanging on to the ear, because the kid had some kind of fat plastic spike through it.

"Uh," the kid said.

"You got a sinus problem?"

"No."

"You could have." He let go of the ear. The kid stood very still. "You aren't going to move, are you?"

"No . . ."

Rydell removed the Ray-Bans, tossing them over his right shoulder. "I'm getting sick of people grinning at me because they know shit I don't. Understand?"

"Okay."

" 'Okay' what?"

"Just . . . okay?"

"Okay is: where are the cables?"

"Under the counter."

"Okay is: where did they come from?"

"Power's standard but lab grade: transformer, current-scrubber. The other, I can't tell you—"

Rydell moved the tool a fraction of an inch, and the kid's eyes widened. "Not okay," Rydell said.

"I don't know! Know we had to have it assembled to spec, in Fresno. I just work here. Nobody tells me who pays for what." He took a deep, shuddering breath. "If they did, somebody like you'd come in and make me tell, right?"

"Yeah," Rydell said, "and that means people are liable to come in and *torture* your ass into telling them things *you don't even know . . .*"

"Look in my shirt pocket," the kid said carefully. "There's an address. Get on there, talk to whoever, maybe they'll tell you."

Rydell gently patted the front of the pocket, making sure there wouldn't be any used needles or other surprises. The massive pad of muscle behind the pocket gave him pause. He slid two fingers in and came up with a slip of cardboard torn from something larger. Rydell saw the address of a website. "The cable people?"

"Don't know. But I don't know why else I'd be supposed to give it to you."

"And that's all you know?"

"Yes."

"Don't move," said Rydell. He removed the tool from the kid's nostril. "Cables under the counter?"

"Yes."

"I don't think I want you to reach under there."

"Wait," said the kid, raising his hands. "I gotta tell you: there's a 'bot under there. It's got your cables. It just wants to give 'em to you, but I didn't want you to get the wrong idea."

"A 'bot?"

"It's okay!"

Rydell watched as a small, highly polished steel claw appeared, looking a lot like a pair of articulated sugar tongs his mother had owned. It grasped the edge of the counter. Then the thing chinned itself, one-handed, and Rydell saw the head. It got a leg up and mounted the counter, pulling a couple of heat-sealed plastic envelopes behind it. Its head was disproportionately small, with a sort of wing-like projection or antenna sticking up on one side. It was in that traditional Japanese style, the one that looked as though a skinny little shiny robot was dressed in oversized white armor, its forearms and ankles wider than its upper arms and thighs. It carried the transparent envelopes, each one containing a carefully wound cable, across the counter, put them down, and backed up. Rydell picked them up, shoved them into the pocket of his khakis, and did a pretty good imitation of the robot, backing up.

As the kid's Ray-Bans came into his peripheral vision, he saw that they hadn't broken.

When he was in the doorway, he tossed the black driver to the kid, who missed catching it. It hit the Heavy Gear II poster and dropped out of sight behind the counter.

RYDELL found a laundromat-café combination, called Vicious Cycle, that had one hotdesk at the back, behind a black plastic curtain. The curtain suggested to him that people used this to access porn sites, but why you'd want to do that in a laundromat was beyond him.

He was glad of the curtain anyway, because he hated the idea of people watching him talk to people who weren't there, so he generally avoided accessing websites in public places. He didn't know why using the phone, audio, wasn't embarrassing that way. It just wasn't. When you were using the phone you didn't actually *look* like you were talking to people who weren't there, even though you were. You were talking to the phone. Although, now that he thought about it, using the phone in the earpiece of the Brazilian glasses would look that way too.

So he pulled the curtain shut and stood there in the background rumble of the dryers, a sound he'd always found sort of comforting. The glasses were already cabled to the hotdesk. He put them on and worked the rocker-pad, inputting the address.

There was a brief and probably entirely symbolic passage through some kind of neon rain, heavy on the pinks and greens, and then he was there.

Looking into that same empty space that he'd glimpsed in Tong's corridor: some kind of dust-blown, sepulchral courtyard, lit from above by a weird, attenuated light.

This time though, he could look up. He did. He seemed to be standing on the floor of a vast empty air shaft that rose up, canyon-like, between walls of peculiarly textured darkness.

High above, a skylight he guessed to be the size of a large swimming pool passed grimy sunlight through decades of soot and what he took, at this distance, to be drifts of something more solid. Black iron mullions divided long rectangles, some of them holed, as by gunfire, through what he guessed was archaic wire-cored safety glass.

When he lowered his head, they were there, the two of them, seated in strange, Chinese-looking chairs that hadn't been there before.

One of them was a thin, pale man in a dark suit from no particular era, his lips pursed primly. He wore glasses with heavy, rectangular frames of black plastic and a snap-brim hat of a kind that Rydell knew only from old films. The hat was positioned dead level on his head, perhaps an inch above the black frames. His legs were crossed, and Rydell saw that he wore black wingtip oxfords. His hands were folded in his lap.

The other presented in far more abstract form: an only vaguely human figure, the space where its head should have been was coronaed in a cyclical and on-going explosion of blood and matter, as though a sniper's victim, in the instant of impact, had been recorded and looped. The halo of blood and brains flickered, never quite attaining a steady state. Beneath it, an open mouth, white teeth exposed in a permanent, silent scream. The rest, except for the hands, clawed as in agony around the gleaming arms of the chair, seemed constantly to be dissolving in some terrible fiery wind. Rydell thought of black-and-white footage, ground zero, slo-mo atomic hurricane.

"Mr. Rydell," said the one with the hat, "thank you for coming. You may call me Klaus. This," and he gestured with a pale, papery-looking hand, which immediately returned to his lap, "is the Rooster."

The one called the Rooster didn't move at all when it spoke, but the open mouth flickered in and out of focus. Its voice was either the sound-collage from Tong's or another like it. "Listen to me, Rydell. You are now responsible for something of the utmost importance, the greatest possible value. Where is it?"

"I don't know who you are," Rydell said. "I'm not telling you anything."

Neither responded, and then Klaus coughed dryly. "The only proper answer. You would be wise to maintain that position. Indeed, you have no idea who we are, and if we were to reappear to you at some later time, you would have no way of knowing that we were, in fact, us."

"Then why should I listen to you?"

"In your situation," said the Rooster, and its voice, just then, seemed composed primarily of the sound of breaking glass, modulated into the semblance of human speech, "you might be advised to listen to anyone who cares to address you."

"But whether or not you choose to believe what you are told is another matter," said Klaus, fussily adjusting his shirt cuffs and refolding his hands.

"You're hackers," Rydell said.

"Actually," said Klaus, "we might better be described as envoys. We represent," he paused, "another country."

"Though not, of course," said the perpetually disintegrating Rooster, "in any obsolete sense of the merely geopolitical—"

" 'Hacker,' " interrupted Klaus, "has certain criminal connotations—"

"Which we do not accept," the Rooster cut in, "having long since established an autonomous reality in which—"

"Quiet," said Klaus, and Rydell had no doubt where the greater authority lay. "Mr. Rydell, your employer, Mr. Laney, has become, for want of a better term, an ally of ours. He has brought a certain situation to our attention, and it is clearly to our advantage to come to his aid."

"What situation is that?"

"That is difficult to explain," Klaus said. He cleared his throat. "If indeed possible. Mr. Laney is possessed of a most peculiar talent, one which he has very satisfactorily demonstrated to us. We are here to assure you, Mr. Rydell, that the resources of the Walled City will be at your disposal in the coming crisis."

"What city," Rydell asked, "what crisis?"

"The nodal point," the Rooster said, its voice like the trickle of water far down in some unseen cistern.

"Mr. Rydell," said Klaus, "you must keep the projector with you at all times. We advise you to use it at the earliest opportunity. Familiarize yourself with her."

"With who?"

"We are concerned," Klaus went on, "that Mr. Laney, for reasons of health, will be unable to continue. We number among us some who are possessed of his talent, but none to such an extraordinary extent. Should Laney be lost to us, Mr. Rydell, we fear that little can be done."

"Jesus," said Rydell, "you think I know what you're talking about?"

"I'm not being deliberately gnomic, Mr. Rydell, I assure you. There is no time for explanations now, and for some things, it seems, there may actually *be* no explanations. Simply remember what we have told you, and that we are here for you, at this address. And now you must return, immediately, to wherever you have left the projector."

And they were gone, and the black courtyard with them, compacted into a sphere of pink and green fractal neon that left residuals on Rydell's retinas, as it shrank and vanished in the dark behind the Brazilian sunglasses.

30. ANOTHER ONE

FONTAINE had spent most of the late afternoon on the phone, trying to lay Clarisse's creepy Japanese baby dolls off on a decreasingly likely list of specialist dealers.

He knew it wasn't the thing to do, in terms of realizing optimum cash, but dolls weren't one of his areas of expertise; besides, they gave him the horrors, these Another One replicas.

Specialist dealers wanted low wholesale, basically, so they could whip the big markup to collectors. If you were a collector, Fontaine figured, specialist dealers were nature's way of telling you you had too much money to begin with. But there was always a chance he'd find one who knew somebody, one specific buyer, to go to. That was what Fontaine had been hoping for when he'd started dialing.

But now it was eight calls later, and he was reduced to talking to this Elliot, in Biscayne Bay, Florida, who he knew had once been put under electronic house arrest for something involving counterfeit Barbies. That was a federal rap, and Fontaine ordinarily avoided people like that, but Elliot did seem to have a line on a buyer. Although he was, as you'd naturally expect, cagey about it.

"Condition," Elliot said. "The three salient points here are condition, condition, and condition."

"Elliot, they look great to me."

" 'Great' is not on the NAADC grading scale, Fontaine."

Fontaine wasn't sure, but he thought that might be the National Association of Animatronic Doll Collectors. "Elliot, you know I don't know how to rate condition on these things. They've got all their fingers and toes, right? I mean, the fucking things look *alive*, okay?"

Fontaine heard Elliot sigh. He'd never met the man. "My client," said Elliot, speaking slowly, for stress, "is a *condition queen*. He wants them minty. He wants them mintier than minty. He wants them mint in box. He wants them new old stock."

"Hey, look," Fontaine said, remembering what Clarisse had said, "you don't get these things unused, right? The grandparents bought them as, like, surrogate offspring, right? They were big-ticket items. They got used."

"Not always," said Elliot. "The most desirable pieces, and my client owns several, are replicas ordered just prior to the unexpected death of the grandchild."

Fontaine took the phone from his ear, looking at it as though it were something dirty. "Fucking hell," Fontaine said, under his breath.

"What's that?" Elliot asked. "What?"

"Sorry, Elliot," Fontaine said, putting the phone back to his ear, "gotta take one on the other line. I'll get back to you." Fontaine broke the connection.

He was perched on a tall stool behind the counter. He leaned sideways to look at the Another One dolls in their bag. They looked horrible. They were horrible. Elliot was horrible. Clarisse was horrible too, but now Fontaine lapsed into a brief but intensely erotic fantasy involving none other, with whom he had not been conjugal in some while. That this fantasy literally involved Clarisse exclusively, he took to be significant. That it produced an actual erectile response, he took to be even more significant. He sighed. Adjusted his trousers.

Life, he reflected, was rough as a cob.

Through the sound of rain sluicing down around his shop (he'd rigged gutters) he could hear a faint but rapid clicking from the back room and noted its peculiar regularity. Each one of those clicks, he knew, represented another watch. He'd shown the boy how to call up auctions on the notebook, not Christie's or Antiquorum, but the living messy scrum of the net auctions. He'd shown him how to bookmark too, because he thought that picking what he liked might be fun.

Fontaine sighed again, this time because he had no idea what he would do about the boy. Having taken him in because he'd wanted a closer look at—well, had wanted, did want—the Jaeger-LeCoultre military, Fontaine would have found it impossible to explain to anyone why he had subsequently fed him, gotten him showered, bought him fresh clothes, and shown him how to use the eyephones. Actually he couldn't explain it to himself. He was not inclined to charity, he didn't think, but sometimes he found himself moving as if to right a particular wrong in the world. And this never made sense to Fontaine, really, because what he made right, he made right only for a little while, and nothing ever really changed.

This boy now, he very likely had some sort of brain damage, and most likely congenital, but Fontaine believed that trouble had no first cause. There was sheer bad luck, he knew that, but often as not he'd seen how cruelty or neglect or hard-luck genetics came twining up through the generations like a vine.

Now he dug down deep, into the pocket of his tweed slacks, where he was keeping the Jaeger-LeCoultre. By itself, of course, so that nothing else would scratch it. He pulled it out now and considered it, but the tenor of his thoughts prevented the momentary distraction, the small pleasure, he'd hoped to take from it.

But how on earth, he wondered, had the boy gotten hold of something like this, such an elegant piece of serious collector's ordnance?

And the workmanship of the strap worried him. He'd never seen anything quite like it, for all that it was very simple. An artisan had sat down with the watch, whose lugs were closed not by spring bars but permanently soldered rods of stainless steel, integral parts of the case, and cut and glued and hand stitched however many pieces of black calf leather. He examined the inside of the strap, but there was nothing, no trademark or signature. "If you could talk," Fontaine said, looking at the watch.

And what would it tell him? he wondered. The story of how the boy had gotten it might turn out to be not the most unlikely adventure it had had. Briefly he imagined it on some officer's wrist out in the Burmese night, a star shell bursting above a jungle hillside, monkeys screaming . . .

Did they have monkeys in Burma? He did know the British had fought there when this had been issued.

He looked down through the scratched, greenish glass that topped the counter. Watches there, each face to him a tiny and contained poem, a pocket museum, subject over time to laws of entropy and of chance. These tiny mechanisms, their jeweled hearts beating. Wearing down, he knew, through the friction of metal on metal. He sold nothing unserviced, everything cleaned and lubricated. He took fresh stock to a sullen but highly skilled Pole in Oakland to be cleaned, oiled, and timed. And he did this, he knew, not to provide a better, more reliable product, but to ensure that each one might better survive in an essentially hostile universe. It would've been difficult to admit this to anyone, but it was true and he knew it.

He put the Jaeger-LeCoultre back in his pocket and slid from the stool. Stood staring blankly into a glass-fronted cabinet, the shelf at eye level displaying military Dinky Toys and a Randall Model 15 "Airman," a stocky-looking combat knife with a saw-toothed spine and black Micarta grips. The Dinky Toys had been played with; dull gray base metal showed through chipped green paint. The Randall was mint, unused, unsharpened, its stainless steel blade exactly as it left the grinding belt. Fontaine wondered how many such had in fact never been used. Totemic objects, they lost considerable resale value if sharpened, and it was his impression that they circulated almost as a species of ritual currency, quite exclusively masculine. He had two currently in stock, the other a hiltless little leaf-point dirk said to have been designed for the US Secret Service. Best dated by the name of the maker on their saddle-sewn sheaths, he estimated them both to be about thirty years old. Such things were devoid of much poetry for Fontaine, although he understood the market and how to value a piece. They spoke to him mainly, as did the window of any army surplus store, of male fear and powerlessness. He turned away now, seeing the dying eyes of a man he'd shot in Cleveland, possibly in the year one of those knives had been made.

He locked the door, put the CLOSED sign up, and went into the back room where he found the boy still seated, cross-legged, as he'd left him, his face hidden by the massive old eyephones cabled to the open notebook in his lap.

"Hey," Fontaine said. "How's fishin'? You been finding anything you think we should bid on?"

The boy continued to monotonously click a single key on the notebook, the eyephones bobbing slightly in time.

"Hey," Fontaine said. "You gonna get netburn."

He squatted beside the boy, wincing at the pain it brought to his knees. He rapped once on the gray cowl of the eyephones, then gently removed them. The boy's eyes blinked furiously, swimming in the vanished light of the miniature video screens. His hand clicked the notebook a few times, then stopped.

"Let's see what you found," Fontaine said, taking the notebook from him. He absently touched a few keys, curious to see what the boy might have bookmarked.

He was expecting auction pages, each one with a scan and description of a given watch on offer, but what he found instead were numbered lists of articles that came up in an archaic font meant to recall typewriters.

He studied one list, then another. He felt something like cold air across the back of his neck and thought for a second that the front door was open, but then he remembered locking it.

"Shit," Fontaine said, pulling up more of these lists. "Shit, how'd you get this?"

These were bank records, confidential tallies of the contents of safety deposit boxes in banks of the brick-and-mortar sort, all apparently in midwestern states. And each list he saw contained at least one watch, very likely part of someone's estate, and very likely forgotten.

A Rolex Explorer in Kansas City. Some sort of gold Patek in a small town in Kansas.

He looked from the screen to the boy, aware of being privy to something profoundly anomalous.

"How'd you get into these files?" he asked. "This stuff is private. Should be impossible. *Is* impossible. How'd you do it?"

And only that absence behind the brown eyes, staring back at him, either infinitely deep or of no depth at all, he couldn't tell.

31. VIEW FROM A HELLWARD STANCHION

HE dreams a vast elevator, descending, its floor like the ballroom of some ancient liner. Its sides are open, in part, and he finds her there at the rail, beside an ornate cast-iron stanchion worked in cherubs and bunches of grapes, their outlines softened beneath innumerable coats of a black enamel glossy as wet ink.

Beyond the black stanchion and the aching geometry of her profile, a darkened world spreads to every horizon, island continents blacker than the seas in which they swim, the lights of great yet nameless cities reduced to firefly glimmers at this height, this distance.

The elevator, this ballroom, this waltzing host unseen now but sensed as background, as necessary gestalt, descends it seems down all his days, in some coded iteration of the history that brings him to this night.

If it is night.

The knife's plain haft, against his ribs, through a starched evening shirt.

The handles of a craftsman's tools bespeak an absolute simplicity, the plainest forms affording the greatest range of possibilities for the user's hand.

That which is overdesigned, too highly specific, anticipates outcome; the anticipation of outcome guarantees, if not failure, the absence of grace.

And now she turns to him, and she is in that instant all she ever was to him, and something more, for he is aware in that same instant that this is a dream, this mighty cage, descending, and she is lost, as ever, and now he opens his eyes to the gray and perfectly neutral ceiling of the bedroom on Russian Hill.

He lies dead straight, atop the blanket of gray lambs wool made up in military fashion, in his gray flannel shirt with its platinum links, his black trousers, his black wool socks. His hands are folded on his chest like the hands of a medieval effigy, a knight atop his own sarcophagus, and the telephone is ringing.

He touches one of the platinum cuff links, to answer.

"It isn't too late, I hope," says the voice.

"For what?" he asks, unmoving.

"I needed to talk."

"Do you?"

"More so, lately."

"And why is that?"

"The time draws near."

"The time?" And he sees again the view from the huge cage, descending.

"Can't you feel it? You with your right place at the right time. You with your letting things unfold. Can't you feel it?"

"I do not deal in outcomes."

"But you do," the voice says. "You've dealt a few for me, after all. You become an outcome."

"No," the man says, "I simply discover that place where I am supposed to be."

"You make it sound so simple. I wish that it were that simple for me."

"It could be," the man says, "but you are addicted to complexity."

"More literally than you know," says the voice, and the man imagines the few square inches of satellite circuitry through which it comes to him. That tiniest and mostly costly of principalities. "It's all about complexity now."

"It is about your will in the world," the man says and raises his arms, cupping the back of his head in his hands.

There follows a silence.

"There was a time," the voice says at last, "when I believed that you were playing a game with me. That all of that was something you made up for me. To annoy me. Or amuse me. To hold my interest. To ensure my patronage."

"I have never been in need of your patronage," the man says mildly.

"No, I suppose not," the voice continues. "There will always be those who need certain others not to be, and will pay to make it so. But it's true: I took you to be another mercenary, one with an expressed philosophy perhaps, but I took that philosophy to be nothing more than a way you had discovered of making yourself interesting, of setting yourself apart from the pack."

"Where I am," the man says to the gray neutral ceiling, "there is no pack."

"Oh, there's a pack all right. Bright young things guaranteeing executive outcomes. Brochures. They have brochures. And lines to read between. What were you doing when I called?"

"Dreaming," the man says.

"I wouldn't have imagined, somehow, that you dream. Was it a good dream?"

The man considers the perfect blankness of the gray ceiling. Remembered geometry of facial bone threatens to form there. He closes his eyes. "I was dreaming of hell," he says.

"How was it?"

"An elevator, descending."

"Christ," says the voice, "this poetry is unlike you." Another silence follows.

The man sits up. Feels the smooth, dark polished wood, cool through his black socks. He begins to perform a series of very specific excercises that involve a minimum of visible movement. There is stiffness in his shoulders. At some distance he hears a car go past, tires on wet pavement.

"I'm not very far from you at the moment," the man says, breaking the silence. "I'm in San Francisco."

Now it is the man's turn for silence. He continues his exercises, remembering the Cuban beach, decades ago, on which he was first taught this sequence and its variations. His teacher that day the master of a school of Argentine knife-fighting most authoritatively declared nonexistent by responsible scholars of the martial arts.

"How long has it been," the voice asks, "since we've spoken, face-to-face?"

"Some years," says the man.

"I think I need to see you now. Something extraordinary is on the verge of happening."

"Really," says the man, and no one sees his brief and wolfish smile, "are you about to become contented?"

A laugh, beamed down from the secret streets of that subminiature cityscape in geosynchronous orbit. "Not that extraordinary, no. But some very basic state is on the brink of change, and we are near its locus."

"We? We have no current involvement."

"Physically. Geographically. It's happening here."

The man moves into the final sequence of the exercise, remembering flies on the instructor's face during that initial demonstration.

"Why did you go to the bridge last night?"

"I needed to think," the man says and stands.

"Nothing drew you there?"

Memory. Loss. Flesh-ghost in Market Street. The smell of cigarettes in her hair. Her winter lips chill against his, opening into warmth. "Nothing," he says, hands closing on nothing.

"It's time for us to meet," the voice says.

Hands opening. Releasing nothing.

32. LOWER COMPANIONS

THE back of the van collected a quarter-inch of water before the rain quit. "Cardboard," Chevette told Tessa.

"Cardboard?"

"We'll find some, dry. Boxes. Open 'em out, put down a couple of layers. Be dry enough."

Tessa clicked her flashlight on and had another look. "We're going to sleep in that puddle?"

"It's interstitial," Chevette told her.

Tessa turned the light off, swung around. "Look," she said, pointing with the flashlight, "at least it isn't pissing down now. Let's go back to the bridge. Find a pub, something to eat, we'll worry about this later."

Chevette said that would be fine, just as long as Tessa didn't bring God's Little Toy, or in any other way record the rest of the evening, and Tessa agreed to that.

They left the van parked there, and walked back along the Embarcadero, past razor wire and barricades that sealed (ineffectually, Chevette knew) the ruined piers. There were dealers in the shadows there, and before they'd gotten to the bridge they were offered speed, plug, weed, opium, and dancer. Chevette explained that these dealers weren't sufficiently competitive to take and hold positions farther along, nearer the bridge. Those were the coveted spots, and the dealers along the Embarcadero were either moving toward or away from that particular arena.

"How do they compete?" Tessa asked. "Do they fight?"

"No," said Chevette, "it's the market, right? The ones with good shit, good prices, and they turn up, well, the users want to see *them*. Somebody came with bad shit, bad prices, the users drive 'em off. But you can see them change, when you live here; see 'em every day, most of that stuff, if they're using themselves, it'll take 'em down. Wind up back down here, then you just don't see 'em."

"They don't sell on the bridge?"

"Well," Chevette said, "yeah, they do, but not so much. And when they do, they're quieter about it. You don't get offered on the bridge, so much, not if they don't know you."

"So how is it like that?" Tessa asked. "How do people know not to? Where does the rule come from?"

Chevette thought about it. "It isn't a rule," she said. "It's just you aren't supposed to *do* it." Then she laughed. "I don't know: it's just like that. Like there aren't too many fights, but the ones there are tend to be serious, and people get hurt."

"How many people actually live out here?" Tessa asked as they walked up the ramp from Bryant.

"I don't know," Chevette said. "Not sure anyone does. Used to be, everyone who did anything here, who had a business going, they lived here. 'Cause you have to. Have to be in possession. No rent or anything. Now, though, you get businesses that are run like businesses, you know? That Bad Sector we were in. Somebody owns all that stock, they built that storefront, and I bet they pay that sumo boy to sleep in the back, hold it down for them."

"But you didn't work here, when you lived here?"

"Nah," Chevette said, "I was messin', soon as I could. Got myself a bike and I was all over town."

They made their way into the lower level, past boxes of fish on ice, until they came to a place Chevette remembered on the south side. It had food sometimes, sometimes music, and it had no name.

"They do good hot wings in here," Chevette said. "You like hot wings?"

"I'll let you know after I've had a beer." Tessa was looking around at the place, like she was trying to decide how interstitial it was.

It turned out they had an Australian beer Tessa really liked, called a Redback, came in a brown bottle with a red spider on it, and Tessa explained that these spiders were the Australian equivalent of a black widow, maybe worse. It was a good beer though, Chevette had to agree, and after they'd both had one, and ordered another, Tessa ordered a cheeseburger, and Chevette ordered a plate of hot wings and a side of fries.

This place really smelled like a bar: stale beer, smoke, fry grease, sweat. She remembered the first bars she'd ever gone into, places along rural highways back up in Oregon, and they'd smelled like this. The bars Carson had taken her to in LA hadn't smelled like anything much. Like aromatherapy candles, sort of.

There was a stage down at one end, just a low black platform raised about a foot above the floor, and there were musicians there, setting up, plugging things in. There was some kind of keyboard, drums, a mike stand. Chevette had never been that much into music, not any particular kind, although in her messenger days she'd gotten to like dancing in clubs, in San Francisco. Carson, though, he'd been very particular about what music he liked, and had tried to teach Chevette to appreciate it like he did, but she just hadn't gotten with it at all. He was into this twentieth-century stuff, a lot of it French, particularly this Serge Something, really creepy-ass, sounded like the guy was being slowly jerked off while he sang, but like it really wasn't even doing that much for him. She'd bought this new Chrome Koran, "My War Is My War," sort of out of self-defense, but she hadn't even liked it that much herself, and the one time she'd put it on, when Carson was there, he'd looked at her like she'd shit on his broadloom or something.

These guys, now, setting up on the little stage, they weren't bridge people, but she knew that there were musicians, some of them famous, who'd come out and record on the bridge just so they could say they had.

There was a big man up there, with a white, stubbly face and a sort of mashed-up cowboy hat on the back of his head. He was fiddling with an unplugged guitar and listening to a smaller man in jeans, wearing a belt buckle like an engraved silver dinner platter.

"Hey," Chevette said, indicating the bottle-blonde man with the belt buckle, "this girl gets molested in the dark, tells 'em it was a mesh-back did it. 'Well,' they say, 'how you know it was, if it was dark?' ' 'Cause he had a tiny little dick and a great big belt buckle!' "

"What's a meshback?" Tessa tilted back the last of her beer.

"Redneck, Skinner called 'em," Chevette said. "It's from those nylon baseball caps they used to wear, got black nylon mesh on the back, for ventilation? My mother used to call those 'gimme' hats . . ."

"Why?" Tessa asked her.

" 'Gimme one them hats.' Give 'em away free with advertising on them."

"Country music, that sort of thing?"

"Well, more like Dukes of Nuke 'Em and stuff. I don't think that's country music."

"It's the music of a disenfranchised, mostly white proletariat," Tessa said, "barely hanging on in post-post-industrial America. Or that's what they'd say on Real One. But we have that joke about the big buckles in Australia, except it's about pilots and wristwatches."

Chevette thought the man with the belt buckle was staring back at her, so she looked in the other direction, at the crowd around the pool table, and here there actually were a couple of the meshbacked hats, so she pointed these out to Tessa by way of illustration.

"Excuse me, ladies," someone said, a woman, and Chevette turned to face directly into the line of fire of some very serious bosom, laced up into a shiny black top. Huge cloud of blowsy blonde hair a la Ashleigh Modine Carter, who Chevette thought of as a singer meshbacks would listen to, if they listened to women, which she wasn't certain they did. The woman put two freshly opened Redbacks down on their table. "With Mr. Creedmore's compliments," she said, beaming at them.

"Mr. Creedmore?" Tessa asked.

"Buell Creedmore, honey," the woman said. "That's him over there getting ready to do the sound check with the legendary Randy Shoats."

"Is he a musician?"

"He's a singer, honey," the woman said and seemed to look more closely at Tessa. "You A&R?"

"No," Chevette said.

"Damn," the woman said, and Chevette thought for a second she might take the beers back. "I thought you might be from an alternative label."

"Alternative to what?" Tessa asked.

The woman brightened. "Buell's singing, honey. It isn't like what you probably think of as country. Well, actually, it's a 'roots' thing. Buell wants to take it back, back there past Waylon and Willie, to some kinda dark 'primal kinda heartland.' Kinda. Thing." The woman beamed, eyes slightly unfocused. Chevette got the feeling that all of that had been memorized, and maybe not too well, but that it was her job to get it out.

"Randy, he was teaching Buell one earlier, called 'There Was Whiskey and Blood on the Highway, but I Didn't Hear Nobody Pray.' That's a hymn, honey. Very traditional. Give me goosebumps to hear it. I think it's called that, anyway. But tonight's set is going to be 'more upbeat, electric.' "

"Cheers," Tessa said, "ta for the lager."

The woman looked puzzled. "Oh. You're welcome, honey. Please do stick around for the set. It's Buell's Northern California debut, and the first time he's actually sung with his Lower Companions."

"His what?" Chevette asked.

" 'Buell Creedmore and his Lower Companions.' I think it's a biblical reference, though I can't quote you chapter and verse." The woman pointed her straining bosom toward the stage and resolutely followed it in that direction.

Chevette didn't really want another beer. "She bought us these because she thought we were A&R." She knew about that because of Carson. A&R were the people in the music business who found and developed talent.

Tessa took a pull on her beer and watched the woman, who'd stopped to talk to one of the boys from the pool table, one of the ones who was actually wearing a meshbacked cap. "Do people like her live here?"

"No," Chevette said, "there's clubs in the city for this kind of thing, or sort of like it, but I've never seen a crowd like this out here before."

The sound check consisted of the man with the squashed cowboy hat playing guitar and the man with the belt buckle singing. They stopped and started a few times, on the one song they did, for various twiddlings of knobs, but the guitarist could really play (Chevette got the feeling he wasn't really letting it out yet, what he could do) and the singer could sing. It was a song about being sad and being tired of being sad.

The bar, meanwhile, was starting to fill up, with what looked to be a bunch of locals, regulars, and a bunch who weren't, who were here to hear the band. The locals tended to tattoos, facial piercings, and asymmetrical haircuts, while the visitors tended to hats (meshback and cowboy, mostly), jeans, and (on the men, anyway) guts. The guts tended to be the kind that looked as though they had moved in while their owners were unaware and had taken up residence on otherwise fat-free frames. The kind of gut that hangs over the top of a pair of jeans with a reasonably small waistband, swelling the front of a flannel shirt but cinched back in, below, with one of those big buckles.

She'd started on Creedmore's Redback out of boredom, when she spotted the singer himself headed their way. He had borrowed someone's meshbacked cap and pulled it on backward, over his weirdly wet-looking bleach-blonde hair. He was wearing an electric-blue cowboy shirt with the store creases still in it, horizontal across the chest, and the white pearlized snaps open halfway down the front, revealing a pale, white, decidedly concave chest that wasn't at all the color of his face, which she figured was painted on. He had what looked like tomato juice in each hand, in a tall glass with ice. "How do," he said. "Saw that Maryalice over here. Thought I'd bring the old girl a drink. I'm Buell Creedmore. You ladies enjoyin' your beer?"

"Yes, thanks," said Tessa and looked in the opposite direction. Creedmore did a quick, and to Chevette very obvious, piece of mental calculation, Chevette coming up as the one more likely to be profitably hit on. "You hear about us in the city here or over in Oakland?"

"We're just here for the hot wings," Chevette said, indicating the plate of chicken bones in front of her.

"They any good?"

"They're okay," Chevette said. "But we're just leaving."

"Leaving?" Creedmore took a big swig of his tomato juice. "Hell, we're on in ten. You oughta stay 'n' hear us." There was some weird-looking, greenish-sandy stuff, Chevette saw, around the rims of the glasses, and now some of this was stuck on Creedmore's upper lip.

"What you doin' with those Caesar's, Buell?" It was the big guitarist. "Now you promised me you wouldn't drink before the set."

"For Maryalice," Creedmore said, gesturing with a glass, "and this here's for the pretty lady." He put the one he'd had the swig from down in front of Chevette.

"So how come you got that garlic salt on your mouth?" the big man asked.

Creedmore grinned and wiped the back of his hand across his mouth. "Nerves, Randy. Big night. Gonna be okay . . ."

"It better be, Buell. I don't see some evidence you can hold your liquor, be the last gig you ever play with me." The guitarist took the drink out of Creedmore's hand, took a sip, made a face, and walked off, taking the drink with him.

"Sons of bitches," Creedmore said.

And it was at this point that Chevette saw Carson enter the bar.

Recognition, on her part, was instantaneous and one-hundred-percent positive. It was not Carson as dressed for lounges that smelled like aromatherapy, but Carson dressed for the knowing exploration of the lower reaches.

Chevette had actually been with him when he bought this outfit, so she'd had to hear about how the jacket was Alaskan steerhide (Alaskan steers having thicker hides, due to the cold winters), and a museum-grade reproduction of a 1940s original. The jeans were nearly as expensive, and more complicated in their sourcing, the denim woven in Japan on ancient, lovingly maintained American looms and then finished in Tunisia to the specifications of a team of Dutch designers and garment historians. This was the kind of stuff that Carson cared deeply about, this absolutely authentic fake stuff, and when Chevette saw him step through that entrance, she had absolutely no doubt that it was him.

And also, though she couldn't have said exactly how, she knew that she was in trouble. Maybe, she'd think later, it had been because he hadn't known she was looking, so he hadn't really been bothering to be the guy he had always pretended to be when he was with her, when he'd known she was looking.

It was like seeing a different guy, a very scary, very cold, very angry guy, and knowing it was Carson. Carson turning to scan the bar—

What she did next surprised her. It must have surprised Creedmore even more. The top of the huge silver buckle made a convenient handle. She grabbed it, pulled, and brought him down, loose-kneed, to kiss his mouth, throwing her arms around his neck and hoping the back of his head, in the backward meshback hat, was between her face and Carson's.

Creedmore's ready enthusiasm was, unfortunately, about what she'd have expected, had she had the time to think.

33. DURIUS

RYDELL was midway back, through that lower-level crunch, when his sunglasses rang. He got his back to the nearest wall, took them out, opened them, put them on.

"Rydell?"

"Yeah?"

"Durius, man. How are you?"

"Fine," Rydell said. The glasses were acting up; weirdly elongated segments of Rio street maps were scrolling down his field of vision. "How are you?" He heard the whine of a drill or power driver, somewhere in LA. "You at the Dragon?"

"Yeah," Durius said, "we got major construction under way here."

"What for?"

"Don't know," Durius said. "They're putting in a new node, back by the ATM. Where they had the baby food and child care products before, you know? Park won't say what it is; don't think he knows. All the branches gettin' 'em, whatever they are. How's your ride up? How's that Creedmore?"

"I think he's an alcoholic, Durius."

"No shit," Durius said. "How's the new job?"

"Well," Rydell said, "I don't think I've figured out much about it yet, but it's getting interesting."

"That's good," Durius said. "Well, just wanted to see how you're doing. Praisegod, she says hi. Wants to know if you like the glasses."

The Rio street maps shuddered, contracted, stretched again.

"Tell her they're great," Rydell said. "Tell her thanks."

"Will do," said Durius. "You take care."

"You too," Rydell said, the maps vanishing as Durius hung up.

Rydell removed the glasses and put them away.

Beef bowl. Maybe he could grab some Ghetto Chef Beef Bowl on the way back.

Then he thought about Klaus and the Rooster and decided he'd better check on the thermos first.

34. MARKET DISCONTINUITIES

"WHAT'S this look like to you, Martial?" Fontaine asked his lawyer, Martial Matitse, of Matitse Rapelego Njembo, whose premises consisted of three notebooks and an antique Chinese bicycle.

Martial made tooth-sucking noises on the other end of the line, and Fontaine knew he was looking at the lists the boy had pulled up. "They seem to be lists of the contents of safety deposit boxes, as required under state law in various jurisdictions. Antiterrorist legislation. Keeps people from stashing drug precursors, nuclear warheads, like that. Plus it was supposed to help prevent money laundering, but that was when money could still be big stacks of green paper. But if I were you, Fontaine, I would be asking my lawyer a different question. To wit: am I not breaking the law by being in possession of these documents?"

"Am I?" Fontaine asked.

Martial maintained telephone silence for a few seconds. "Yes," he said, "you are. But it depends on how you got them. And I have just determined that the actual owners of the listed properties, in every case, are dead."

"Dead?"

"Entirely. These are probate documents. Still protected by law, but I would say that some items on these lists are property, to be auctioned off as the various estates are executed."

Fontaine looked over his shoulder and saw the boy, still seated on the floor, down his third iced-guava smoothie.

"How did you get these?" Martial asked.

"I'm not sure," Fontaine said.

"You aren't supposed to be able to decrypt files like this," Martial said. "Not unless you're the fed. If someone else does the decryption, it's merely a privacy issue insofar as you're concerned. But if you're doing this yourself, or are knowingly party to it, you are in possession of or are party to possession of proscribed technology, which can earn you a stay in one of those extremely efficient prisons the private sector has done such a fine job of building and maintaining."

"I'm not," said Fontaine.

"Be that as it may," said Martial, "if you were, you might be able, through judicious application, and with all due secrecy, to use said technology to reveal certain lucrative market discontinuities. Follow me, Fontaine?"

"No," said Fontaine.

"Put it this way: if you have a way of getting hold of documents nobody else can, you might want to talk about it with someone who'd have an idea of exactly which documents might be most lucratively obtained."

"Hey, Martial, I'm not into—"

"Fontaine, please. Anyone who sells secondhand cutlery and old rat-sucked toys, I understand it's an avocation. A calling. You are not in it for the money, I know. However, if you have a back channel into something else, I advise you to consult with your lawyer, me, at your very earliest. Hear me?"

"Martial, I don't—"

"Clarisse has been making inquiries of another partner in our firm, Fontaine. I tell you that in confidence."

Fontaine was not happy to hear it.

"She is talking divorce, my friend."

"Gotta go, Martial. Customers."

Fontaine hung up. Martial's news about Clarisse was not all that new to Fontaine, but he had been so far successful in avoiding thinking about it.

He became aware of a soft, steady clicking and turned to see that the boy had put the eyephones back on.

35. ON AUTOMATIC

CHEVETTE hadn't closed her eyes when she'd pulled Creedmore down and kissed him, but with her arms locked around his neck, to hold him there and hide her from Carson, she couldn't see past the sleeve of Skinner's jacket. What she could see, past an out-of-focus view of Creedmore's cheekbone and left ear, was an adrenaline-sharp shot of Carson's progress through the crowd. This was sufficiently arresting that she had managed to ignore Creedmore's response, which had his tongue trying apparently to subdue hers with a so-far unsuccessful combination of speed and leverage, and his hands, up under Skinner's jacket, hunting frantically for nipple.

The crystal-clear shot of Carson was eclipsed by a close-up of Tessa, eyes wide with amazement and about to burst out laughing, just as Creedmore found one of the nipples he was after, and Chevette, in pure reflex, let go of his neck with her left arm and punched him, as hard and as discreetly as possible, in the ribs, going in with all the knuckle she could leverage.

Creedmore's eyes flew open, blue and bloodshot, and Chevette let go of him, ducked off her chair, and rolled under the table, all on automatic now. She thought she heard Creedmore's head hit the table as he tried to follow her, but now that he didn't have his mouth actually on hers, she was aware of the taste of it, and something naggingly familiar there, but that was just something her mind was doing while her body took her out of there the quickest way it saw. Which was a scramble on hands and knees, still under the table; out on the floor, still crouching but getting up speed; sprinting, still bent low, arms up to block anyone who might try to stop her; out through the door.

Where instinct, something, some recollection, took her right, toward Oakland.

And she didn't slow down until she felt it was safe to, but by then she'd realized what the taste in Creedmore's mouth was: dancer, and she wondered how much of that she'd taken on. Not much, probably, but she could feel it in the pounding of her heart, see it in a faint aura around every source of light now, and know it in the fact that none of what had just happened actually bothered her, very much.

Trouble could look abstract, on dancer.

Carson, she thought, was trouble, and seeing the look on his face then, a look she'd suspected, she now thought, but had never quite managed to catch there, had made her scared of him. She'd been scared of him since the time he'd hit her, but she hadn't understood it in quite the same way. He hadn't really hurt her much, not physically, when he'd hit her. She was coming from a place where she'd seen people maimed, hurt really bad, and this cute media boy, who didn't even know how to punch, how dangerous was that?

But now she saw, the residual drug in Creedmore's saliva having its effect, that what she'd been afraid of wasn't that he'd hit her that time, or the possibility he'd do it again, but some instinctive, underlying recognition that there was something wrong, something way worse. That he was bad news and covered it up. Always, more carefully even than he chose his clothes.

And Tessa, when Chevette had had the conversation with her that had resulted in her moving to Malibu, had said that she envied men the inability to get it up, when there was something wrong. Even if they don't consciously know, Tessa said, it won't happen. But we don't have that, so something can be just as wrong as can be, and we still stay. But you can't stay if he's hit you, because he'll do it again.

Walking on, toward Treasure now, the bridge gone spectral, monochrome, and maybe that was the dancer too, she didn't know.

"Out of control," she said. That was how she felt her life was now. She was just reacting to things. She stopped. Maybe she was just reacting to Carson.

"Hey. Chevette."

Turning to see a face she knew, though she couldn't put a name to it. Ragged pale hair above a thin hard face, bad scar snaking his left cheek. A sometime messenger from her Allied days, not part of her crew but a face from parties. "Heron," the name came to her.

"I thought you were gone," Heron said, displaying broken teeth.

Maybe something broken in his head too, it struck her. Or maybe just some substance, tonight.

"I was," Chevette said.

"Where?"

"SoCal."

"You ride down there? Messenger?"

"No," she said.

"I can't ride now," Heron said and swung his left leg, rigid, forward, catching his weight on it, something wrong there with his knee. "Tangled with a cage." A car, and she thought how long it had been since she'd heard that.

"You get insurance?"

"Shit no, cage from DoJ City." The Department of Justice. "I got lawyers on it, but . . ." Crooked shrug. "One of my lawyers, Njembo, you know those three guys? Refugees from the African Union, right? Njembo, he knows that Fontaine. You know Fontaine, right?"

"Yeah," Chevette said, glancing back over her shoulder. "He still out by Oakland, wives and kids?"

"No," Heron said, "no, he's got a shop, just up there." He pointed. "Sleeps there. Sells stuff to tourists. Njembo says his wives are after his ass." He squinted at her, the scar on his cheek catching the light. "You look good. Hair's different."

Something in that flash of scar catching in the edge of Creedmore's spit-high; she shivered, the dancer dealing her cards of Carson walking this way, that same expression on his face, hands in the pockets of his leather jacket.

"Good to see you, Heron."

"Yeah," he said, something sullen and untrusting, maybe longing, evident there, and again the crooked shrug, maybe just to shake some pain from his shoulders. He looked down and set off back the way she'd come, and she saw how twisted the accident had left him, hobbling, swinging his stiff leg as he went.

She zipped up Skinner's jacket and went looking for Fontaine's shop, wondering if she'd know it if she found it.

36. FAMOUS ASPECT

RYDELL bought a white foam take-out beef bowl from Ghetto Chef, then had to figure out how to get up the ladder one-handed, without spilling it.

Climbing a ladder with something hot in one hand was one of those things that you never ordinarily thought about, but that turned out to be difficult. You can't safely tuck a hot beef bowl under your arm, and when you climb with only one hand, you've got to move that hand fast, keep catching those rungs.

But he got up there, didn't spill any, and then he put it down while he unlocked the two-by-four and chicken-wire security grid. This had a chrome-plated Nepalese padlock on either side, and he'd found the keys, earlier, hanging on a nail. It was one of those deeply pointless arrangements, in terms of security, because anyone who wanted in could boltcut the padlocks, pry their hasps out of the wood, or just yank the chicken wire until the staples pulled out. On the other hand, if you went out, left it unlocked, and somebody took your stuff with no effort at all, he guessed you'd feel even stupider.

When he got it open, he settled down on the foot of the bed with his beef bowl and the plastic spoon they'd given him. He was just inhaling the steam when it came to him he should check on the thermosthing. The projector, Laney had called it. He sighed, put his beef bowl down, and got up (well, he had to crouch).

The GlobEx box was in the cabinet there, beside his bag, and the spun-metal cylinder was in the GlobEx box.

He sat back down, with the GlobEx box next to him on the bed, and got to work on his beef bowl, which was worth waiting for. It was strange how this kind of shaved, basically overcooked mystery meat, which he guessed really was, probably, beef, could be tastier, under the right circumstances, than a really good steak. He ate the whole thing, every last grain of rice and drop of broth and figured the tourist-trap map had put their three stars and a half in the right place.

Then he opened the GlobEx box and got the thermos-thing out. He looked at the FAMOUS ASPECT sticker again, and it didn't tell him any more than it had before. He stood the thing up on its base, on the green-and-orange carpet, and crawled back up the bed to get the switchblade. He used that to slice open the plastic envelopes containing the two cables and sat there looking at them.

The one that was standard power just looked like what you used to run a notebook off the wall, he thought, although the end that went into the thermos looked a little more complicated than usual. The other one though, the jacks on either end looked serious. He found the socket that one end of this obviously went into, but what was the other end supposed to fit? If the sumo kid was telling the truth, this was a custom cable, required to jack this thing into something that it might not usually be required to jack to. This one was optical, it looked like.

The power cable, that was easy. What took a while was finding a socket up here, but it turned out there was one (well, actually the end of an industrial-grade yellow extension cord) in the storage cabinet.

No control on the thing, that he could see, no switches. He plugged the power cable into the wall socket, then sat on the bed, the other end in his hand, looking at the silvery cylinder.

"Hell," he said and plugged the cable into the cylinder. Just as he did, he had the clearest possible vision of the thing being, absolutely and no doubt, brimful of plastic explosive and a detonator, just waiting for this juice—

But, no, if it had been, he'd be dead. He wasn't.

But the cylinder wasn't doing anything either. He thought he could hear a faint hum from it, and that was it.

"I don't get it," Rydell said.

Something flickered. Neon butterfly. Torn wings.

And then this girl was there, kneeling, right up close, and he felt his heart roll over, catch itself.

The how of her not being there, then being there. Something hurt in his chest, until he reminded himself to breathe.

If Rydell had had to describe her, he would've said beautiful, and been utterly frustrated in the attempt to convey how. He thought she had to be one of Durius' examples of hybrid vigor, but saying which races had been mixed was beyond him.

"Where are we?" she asked.

He blinked, uncertain as to whether she saw and addressed him, or someone else, in some other reality. "Bed-and-breakfast," he said, by way of experiment. "San Francisco-Oakland Bay."

"You are Laney's friend?"

"I— Well. Yeah."

She was looking around now, with evident interest, and Rydell felt the hairs stand up along his arms, seeing that she wore an outfit that exactly mirrored his own, though everything she wore fit her perfectly, and of course looked very different on her. Loose khakis, blue workshirt, black nylon jacket with a Velcro rectangle over the heart, where you stuck the logo of your company. Right down to black socks (with holes? he wondered) and miniature versions of the black Work-'N'-Walks he'd bought for Lucky Dragon. But the hair on his arms was up because he *knew,* he had seen, he had, that in the first instant of her being there, she'd crouched before him naked.

"I am Rei Toei," she said. Her hair was coarse and glossy and roughly but perfectly cut, her mouth wide and generous and not quite smiling, and Rydell put out his hand and watched it pass right through her shoulder, through the pattern of coherent light he knew she must be. "This is a hologram," she said, "but I am real."

"Where are you?" Rydell asked, withdrawing his hand.

"I'm here," she said.

"But where are you really?"

"Here. This is not a broadcast hologram. It is generated by the Famous Aspect unit. I am here, with you. Your room is very small. Are you poor?" She crawled past Rydell (he supposed she could've crawled through him, if he hadn't moved aside) to the head of his bed, examining the salt-caked hemisphere of plastic. Rydell could see now that she literally was a source of illumination, though somehow it reminded him of moonlight.

"It's a rented room," Rydell said. "And I'm not rich."

She looked back at this. "I meant no offense."

"That's okay," Rydell said, looking from her to the projector and back. "I mean, a lot of people, they'd think I'm poor."

"But more would think you rich."

"I don't know about that—"

"I do," she said. "There are, literally, more humans alive at this moment who have measurably less than you do. You have this sleeping place, you have clothing, I see you have eaten. What is your name?"

"Berry Rydell," he said, feeling a strange shyness. But he thought he at least knew who she was, or was supposed to be. "Look, I recognize you. You're that Japanese singer, the one who isn't . . . I mean, the one who—"

"Doesn't exist?"

"I didn't say that. I mean, weren't you supposed to be married to that Irish guy, Chinese, whatever? In that band?"

"Yes." She'd stretched out on the bed, on her stomach, hands propping her chin a few inches from the occluded plastic bubble. (Rydell had a flash of that seen from the water below, like the glaucous eye of some behemoth.) "But we did not marry, Berry Rydell."

"How do you know Laney?" he asked her, hoping to bring it around to some footing that he could stand on as well, whatever that might be.

"Laney and I are friends, Berry Rydell. Do you know where he is?"

"Not exactly," Rydell said, which was true.

She rolled over, gorgeous and quite literally glowing, in her incongruous mirroring of what he wore, which looked, on her, like the first and purest expression of some irresistible new fashion, and fixed him with a sorrowful stare. He would, in that moment, have happily and willingly locked eyes with her for however long she wanted and have sat there, effectively, forever. "Laney and I have been separated. I do not understand why, but I must trust that it is for our mutual and eventual good. Who gave you the projector, Berry Rydell?"

"I don't know," Rydell said. "It was shipped here GlobEx, but in Laney's name. Address in Melbourne, company called Paragon-Asia."

She raised her eyebrows. "Do you know why we are together in San Francisco, Berry Rydell?"

"No," he said, "do you?"

"Laney believes that the world will end soon," she said, and her smile was luminous.

He couldn't help but smile back. "I think we went through that one when the century rolled over."

"Laney says that that was only a date. Laney says that this is the real thing. But I have not spoken with him in weeks, Berry Rydell. I do not know how much closer we are now, to the nodal point."

37. A LITTLE SHIT MONEY

BOOMZILLA, with a little shit money tonight, debit chip he got off those truck bitches, goes down to Lucky Dragon. That's where he goes when he gets money, because they got all the shit.

Food he likes there, because it's not bridge food; food like on TV, out of a package. And everything: shit to look at, the games they got in there. Best place.

Someday he'll have his shit together right. He'll live in a house, and it will be clean as Lucky Dragon. All lit up like that, and he'll get those camera balloons like the truck bitches. Watch everybody's ass and nobody fuck with him.

Gets the chip out, walking up to the front, because if he has it in his hand, shows it to the security, security'll let him in. Security wants to know you're a player. Otherwise, you'd steal. Boomzilla understands that.

Tonight is different. Tonight a big white truck in front of Lucky Dragon. Biggest, cleanest truck he's ever seen. No writing on it, SoCal plates, couple of securities standing out by it. Boomzilla wonders if this what they bring the new games in? Never seen this before.

So in the doors, holding up his chip, and heads over, like he does, first to the candy.

Boomzilla likes this Jap candy that's like a little drug lab. You mix these different parts, it fizzes, gets hot, cools. You do this extrusion-molding thing and watch it harden. When you eat it, it's just candy, but Boomzilla likes making it.

Gets six of those, pissed there's no grape, and a couple or two chocos. Spends a good long time by the machine that makes magazines, watching screens, all the different shit you can get put in your magazine. Then back to get his noodles, kind you add water and pull the string.

Back there, deciding between beef and chicken, he sees they've unfastened a whole piece of Lucky Dragon wall. Next to GlobEx and the cash machine.

So he thinks this is what the white truck is about, some new thing to put in there, and he wonders if it's maybe a game.

White men in white paper suits working on the section of wall.

Watches them, then goes back to the front, shows his shit. Checker runs his shit over the window that counts, takes Boomzilla's chip and debits it. There goes his shit money.

Takes his bag outside and finds a curb to sit on. Pretty soon he'll start making the first candy. Red one.

He looks past the white truck to the screens there, by the front, and he notices white trucks on half the screens. So all over the world now, these white trucks sitting outside Lucky Dragons, so it must mean something new is being put in all of them tonight.

Boomzilla unseals the candy and studies the multistage but entirely nonverbal instructions.

Gotta get it right.

38. VINCENT BLACK LIGHTNING

FONTAINE'S shop must be this narrow purple one with its high thin window caulked with enough silicone to frost a wedding cake. The whole front of the place had been painted the same flat purple, blistered now by sun and rain, and she had some faint memory of its earlier incarnation as something else, used clothing maybe. They'd put that purple over everything: over the droops and gobs of silicone, over the hardware on the old wooden door with its upper panels replaced with glass.

If this was Fontaine's place, he hadn't bothered naming it, but that was like him. And the few things displayed in the window, under the beam of an antique Tensor, were like him as well: a few old-fashioned watches with their dials going rusty, a bone-handled jackknife someone had polished till it shone, and some kind of huge ugly telephone, sheathed in ridged black rubber. Fontaine was crazy about old things, and sometimes, before, he'd bring different pieces over, show them to Skinner.

Sometimes she'd thought he'd just done that to get the old man started, and then Skinner's own stories would come out. He hadn't been much for stories, Skinner, but turning some battered treasure of Fontaine's in his hands, he'd talk, and Fontaine would sit and listen, and nod sometimes, as though Skinner's stories confirmed some long-held suspicion.

Made privy to Skinner's past, Fontaine would then handle the objects himself with a new excitement, asking questions.

Fontaine lived in the world of things, it had seemed to her, the world of the things people made, and probably it was easier for him to approach them, people, through these things. If Skinner couldn't tell Fontaine a story about something, Fontaine would make up his own story, read function in the shape of something, read use in the way it was worn down. It seemed to comfort him.

Everything, to Fontaine, had a story. Each object, each fragment comprising the built world. A chorus of voices, the past alive in everything, that sea upon which the present tossed and rode. When he'd built Skinner's funicular, the elevator that crawled like a small cable car up the angled iron of the tower, when the old man's hip had gotten too bad to allow him to easily climb, Fontaine had had a story about the derivation of each piece. He wove their stories together, applied electricity: the thing rose, clicking, to the hatch in the floor of Skinner's room.

Now she stands there, looking into the window, at these watches with their foxed faces, their hands unmoving, and she fears history.

Fontaine will fit her to history in some different way, she knows, and it is a history she has avoided.

Through the thick pane of the door, thick enough to bend light, the way water in a glass does, she sees that the lights are on in a space behind the shop. Another door there, not quite closed.

CLOSED/CERRADO says the dog-eared cardboard sign hung inside the glass on a suction-cup shower hook.

She knocks.

Almost immediately the inner door is opened, a figure silhouetted there against brightness.

"Hey, Fontaine. Chevette. It's me."

The figure shuffles forward, and she sees that it is in fact him, this angular black man whose graying hair is twisted into irregular branches that hang like the arms of a dusty houseplant in need of water. As he rounds the flat gleam of a glass-topped counter, she sees that he holds a gun, the old-fashioned kind with the cylinder that turns as the bullets are fired manually, one at a time. "Fontaine? It's me."

He stops there, looking. Takes a step forward. Lowers the pistol. "Chevette?"

"Yeah?"

"Hold on." He comes forward and peers at her, past her. "You alone?"

"Yes," she says, glancing to either side.

"Hold on—" a rattling of locks, bolts undone, and at last the door opens, and he blinks at her, mystified. "You back."

"How are you, Fontaine?"

"Fine," he says, "fine," and steps back. "Come in."

She does. The place smells of machine oil, metal polish, burnt coffee. A thousand things gleam from the depths of Fontaine's history reef.

"Thought you were in LA," he says.

"I was. I'm back . . ."

He closes the door and starts locking it, an elaborate process but one
he can do in the dark, in his sleep perhaps. "Old man's gone. You know?"

"I know," she says. "How?"

"Just old," he says, tucking his pistol away now. "Wouldn't get out
of bed, finally. Curled up there like a baby. Clarisse she came to nurse
him. She been a nurse, Clarisse. Says when they turn to face the wall,
that means it's over soon."

Chevette wants so badly to say something, but it will not come.

"I like your hair, girl," Fontaine says, looking at her. "Not so fierce
now."

"IT'S changing," Fontaine says, meaning the bridge and how they live on
it. He's told her about the tendency to build these shops, how most of
them are built with nonresident money, the owners hiring people to live
there and maintain possession. "That Lucky Dragon," he says, cupping
a white china mug of his bitter, silted coffee, "that's there because someone decided the money was there for it to make. Tourists buying what
they need to come out here. That wouldn't have happened, before."

"Why do you think it is, that it's changing?"

"It just is," he says. "Things have a time, then they change."

"Skinner," she says, "he lived out his life here, didn't he? I mean,
when this was all what it was. He was here for all of that. Here when
they built it."

"Not his whole life. Just the end of it. That jacket you're wearing,
he got that in England, when he was younger. He lived there and rode
motorcycles. Told me about it. Rode them up to Scotland, rode them all
over. Real old ones."

"He told me a little about it, once," she says. "Then he came back
here and the Little Big One came. Cracked the bridge. Pretty soon he
was out here."

"Here," he says, "I'll show you something." Opening a cabinet.

Brings out a sheath knife, greenish handles inlaid with copper abstracts. Draws it from the waxed brown saddle leather. Blade of Damascus steel, tracked with dark patterns.

The knife of Chevette's memories, its grip scaled with belt-ground segments of phenolic circuit board.

"I saw that made," she says, leaning forward.

"Forged from a motorcycle drive chain. Vincent 'Black Lightning,' 1952. Rode that in England. It was a good forty years old too, then. Said there wasn't ever a bike to match it. Kept the chain till he found this maker." Passes the knife to her. Five inches of blade, five inches of handle. "Like you to have it."

Chevette runs her finger along the flat of the blade, the crocodile pattern of light and dark steel that had been formed as the links were beaten out. "I was thinking about this before, Fontaine. Today. How we went to where the smith worked. Burned coke in an old coffee can."

"Yes. I've seen it done." Hands her the sheath.

"But you need to sell this stuff." Tries to hand it back.

"It wasn't for sale," he says. "I was keeping it for you."

FONTAINE has a strange boy in the shop's back room. Heavy, Hispanic, hair cut short. He sits the whole time, cross-legged, his head in an old eyephone rig that looks like it came out of some military robotics dump. With a worn-out old notebook on his lap. Endlessly, steadily, clicking from one screen to the next.

"Who's this?" she asks when they're back, Fontaine putting on a fresh pot of his terrible coffee. Thinking the boy can hear her.

"I don't know," Fontaine says, turning to regard the boy in the eyephones. "He was outside this morning, breathing on my window."

Chevette looks at Fontaine, not getting it.

"He likes watches," Fontaine says, lighting the butane ring with a spark gun like a toy pistol. "Showed him how to hunt for watches this morning, hasn't done much since." Fontaine crosses to where the boy sits, looks down at him.

"I'm not sure how much he understands English, " Fontaine says. "Or he understands it, but it gets through funny."

"Spanish maybe?"

"I had big Carlos by here," Fontaine says. "Didn't seem to make much difference."

"You live here now, Fontaine?"

"Yeah," he says. "Not getting along with Clarisse."

"How's your kids?"

"They're okay. Hell, Tourmaline's okay too, by anybody's standards but her own. I mean, not to live with, understand, but her health's pretty good."

Chevette picks up the sheathed Damascus boot knife and tries it in the inner, zippered pocket of Skinner's jacket. It fit, if you zipped the pocket shut, as far as you could, to hold it upright. "What's he doing with your notebook?"

"He's hunting watches. I started him looking on the net auctions, but now he's looking everywhere. Gets places I don't understand how he does."

"He gonna live here?"

Fontaine frowns. "I hadn't planned on it."

Chevette stands up, stretches, seeing the old man, Skinner, in memory, sitting up in his bed in the room atop the cable tower. What dancer she'd gotten off Creedmore has long since worn off, leaving an edge of tiredness. Long day. Very long day. "We're sleeping in a van down the foot of Folsom," she says.

"You and who?"

"Tessa. Friend of mine."

"Know you're welcome here."

"No," she says, "Tessa'll be worried. I'm glad I saw you, Fontaine." She zips the jacket. "Thank you for keeping his knife." Whatever history it was she'd felt herself dodging, she hasn't found it. She just feels tired now; otherwise, she doesn't seem to feel.

"Your knife. Made it for you. Wanted you to have it. Told me." Looking up from beneath his sparse gray dreadlocks now. And gently says: "Asked us where you were, you know?"

Her fit with history, and how that hurts.

39. PANOPTICON

LANEY'S progress through all the data in the world (or that data's progress through him) has long since become what he is, rather than something he merely does.

The Hole, that blankness at the core of his being, ceases to trouble him here. He is a man with a mission, though he readily admits to himself that he has no real idea what that mission may finally be.

This all began, he reflects, knocking back his cough syrup in the amniotic darkness of his cardboard hutch, with his "interest" in Cody Harwood. The first prickings of the so-called stalker syndrome thought to eventually afflict every test subject ever dosed with 5-SB. His initial reaction, of course, had been denial: this couldn't be happening to him, not after all these years. He was *interested* in Harwood, and for good reason; his awareness of the nodal points, the points from which change was emerging, would repeatedly bring Harwood to his attention. It was not so much that he was focusing on Harwood, as that things *swung* toward Harwood, gently yet unavoidably, like the needle of a compass.

His life, at that point, had been in stasis: employed by the management of Lo/Rez, the pop group, to facilitate the singer Rez's "marriage" to the Japanese virtual star Rei Toei, Laney had settled into a life in Tokyo that centered around visits to a private, artificially constructed island in Tokyo Bay, an expensive nub of engineered landfill upon which Rez and Rei Toei intended to bring forth some sort of new reality. That Laney had never been able to quite grasp the nature of this reality hadn't surprised him. Rez was a law unto himself, very possibly the last of the pre-posthuman megastars, and Rei Toei, the idoru, was an emergent system, a self continually being iterated from experiential input. Rez was Rez, and thereby difficult, and Rei Toei was that river into which one can never step twice. As she became more herself, through the inputting of experience, through human interaction, she grew and changed. Rez hadn't, and a psychologist employed by the band's management had confided in Laney that Rez, whom the psychologist char-acterized as having narcissistic personality disorder, wasn't likely to. "I've met a lot of people, particularly in this industry," the psychologist had said, "who *have* that, but I've never met one who had *had* it."

So Laney had climbed, each working day, from a Tokyo dock into an inflatable Zodiac. To skim across the gray metallic skin of the bay to that nameless and perfectly circular island, and there to interact with ("teach" was not the word, somehow) the idoru. And what he had done, although neither of them had planned it, was to take her with him, into that flow of information where he was most at home (or, really, farthest from his inner Hole). He had shown her, as it were, the ropes, although they were not ropes that he or anyone else had names for. He had shown her nodal points in that flow, and they had watched together as change had emerged from these into the physical world.

And he had never asked her how it was, exactly, that she intended to "marry" Rez, and he doubted that, in any ordinary sense, she knew. She simply continued to emerge, to be, to be *more*. More present. And Laney fell in love with her, although he understood that she had been designed for him (and for the world) to fall in love with. As the ampli-fied reflection of desire, she was a team effort; to the extent that her designers had done their jobs properly, she was a waking dream, a love object sprung from an approximation of the global mass unconscious. And this was not, Laney understood, a matter of sexual desire exclu-sively (though of course he felt that, to his great confusion) but of some actual and initially painful opening of his heart.

He loved her, and in loving her understood that his most basic sense of what that word might mean had changed, supplanting every previous concept. An entirely new feeling, and he had held it close, sharing it with no one, least of all the idoru.

And it had been toward the end of this that Cody Harwood, shy and smiling and gently elusive, someone Laney had never felt the least inter-est in, had begun to obsess him. Harwood, most often depicted as a twenty-first-century synthesis of Bill Gates and Woody Allen, had never previously been any more to Laney than a vague source of irritation, one of those familiar icons who loom regularly on the horizons of media, only to drop away until they next appear. Laney had had no opinion of Harwood, other than that he felt he had been glimpsing him all his life, and didn't quite know why, and was vaguely tired of it.

But as he spent more time cruising the aspects of the flow that were concerned with Harwood, and with the activities of his firm, Harwood Levine, it had begun to become apparent that this was a locus of nodal points, a sort of meta-node, and that, in some way he had been unable to define, something very large was happening here. His compulsive study of Harwood and things Harwoodian had led him to the recognition that history too was subject to the nodal vision, and the version of history that Laney came to understand there bore little or no relation to any accepted version.

He had been taught, of course, that history, along with geography, was dead. That history in the older sense was an historical concept. History in the older sense was narrative, stories we told ourselves about where we'd come from and what it had been like, and those narratives were revised by each new generation, and indeed always had been. History was plastic, was a matter of interpretation. The digital had not so much changed that as made it too obvious to ignore. History was stored data, subject to manipulation and interpretation.

But the "history" Laney discovered, through the quirk in his vision induced by having been repeatedly dosed with 5-SB, was something very different. It was that *shape* comprised of every narrative, every version; it was that shape that only he (as far as he knew) could see.

At first, discovering this, he had attempted to share it with the idoru. Perhaps, if shown, she, this posthuman emergent entity, would simply start to see this way as well. And he had been disappointed when she had finally told him that what he saw was not there for her; that his ability to apprehend the nodal points, those emergent systems of history, was not there, nor did she expect to find it with growth. "This is human, I think," she'd said, when pressed. "This is the result of what you are, biochemically, being stressed in a particular way. This is wonderful. This is closed to me."

And shortly after that, as her growing complexity continued to widen the distance he already knew she felt toward Rez, she had come to him and asked him to interpret the data as it flowed around herself and Rez. And he had done this, though reluctantly, out of love. Knowing somehow he would be saying good-bye to her in the process.

The flow around Rez and Rei was ripe with nodal points, particularly at those junctures where queerly occulted data poured steadily in from the Walled City, that semi-mythical otherwhere of outlaw iconoclasts. "Why have you connected with these people?" he'd asked. "Because I need them," she'd said, "I don't know why, but I know that I do. The situation does."

"Without them," he'd said, "you might not *have* a situation."

"I know." Smiling.

But as his obsession with Harwood had deepened, Laney had grown less comfortable with his trips to the island and their forays together into the fields of data. It had been as though he did not wish her to see him this way, his concentration warped from within, bent toward this one object, this strangely banal object. The sense of Harwood, of the information cloud he generated, swarmed in Laney's dreams. And one morning, waking in the Tokyo hotel in which Lo/Rez kept him billeted, he had decided not to go to work.

And sometime after that, he knew from Yamazaki, and from his own observation of the flow, the idoru had departed Tokyo as well. He had his own theories about that, about her conversations with the denizens (they would have insisted on the term, he thought) of the digitally occluded Walled City, and now, evidently, she was in San Francisco.

Although he had known she would be, because of course she had to be. Because San Francisco, he could see in the shape of things, was where the world ended. Was ending. And she was a part of that, and so was he, and Harwood as well.

But something would be decided (was being decided) there. And that was why he dared not sleep. Why he must send the Suit, immaculate and malodorous, with his ankles tarred black, for Regain and more of the blue syrup.

SOMETIMES, now, beyond the point of exhaustion, he has started to enter, for what may be seconds but can feel like hours or days, some new mode of being.

It is as though he becomes a single retina, distributed evenly across the inner surface of a sphere. Unblinking, he stares, globally, into that eye, seeing that with which he sees, while from a single invisible iris appear individual, card-like images of Harwood, one after another.

Yamazaki has brought him pillows and fresh sleeping bags, bottles of water, an unused change of clothes. He is vaguely aware of these things, but when he becomes the eye that looks in upon itself, and upon the endless string of images, he has no awareness beyond that interiority, infinite and closed.

And part of him asks himself if this is an artifact of his illness, of the 5-SB, or if this vast and inward-looking eye is not in fact some inner aspect of that single shape comprised of every bit of data in the world?

This last he feels is at least partly confirmed by his repeated experience of the eye everting, turning itself inside out, in Moebius spasm, at which point he finds himself, invariably, staring at that indescribable shape.

But now, when he *is* the eye, *he is starting to be aware of someone else watching.* Someone else is very interested in those images of Harwood. He feels them register each one.

How can that be?

THE vintage plastic Gunsmith Cats alarm watch pulls him from the flow. He finds it in the dark and turns off the alarm. He wonders where it came from. The old man?

It is time to phone Rydell in San Francisco. He moves his fingers delicately over the disposables on the cardboard shelf, feeling for the used one with ten minutes left.

40. YELLOW RIBBON

REI Toei could make herself very small.

Six inches tall, she sat on Rydell's pillow, in the salt-frosted plastic dome of his room at the bed-and-breakfast, and he felt like a child.

When she was small, the projection seemed more concentrated; she was brighter, and it made him think of fairies in old anime, those Disney things. She could as easily have had wings, he thought, and fly around, trailing glowing dust if she wanted. But she only sat there, even more perfect at six inches tall, and talked with him.

And when he'd close his eyes, not intending to sleep but only to rest them, he could hear that her voice was actually coming from the projector at the foot of his bed. She was telling him about Rez, the singer she'd wanted to marry, and why that hadn't worked, but it was difficult to follow. Rez had been very interested in Rez, Rydell gathered, and not much else, and Rei Toei had become more interested in other people (or, he guessed, if you were her, in other things). But he kept slipping out of focus, falling asleep really, and her voice was so beautiful.

Before he'd stretched out here, and she'd shown him how she could get small, he'd pulled the chicken-wire gate into place and spread the curtains that were thumbtacked to it, some kind of faded nubby fabric printed with a pattern of ornate keys and strange, long-necked cats (he thought they were).

He didn't know how long the sunglasses had been ringing, and it took him several rings to locate his jacket in the dark. He was fully dressed, shoes and all, otherwise, and he knew he'd been deep asleep.

"Hello?" He put the glasses on with his left hand. With his right he reached up and touched the ceiling. It's paneling gave, slightly, when he did that, so he didn't do it again.

"Where are you?" It was Laney.

"Bed-and-breakfast," Rydell told him. With the sunglasses on, it was totally dark. He watched the low spark of his own optic nerve, colors without names.

"Did you get the cables?"

"Yeah," Rydell said. He remembered being harsh with the sumo kid and felt stupid. He'd lost it. That claustro thing he got in crowds sometimes. Tara-May Allenby had told him that was called agoraphobia, and it meant "fear of the mall," but it wasn't actually malls that did it to him. But he couldn't stand those little under-lip beards either. "Two of them."

"Use them yet?"

"Just the power," Rydell said. "The other one, I don't know what it jacks with."

"Neither do I," said Laney. "Is she there?"

"She was," Rydell said, looking around in the dark for his fairy star, then remembering he was wearing sunglasses.

His hand found a switch that dangled from a wire near his head. He clicked it. A bare fifty-watt bulb came on. He slid the glasses down his nose and peered over them, finding the projector still there and still plugged in. "The thermos-thing's still here."

"Don't let that out of your sight," Laney said. "Or the cables. I don't know what we need her to do there, but it's all around her."

"What's all around her?"

"The change."

"Laney, she said you told her the world was going to end."

"Is going to end," Laney corrected.

"Why'd you tell her that?"

Laney sighed, the deep end of his sigh becoming a cough, which he seemed to choke off. "As we *know* it, okay?" he managed. "As we know it. And that's all I or anyone else can tell you about that. It's not what I want you thinking about. You're working for me, remember?"

And you're crazy, Rydell thought, but I've got your credit chip in my pocket. "Okay," he said, "what's next?"

"You have to go to the site of a double homicide, one that took place last night, on the bridge."

"What do you want me to try to find out?"

"Nothing," Laney said. "Just look like you're trying to find something out. Pretend. Like you're investigating. Call me when you're ready to go, I'll give you the GPS fix for the spot."

"Hey," Rydell said, "what if I do find something out?"

"Then call me."

"Don't hang up," Rydell said. "How come you haven't been in touch with her, Laney? She said you two were separated."

"The people who, well, 'own' her, that's not quite the term, really, but they'd like to talk to me, because she's missing. And the Lo/Rez people too. So I need to be incommunicado at the moment, as far as they're concerned. But she hasn't tried to reach me, Rydell. She'll be able to, when she needs to." He hung up.

Took the glasses off, left them folded on the pillow, and crawled to the end of the bed. "Hey," he said to the thermos-thing, "you there?" Nothing.

He started getting himself together. He unpacked his duffel, used the switchblade to cut a couple of slits in it, took off his nylon belt and threaded it through the slits, using it as a strap, so he could sling the bag over his shoulder.

"Hey," he said again to the thermos-thing, "you there? I'm gonna unplug you now." He hesitated, did. He put it in the duffel, along with the power cable, the other cable, and his Lucky Dragon fanny pack, this last because the thing had already saved his ass once, and it might be lucky. He put his nylon jacket on, put the sunglasses in his pocket, and, as an afterthought, gingerly put the switchblade in his right front trouser pocket. Then he imagined it opening there, thought about its lack of a safety catch, and, even more gingerly, fished it out and put it in the side pocket of his jacket.

AND found the place without too much trouble, though Laney's mode of GPS-by-phone was pretty basic. Laney had a fix on the spot (Rydell had no idea how) but no map of the bridge, so he triangulated Rydell's sunglasses somehow and told him to walk back toward San Francisco, lower level, keep walking, keep walking, getting warmer. Okay, turn right.

Which had left Rydell facing a blank plywood partition plastered with rain-stained handbills, in a European language he didn't recognize, for a concert by someone named Ottoman Badchair. He described this to Laney.

"That isn't it," Laney said, "but you're really close."

There was a shop next door, closed, and he couldn't figure out what it sold when it was open, and then a gap. Rolls of plastic back in there. Lumber. Someone was building another shop, he thought. If this was it, the crime scene, there ought to be a yellow plastic ribbon with SFPD stapled up, but then he remembered that the police didn't come out here all that much, and he wondered what they did when they had a body to dispose of. Flipping them over the side wouldn't make the city too happy, although of course there was no way the city could prove a particular corpse had come off the bridge. Still, it bothered Rydell that there wasn't any yellow ribbon. He guessed he thought of it as a mark of respect.

He moved in, edging past the rolls of plastic, climbing over a low stack of plywood, and spotted, in the harsh light slung from the scavenged fluorescents closer to the pedestrian stroll, two frosty-looking white marks, something aerosoled over two darker stains, and he knew what that was. Kil'Z, this stuff you sprayed where bodily fluids had gotten out, in case the person who'd lost them was seropositive. He knew what Kil'Z looked like over blood, and this was that.

Not much of a crime scene. He stood there staring down at it and wondering how Laney expected him to look like he was conducting an investigation. He put the duffel with Rei Toei's projector down on the rolls of plastic.

Kil'Z residue was fairly waterproof, so the rain hadn't washed it away. But then he knew that the victims, whoever they had been, had died the night before.

He felt like an idiot. He really had wanted to be a cop once, and he'd dreamed of crossing the yellow line and looking at the scene. And being able to do something. And now here he was.

He took out the glasses and called Laney. But now Laney, in whatever fine hotel he might be in, in Tokyo, wouldn't answer.

"No shit, Sherlock," Rydell said to himself, listening to a phone ring in Tokyo.

41. TRANSAM

"**HIS** name is Rydell," Harwood says. "Image matching gave us that immediately. He was briefly associated with *Cops in Trouble*."

"Associated with whom?" The knife, with its sheath and harness, was secured in a twilit alcove off the central elevator stack, approximately eight hundred feet below.

"*Cops in Trouble*," Harwood says. "A cultural treasure. Don't you watch television?"

"No." He is looking east, from the forty-eighth and ultimate floor of the city's tallest building, toward the shadow of the ruined Embarcadero, the gypsy glow of the bridge, the feral darkness of Treasure Island.

Stepping closer to the window, he touches his belt. Stitched between two layers of black calf is concealed a ribbon of a very particular, very expensive material. Under certain circumstances, it ceases to behave as though it were some loosely woven, tissue-thin fabric, something a child might accidentally pull to pieces, and becomes instead thirty inches of something limber, double-edged, and very sharp. Its texture, in that state, its sleek translucency, has reminded him of fresh cuttlebone.

"You do have a sense of humor," Harwood says, behind him. "I know it."

Leaning closer to the window, looking down. Foreshortened perspective up the side of this obelisk, this pyramid so-called, and midway the dark bulge of that Japanese material, placed to counter old quake damage. This is new, replacing earlier splines of polycarbon, and the subject of architectural and aesthetic scandal. Briefly fascinated, he watches as reflections of the lights of surrounding buildings shudder slightly, the thing's glossy surface tensing in response to winds he cannot feel. The truss is alive.

Turning to face Harwood, who is seated behind a broad dark plain of nonreflective wood, across which an accumulation of architectural models and hillocks of documents suggest the courses of imaginary rivers: a topography in which might be read change in the world beyond the window, if meanings were known, and one were sufficiently concerned with outcomes.

Harwood's eyes are the most present thing about him, the rest giving an impression of existing at one remove, in some other and unspecific dimension. A tall man, he seems to occupy relatively little space, communicating from elsewhere via deliberately constricted channels. He is slender, with that agelessness of the aging rich, his long face free of tension. His eyes, enlarged by archaic lenses, are seldom still. "Why do you pretend to not be interested in this former policeman visiting the site of your recent activities?" On his wrist, gold and titanium catches the light; some multitasking bauble with intricate displays.

"I don't pretend." On the large flatscreen that stands to the left of the desk, four cameras present angles on a tall, sturdy-looking man who stands, chin down, as if brooding. The cameras would be no larger than roaches, but the four images, in spite of inadequate light, offer excellent resolution. "Who placed these cameras?"

"My bright young things."

"Why?"

"Against exactly this eventuality: that someone might visit the site of these two utterly forgettable deaths and stand there, thinking. Look at him. He's thinking."

"He looks unhappy."

"He's trying to imagine you."

"You imagine he is."

"The fact that he's found his way to that spot at all is indicative of knowledge and motive. He knows that two men died there."

Amid the various models on Harwood's desk stands one in glossy red and white, rendered with functioning miniature video screens on the trademark pylon. Tiny images move and change there, in liquid crystal.

"Do you own the company that built this thing?" indicating the model with his index finger.

The eyes behind Hardwood's glasses register surprise, from their peculiar distance. Then interest. "No. We advise them. We are a public relations firm. We did, I believe, advise on impact. We advised the city as well."

"It's horrible."

"Yes," says Harwood, "aesthetically, I agree. And that was an expressed concern of the municipal authorities. But our studies indicated that positioning it there would encourage walk-on tourism, and that is a crucial aspect of normalization."

"Normalization?"

"There is an ongoing initiative to bring the bridge community back into the fold, as it were. But the issue is sensitive. A matter of image really, and that of course is where we come in." Harwood smiles. "A number of major cities have these autonomous zones, and how a given city chooses to deal with the situation can impact drastically on that city's image. Copenhagen, for instance, was one of the first, and has done very well. Atlanta, I suppose, would be the classic example of what not to do." Harwood blinks. "It's what we do now instead of bohemias," he says.

"Instead of what?"

"Bohemias. Alternative subcultures. They were a crucial aspect of industrial civilization in the two previous centuries. They were where industrial civilization went to dream. A sort of unconscious R&D, exploring alternate societal strategies. Each one would have a dress code, characteristic forms of artistic expression, a substance or substances of choice, and a set of sexual values at odds with those of the culture at large. And they did, frequently, have locales with which they became associated. But they became extinct."

"Extinct?"

"We started picking them before they could ripen. A certain crucial growing period was lost, as marketing evolved and the mechanisms of recommodification became quicker, more rapacious. Authentic subcultures required backwaters, and time, and there are no more backwaters. They went the way of geography in general. Autonomous zones do offer a certain insulation from the monoculture, but they seem not to lend themselves to recommodification, not in the same way. We don't know why exactly." The little images shift, flickering.

"They shouldn't have put it there."

Harwood's eyes come in from their private distance. "I don't believe I've ever heard you express so specific an opinion."

No reply.

"You'll have a second chance to see it. I want you to find out what our pensive friend here is thinking about."

"Is this concerned with what you implied when we spoke earlier, that something is on the verge of happening?"

"Yes."

"And what would that be?"

Harwood considers him from the distance behind his glasses. "Do you believe in forces of history?"

"I believe in what brings us to the moment."

"I seem to have come to believe in the moment myself. I believe we are approaching one, drawn to it by the gravity of its strangeness. It is a moment in which everything and nothing will change. I am seeking an outcome in which I will retain viability. I am seeking an outcome in which Harwood Levine will not have become four meaningless sylla-bles. If the world is to be reborn, I wish to be reborn in it, as something akin to what I am today."

Thinking of the possible number and variety of crosshairs that must be trained on him now, hidden telepresent weapons platforms. He is fairly certain, nonetheless, that he could kill Harwood, if the moment required, though he also knows that he would almost certainly prede-cease him, if only by some fraction of a second. "I think you have become more complicated, since we last met."

"Complex," Harwood says, and smiles.

42. RED GHOSTS OF EUROPEAN TIME

FONTAINE makes himself a cup of instant miso on the hotplate. This is what he drinks before bed, a soothing saltiness and bits of seaweed at the bottom. Thinking of Skinner's girl and seeing her again. Usually when people leave the bridge they don't come back. Weirdness around her departure but he forgets what exactly. Not good for the old man but his time nearly done then anyway.

Tick tick of the silent boy under the eyephones, hunting watches. Fontaine pours his miso into a cup missing its handle, savoring the aromatic steam. Tired now, he wonders where the boy can sleep here or if indeed he will. Maybe sit up all night hunting watches. Fontaine shakes his head. The ticking stops.

Carrying his soup, he turns to see what's arrested the ceaseless hunt.

There on the screen of the notebook, in the boy's lap, is a scan of a battered Rolex "Victory," an inexpensive wartime model for the Canadian market, worth a fair bit now but not in this condition. The steel case looks rough and the dial has faded unevenly. Black Arabics from one to twelve are crisp, but the inner chapter, red, European time, is almost gone.

Fontaine sips his miso, looking down, wondering what it is this boy sees to hold him, in the red ghosts of European time.

Then the boy's head sags under the weight of the eyephones, and Fontaine hears him start to snore.

43. LIBIA & PACO

LANEY finds himself on an island in that mind-wide flow he ceaselessly cruises.

It is not a construct, this place, an environment proper, so much as a knotting, a folding-in of information rooted in the substrates of the oldest codes. It is something like a makeshift raft, random pieces thrown together, but it is anchored, unmoving. He knows that it is no accident, that it has been put in his path for a reason.

The reason, he soon finds, is that Libia and Paco wish to speak with him.

They are associates of the Rooster, junior denizens of the Walled City, and present here as a sphere of mercury in zero gravity and a black, three-legged cat, respectively. The sphere of mercury (Libia) has a lovely voice, a girl's, and the three-legged cat, who is also missing one eye and one ear (Paco) has a cunningly modulated growl Laney thinks he remembers from a Mexican cartoon. They are almost certainly from Mexico City, these two, if geography needs to be taken into consideration, and very likely belong to that faction of flaming youth currently opting for the re-flooding of the Federal District's drained lakes, a radical urban reconfiguration that for some reason had obsessed Rei Toei in her final month in Tokyo. She had developed a fascination with large human settlements in general, and Laney had been her guide through certain of the stranger info-prospects presented by what passes, this century, for town planning.

So he hangs here, at the juncture of these old code-roots, in a place devoid of very specific shape or texture, aside from Libia and Paco, and hears them.

"The Rooster tells us you feel someone is watching you watch Cody Harwood," says the sphere of mercury, pulsing as it speaks, its surface reflecting vehicles passing in some busy street.

"It might be an artifact," Laney counters, not sure he should have brought it up with the Rooster, whose paranoia is legendary. "Something the 5-SB generates."

"We think not," says the cat, its one-eyed filthy head propped atop an arrested drift of data. It yawns, revealing grayish-white gums, the color of boiled pork, and a single orange canine. Its one eye is yellow and hate-filled, unblinking. "We have determined that you are, in fact, being observed in your observation."

"But not at the moment," says Libia.

"Because we have constructed this blind," says the cat.

"Do you know who it is?" Laney asks.

"It is Harwood," says Libia, the sphere quivering delicately.

"Harwood? Harwood is watching me watch him?"

"Harwood," says the cat, "dosed *himself* with 5-SB. Three years after you were released from the orphanage in Gainesville."

Laney is suddenly and terribly aware of his physical being, the condition of his body. His lungs failing in a cardboard carton in the concrete bowels of Shinjuku Station.

Harwood. It is Harwood whom he has sometimes imagined as the presence of God.

Harwood, who is . . .

Like him.

Harwood who sees, Laney now sees, the nodal points. Who sees the shapes from which history emerges. And that is why he is at the very heart of the emergent cusp, this newness Laney cannot quite glimpse. Of course Harwood is there.

Because Harwood, in a sense, is causing it.

"How do you know?" he hears himself ask, and wills himself beyond the failing strictures of his body. "Can you be sure?"

"We've found a way in," Libia chimes, the sphere distorting like a topographic learning aid, turning reflections of moving traffic into animated Escher-fragments that fly together, mirroring one another. "The Rooster set us to it, and we did."

"And does he know?" Laney asks. "Does Harwood know?"

"We don't think he's noticed," growls the cat, purple-brown scabs caked on the absence of its ear.

"Watch this," says Libia, making no effort to conceal her pride. The intricately lobed surface of the mirrored shape flows and ripples, and Laney is looking into the gray eyes of a young and very serious-looking man.

"You want us to kill him," the young man says. "Or do I misunderstand you?"

"You understand me," says Harwood, his voice familiar, unmistakable, though he sounds tired.

"You know I think it's a very good idea," says the young man, "but it could be done with greater surety if you gave us time for preparation. I prefer to choose the time and the terrain, if possible."

"Not possible," Harwood says. "Do it when you can."

"You don't have to give me a reason, of course," the young man says, "but you must realize I'm curious. We've suggested his removal since you contracted with us."

"It's time," Harwood replies. "The moment."

Wind catches the young man's dark scarf. It flutters, strobing the image. "What about the other one, the rent-a-cop?"

"Kill him if it seems he's likely to escape. Otherwise, it might be useful if he could be questioned. He's in this too, but I don't see exactly how."

Libia becomes a sphere again, rotating.

Laney closes his eyes and gropes in the close electric dark for the blue cough syrup. He feels the hate-filled yellow eye watching him, but he imagines it as Harwood's.

Harwood knows.

Harwood took the 5-SB.

Harwood is like him.

But Harwood has an agenda of his own, and it is from this agenda, in part, that the situation is emerging.

Laney cracks the seal. Drinks the blue syrup. He must think now.

44. JUST WHEN YOU THINK . . .

THE rain wasn't coming back, Chevette decided, shrugging her shoulders against the weight of Skinner's jacket.

She was sitting on a bench, behind a stack of empty poultry crates, and she knew she should be going somewhere but she just couldn't. Thinking about Skinner dying here, about what Fontaine had said. The knife in the inside pocket, its handle digging into her left collarbone, the way she was slouched. She straightened her back against the plywood behind her and tried to pull herself together.

She had to find Tessa and get back to the van, and she had to do that, if she could, without running into Carson. It was possible, she figured, that he hadn't even seen her run out, even though she was sure somehow that when she'd seen him, he'd been looking for nobody but her. But if he hadn't seen her, and he wouldn't have found her there, then probably that bar would be the last place she should expect to find him now. And if he had seen her, then he wouldn't think she'd go back there either. Which would also put him somewhere else. And it was possible that Tessa, who liked her beers, would be there still, because she sure hadn't been keen on bedding down in the van. Probably Tessa thought that the bar was way interstitial, so it might just be that Chevette, if she was careful about it, could slip in there and get her, and get her back to the van. Carson wasn't too likely to come sniffing around the foot of Folsom, and if he did he was liable to run into the kind of people who'd take him for easy meat.

But it was no good sitting here, this close to chicken crates, because that was a good way to catch lice, and just the thought of it made her scalp itch. She stood up, stretched, smelling the faint ammonia tang of chicken shit, and set off through the upper level toward the city, keeping an eye out for Carson.

Not many people out now, and none of them tourists. The rain could do that, she remembered. Once again she got that feeling that she loved this place but wasn't really a part of it anymore. Kind of twisted in, like a hook, not a big feeling but sharp and deep. She sighed, remembering foggy mornings when she'd come down from the cable tower with her bike over her shoulder and pumped it over to Allied, wondering if Bunny'd have a scratch for her right off, a good ticket to pull, or if he'd give her a deadhead, what they called a pickup outside the city core. She'd liked a deadhead sometimes, because she got to see parts of town she might not have ridden before. And sometimes she'd wind up clean, what they called it when you didn't have any deliveries, and that could be great too, just go over to the Alcoholocaust or one of the other messenger bars and drink espresso until Bunny paged her. It had been pretty good, riding for Allied. She'd never even eaten it, wiped out bad, and the cops weren't as book-happy if you were a girl; you could get away with doing sidewalks and stuff. Not that she could imagine going back to it now, riding, and that brought her mood back, because she didn't know what else she could do. Whatever, she wasn't going to star in any new versions of Tessa's docu.

She remembered this skinny tech named Tara-May, somebody *Cops in Trouble* had sent over to grab footage of poor Rydell, who'd only ever wanted to feature in a segment of that thing. No, she corrected herself, that wasn't fair, because she knew that what Rydell had really wanted was to be a cop, which was what he'd started out to be in Tennessee. But it hadn't worked out, and then his episode hadn't worked out, let alone the mini-series they'd talked about spinning off. Mainly, she supposed, because what Tara-May had shot had convinced the *Cops in Trouble* people that Rydell looked a little on the heavy side on TV. Not that there was any fat on him, he was all muscle and long legs, but when they shot him he didn't look like that. And that had driven him sort of crazy, that and Tara-May always going on about how Chevette should take speech and acting classes, learn all these martial arts, and give up drugs. When Chevette had made it clear she didn't *do* drugs, Tara-May had said that that would make networking a little harder, not having anything to quit, but that there were groups for everything and that was probably the best way to meet people who could help you with your career.

But Chevette hadn't wanted a career, or not the way Tara-May meant it, and Tara-May just hadn't been able to get that. Actually there were a lot of people like Tara-May in Hollywood, maybe even most people were; everybody had something they "really" did. Drivers wrote, bartenders acted; she'd had massages from a girl who was really a stunt double for some actress Chevette had never heard of yet, except she hadn't really ever been called, but they had her number. Somebody had everybody's number, but it looked to Chevette like the game had *all* their numbers, every one, and nobody really was winning, but nobody wanted to hear that, or talk to you much if you didn't buy into what they "really" did.

Now she thought about it, that was part of what had gotten between her and Rydell, because he'd always buy into that, whatever anybody told him they really were. And then he'd tell them how he really wanted to do an episode of *Cops in Trouble,* and how it looked like he actually would, because *Cops in Trouble* was paying his rent now. Which nobody wanted to hear really, because it was a little too real, but Rydell never got that. And then they'd hit on him for phone numbers, names, intros, and start slipping him disks and lists of credits, hoping he was dumb enough to go back and try to show them to producers. Which he was, or anyway good-hearted enough, and that hadn't helped him any with the people at *Cops in Trouble* either.

And that, somehow, was how she'd wound up with Carson. Rydell sitting on the couch in that apartment with the lights off, watching one old *Cops in Trouble* after another, looking lost, and she just hadn't been able to handle it. It had been fine when they'd had things to do together, but when it came to just being together, that hadn't seemed to work, and Rydell going into that sad thing when it had started to look like it wasn't going to work out with the show . . .

But here was the bar, a small crowd around the door now and the sound of music she'd been hearing but not really listening to, which died as she got up close to the crowd.

Place was packed. She slid in sideways between a couple of Mexicans looked like truck drivers, had those steel chisel-toe things tacked to the front of their black cowboy boots. Inside, over the heads of the people packed on the floor, she could see Creedmore with a microphone in his hand, grinning out over the crowd. It was a dancer grin, ten thousand watts of bad electricity, and she saw he had the start of that thing that dancer did to your gums.

People were clapping and whistling for more, and Creedmore, his face running with sweat, looked like he was intending to give it to them.

"Thank you, thank you kindly," she heard Creedmore's amplified voice say. "Now this next number's one I wrote myself, and it's going out soon as our first single, Buell Creedmore and his Lower Companions, and it's called 'Just When You Think You've Got It Dicked . . .'"

Or anyway that was what she thought she heard him say, but then the band kicked in, loud, with the guitarist choking steely serpentine chords out of a big, shiny, old red electric, and she couldn't make out any of the words. Although she had to admit it sounded like Creedmore could sing.

They were jammed in here so tight, it made it hard to keep a lookout for Carson, but on the other hand it wasn't too likely he'd be able to see her either.

She kept moving, as best she could, trying to find Tessa.

45. JACK MOVE

RYDELL had taken a surveillance course, back at the academy, and his favorite part had been going out and following people. It wasn't something you did alone, but with at least one partner, and the more partners the better. You learned how to trade off, somebody taking your place, and how to deak up ahead of the subject so you'd be ready when the next guy needed to trade off. That way the subject never had the same person behind him for too long. There was a definite art to it, and when you got it down it was sort of like a dance.

He hadn't really gotten the chance to put it into practice, in his very brief career as a police officer, or later when he'd worked for IntenSecure, but he felt like he'd been pretty good at it, and it had given him an idea of what it would feel like if you were being followed, and particularly if you were being followed by some people who knew how to do it right.

And that was what he found himself thinking about now, as he shouldered the duffel with Rei Toei's projector in it and prepared to depart this pathetic excuse for a crime scene. If Laney had wanted him to attract someone's attention by standing here, well, he'd stood here. But maybe now, he thought, he was getting that watched feeling because Laney had told him he'd be sure to be noticed if he came here.

Could be nerves. Maybe, but actually he didn't feel nervous, just tired. He'd driven all night up the coast with Creedmore, and all the downtime he'd had today had been when he'd fallen asleep listening to Rei Toei. What he felt like now was going back to his room, checking out the projector to see if she'd come back, then hitting the bed.

But there it was, that prickling at the back of his neck. He turned and looked back, but there was nobody, just the place where the Kil'Z had been sprayed over dried blood.

Guy going by in the direction of Oakland and Rydell's room.

Young guy with dark military-buzzed hair, black coat, black scarf up around his face. Seemed not to see Rydell, just kept walking, hands in his pockets. Rydell fell in behind him, about fifteen feet.

He tried to imagine this place the way it had been before, when it was a regular bridge. Millions of cars had gone through here, this same space where he walked now. It had all been open then, just girders and railing and deck; now it was this tunnel, everything patched together out of junk, used lumber, plastic, whatever people could find, all of it lashed up however anybody could get it to stay, it looked like, and somehow it did stay, in spite of the winds he knew must come through here. He'd been back in a bayou once, in Louisiana, and something about the way it looked in here reminded him of that: there was stuff hanging everywhere, tubing and cables and things whose function he couldn't identify, and it was like Spanish moss in a way, everything softened at the outline. And the light now was dim and sort of underwater-looking, just these banks of scavenged fluorescents slung every twenty feet or so, some of them dead and others flickering.

He walked around a puddle where a vendor had dumped about ten pounds of dirty shaved ice.

Up ahead, he saw the guy with the black scarf turn into a café, one of these tiny little places you got in here, maybe two small tables and a counter that sat four or five. Big blonde boy looked like a weight lifter was coming out as the scarf went in, and the weight lifter made just that little bit of eye contact with Rydell that told him.

They were doing him: the trade-off. He was being tailed, and by at least three people.

Weight lifter started in the direction of Rydell's bed-and-breakfast, Treasure Island, Oakland. Back of his neck as wide as Rydell's thigh. As Rydell passed the café, he looked in and saw the scarf ordering a coffee. Just as normal as pie. So he didn't look behind him, because he knew that if he did that, they'd know. They would. Just like he'd known, when the weight lifter blew it by looking him in the eye.

The belt he'd slung the duffel from was cutting into his shoulder, through his nylon jacket, and he thought about Laney and Klaus and the Rooster, about how they all obviously thought the projector was really important, or valuable. Was that what he was being followed for, or was it about this mystery man of Laney's, his man who wasn't there? Otherwise, he didn't think he had any serious long-term enemies up here, though it was hard to be sure, and he didn't think these guys were ordinary jackers, because it looked to him like they really knew what they were doing.

He reached into the jacket pocket and felt the knife. It was there, and he was glad he had it, though the thought of actually cutting some-body with it bothered him. The thing about knives was that the people who thought they wanted to use them on other people usually had no idea how much *mess* it made. It wasn't like in the movies; cut people bled like stuck pigs. He'd had to deal with a few cut people around the Sunset Lucky Dragon. And it could get tricky because who knew who was seropositive? He and Durius had these goggles they were supposed to put on, to keep people's blood from getting in their eyes, but usually it just happened all at once and they didn't remember the goggles until it was likely too late anyway.

But the main thing about knives, even ones that cut steel-belt radi-als like ripe banana, was that they weren't much good in a gunfight.

Someone had slung up an old anti-shoplifting mirror above a closed stall, and as he approached this he tried to see who might be following him, but there was enough foot traffic in here that he only got a gener-alized sense of people moving.

But what really bothered him now was that he was just doing what they'd probably expect him to: heading back to wherever he was going to spend the night (assuming they didn't already know where that was). And once he got there, what then? He'd be trapped, up in his room, no exit but that ladder, and they'd have him. He guessed he could just keep walking, but he didn't see what that would get him either.

What he needed, he thought, was something he could do that they weren't expecting. Something that put the shoe on the other foot, or any-way he should lose them, whoever they were. Then maybe he could raise Laney and get Laney's take on who they might be.

He'd had an instructor in Knoxville who'd liked to talk about lateral thinking. Which in a way wasn't that far off what Durius meant when he talked about serious users getting lateral, out on the sidewalk outside Lucky Dragon. Just losing it. What it took, sometimes, was just your basic jack move, something nobody, maybe even you, was expecting.

To his right now, he saw he was passing a stretch of wall that was actually canvas, like a sail or an old tent, stretched tight over lumber and maybe half an inch thick with however many coats of paint it had had since it was put up here. Some kind of mural, but he wasn't noticing that.

The switchblade sounded so loud, opening it, that he was sure they'd have heard it, so he just moved, sweeping the ceramic blade down, then sideways, to cut himself a backward "L." Through which he ducked and stepped, as if in a dream, the paint on the canvas crackling as he did so. Into warmth and a different light and these completely unexpected people seated around a table, cards in their hands, mother-of-pearl chips piled on the table in front of them. And one of them, a woman, the nipples of her bare breasts transfixed with surgical steel, the stub of a small cigar wedged into the corner of her mouth, met Rydell's eye and said: "I'll see you one and raise you one."

"Never mind me," Rydell heard himself say, as he saw a man with a tattooed scalp, still holding his hand of cards, raise his other hand, with a gun in it, from beneath the table. And simultaneously he realized that he still had the black knife, open, in his hand. He felt a weird wash of cold down his spine as his feet just kept moving, past the table and the man and the deep and somehow limitlessly large black hole in the winking ring of stainless steel that was the pistol's muzzle.

Through a thick brown velour curtain that smelled of ancient movie houses and he was still moving, apparently intact. Feeling his hand thumb the button, closing and cocking the blade against his hip as he went, something he wouldn't have thought of doing otherwise. Pocketing the knife. In front of him a ladder rough-sawn from two-by-fours. Straight to it and just climbing, as fast as he could.

Took him up through a square hole in a splintered timber deck, narrow walkway between walls cut from peeling billboards, a woman's huge stained paper eye faded there as if staring into infinite distance.

Stop. Breathe. Heart pounding. Listen.

Laughter. The card players?

He started along the walkway, feeling a rising sense of triumph: he'd done it. Lost 'em. Wherever he was, up here, he'd be able to find his way back out, and down, and then he'd see how it went. But he had the projector and he'd lost them and he hadn't gotten his ass shot for interrupting somebody's poker game. "Lateral thinking," he said, congratulating himself, as he reached the end of the walkway and rounded a corner.

He felt the rib crack as the weight lifter hit him and knew that the black glove, like the ones he'd trained with in Nashville, was weighted with lead.

It sent him back against the opposite wall, his head slamming against that, and his whole left side refused to move when he tried.

The weight lifter pulled the black glove back for a roundhouse into Rydell's face. And smiled.

Rydell tried to shake his head.

Faintest look of surprise, maybe confusion, in the other's eyes, his face. Then nothing. The smile gone slack.

The weight lifter went suddenly and very heavily to his knees, swayed, and crashed sideways to the gray timber deck. Revealing behind him this slender, gray-haired man in a long smooth coat the color of old moss, who was replacing something there, the lapel held open with his other hand. Eyes regarding Rydell through gold-rimmed glasses. A deep crease up each cheek, like he smiled a lot. The man adjusted his beautiful coat and lowered his hands.

"Are you injured?"

Rydell drew a ragged breath, wincing as the rib seemed to grate. "Rib," he managed.

"Are you armed?"

Rydell looked into the clear, bright, unmoving eyes. "Knife in my right pocket," he said.

"Please keep it there," the man said. "Are you able to walk?"

"Sure," Rydell said, taking a step and almost falling on the weight lifter.

"Come with me, please," the man said and turned, and Rydell followed.

46. PINE BOX

CREEDMORE was into the climax of his number before Chevette spotted God's Little Toy cruising past overhead. The bar, like a lot of the spaces here on the original deck, didn't have a ceiling of its own, just the bottoms of whatever floor areas had been erected above it, with the result that what passed for a ceiling was uneven and irregular. The management had at some point sprayed all that black, and Chevette might not have noticed the floating camera platform if its Mylar balloon hadn't caught and reflected the stage lights. It was definitely under human control and looked like it might be jockeying to get a close-up of Creedmore. Then Chevette spotted two more of the silver balloons, these parked up in a sort of hollow created by a discontinuity in the floors above.

That meant, she thought, that Tessa had gotten someone to drive her back to the foot of Folsom. Then either she'd driven back or gotten a lift. (She was pretty sure Tessa wouldn't have walked it, not with the balloons anyway.) Chevette hoped the latter, because she didn't want to have to try to find a space to park the van a second time. Whatever Tessa was up to here, they were going to need a place to sleep later.

Creedmore's song ended with a sort of yodeling cry of brainless defiance, which was echoed back, amplified into a terrifying roar, by the meshback crowd. Chevette was amazed by the enthusiasm, not so much that it was for Creedmore as it was for this kind of music. Music was strange that way though; there were people into any damned thing, it seemed like, and if you got enough of them together in one bar, she guessed, you could have a pretty good time.

She was still working her way through the crowd, warding off the odd grope, looking for Tessa, and keeping an eye out for Carson, when Creedmore's friend Maryalice found her. Maryalice had undone a couple of extra increments of bustier, it looked like, and was presenting as very ample indeed. She looked really happy, or anyway as happy as you can look when you're really drunk, which she definitely and obviously was.

"Honey!" she cried, grabbing Chevette by the shoulders. "Where have you been? We got all kinds of free drinks for our industry guests!"

Maryalice clearly didn't remember Chevette having told her that she and Tessa weren't A&R people, but Chevette guessed that there was quite a lot, usually, that Maryalice didn't remember.

"That's great," Chevette said. "Have you seen Tessa? My friend I was here with? She's Australian—"

"Up in the light booth with Saint Vitus, honey. She's getting Buell's whole performance on those little balloon things!" Maryalice beamed. Gave Chevette a big, lipstick-greasy kiss on the cheek and instantly forgot her, face going blank as she turned in what Chevette supposed would be the direction of the bar.

But the light booth, now, she could see that: a sort of oversized matte-black crate tacked up against the angle of the wall, opposite the stage, with a warped plastic window running its length, through which she could see, quite plainly, the faces of Tessa and some bald-headed boy with mean-looking slitty black glasses. Just their two heads in there, like puppet heads. Reached, she saw, by an aluminum stepladder fastened to the wall with lengths of rusting pipe strap.

Tessa had her own special glasses on, and Chevette knew she'd be seeing the output from God's Little Toy, adjusting angle and focus with her black glove. Creedmore had launched into another song, its tempo faster, and people were tapping their feet and bobbing up and down in time.

Couple of men in those meshback caps, drinking beer out of cans, by that ladder, but she ducked under their arms and climbed up, ignoring the one who laughed and swatted her butt with the flat of his hand.

Up through the square hole, her nose level with dusty, beer-soaked brown carpet. "Tessa. Hey."

"Chevette?" Tessa didn't turn, lost in the view in her glasses. "Where'd you go?"

"I saw Carson," Chevette said, climbing up through the hole. "I took off."

"This is amazing footage," Tessa said. "The faces on these people. Like Robert Frank. I'm going to treat it as mono and grain it down—"

"Tessa," Chevette said, "I think we should get out of here."

"Who the fuck are you?" said the baldie, turning. He was wearing a sleeveless tube shirt and his upper arms were no thicker than Chevette's wrists, his bare shoulders looking fragile as the bones of a bird.

"This is Saint Vitus," Tessa said, as if absently bidding to forestall hostilities, attention elsewhere. "He does the lights in here, but he's the sound man at two other clubs on the bridge, Cognitive Dissidents and something else . . ." Tessa's hand dancing with itself in the black control glove.

Chevette knew Cog Diss from before. "That's a dancer bar, Tessa," she said.

"We're going over there after this," Tessa said. "He says it'll just be getting going, and it'll be a lot more interesting than this."

"Anything would," Saint Vitus said with infinite weariness.

"Blue Ahmed cut a single there," Tessa said, "called 'My War Is My War.' "

"It sucked," Chevette said.

"You're thinking of the Chrome Koran *cover*," said Saint Vitus, his voice dripping with contempt. "You've never heard Ahmed's version."

"How the fuck would you know?" Chevette demanded.

"Because it was never *released*," Saint Vitus declared smugly.

"Well, maybe it fucking *escaped*," Chevette said, feeling like she wanted to deck this diz-monkey, and thinking it might not be that hard to do, although you never knew what would happen if somebody tightened on dancer got really upset. All those stories about twelve-year-olds getting so dizzed they'd grab the bumper of a cop car and flip the whole thing, though these usually involved the kids' muscles popping out through their skins, which she sincerely hoped was impossible. Had to be: what Carson called urban legends.

Creedmore's song ended with a steely clash of guitar that drew Chevette's attention to the stage. Creedmore looked completely tightened now, staring triumphantly out as though across a sea of faces in some vast stadium.

The big guitarist unslung his red guitar and handed it to a boy with sideburns and a black leather vest, who passed him a black guitar with a skinnier body.

"This here's called 'Pine Box,' " Creedmore said, as the big guitarist began to play. Chevette couldn't catch the words as Creedmore began to sing, except that it sounded old and doleful and was about winding up in a pine box, by which she took him to mean a coffin, like what they used to bury people in, but she guessed it could just as easily apply to this sound booth she was stuck in here, with Tessa and this asshole. She looked around and saw an old chrome stool with its pad of upholstery split and taped over, so she planted herself on that and decided she was just going to keep quiet until Tessa had taped as much as she wanted of Creedmore's act. Then she'd see about getting them out of here.

47. SAI SHING ROAD

LIBIA and Paco have shown Laney to a barbershop in Sai Shing Road. He has arrived here, of course, with no knowledge of the route involved; Sai Shing is in the Walled City, and he is a visitor, not a resident. The Walled City's whereabouts, the conceptual mechanisms by which its citizens have opted to secede from the human datascape at large are the place's central and most closely held secret. The Walled City is a universe unto itself, a subversive rumor, the stuff of legend.

Laney has been here before, although not to this specific construct, this barbershop, and he dislikes the place. Something in the underlying code of the Walled City's creation induces a metaphysical vertigo, and the visual representation is tediously aggressive, as though one were caught in some art school video production with infinitely high production values. Nothing is ever straightforward, in the Walled City; nothing is ever presented as written, but filtered instead through half a dozen species of carefully cultivated bit rot, as though the inhabitants were determined to express their massive attitude right down into the least fractal texture of the place. Where a clever website might hint at dirt, at wear, the Walled City luxuriates in apparent frank decay, in texture maps that constantly unravel, revealing of other textures, equally moth-eaten.

This barbershop, for instance, is shingled from overlapping tiles of texture, so that they don't quite match up at their edges, deliberately spoiling any illusion of surface or place. And everything here is done in a palette of rain-wet Chinatown neon: pink, blue, yellow, pale green, and the authoritatively faded red.

Libia and Paco depart immediately, leaving Laney to wonder how he, were he to bother, might choose to present himself in this environment: perhaps as a large cardboard carton?

Klaus and the Rooster put an end to this surmise, however, abruptly appearing in two of the shop's four barber chairs. They look as he remembers them, except that Klaus now wears a black leather version of his snap-brim fedora, its brim turned up all around, and the Rooster somehow looks even more like one of Francis Bacon's screaming popes.

"Whole new game here," Laney opens.

"How so?" Klaus appears to suck his teeth.

"Harwood's had 5-SB. And you know it too, because those chilango kids of yours just told me. How long have you known?"

"We operate on a need-to-know basis," the Rooster begins, in full geek-pontificator mode, but Klaus cuts him off: "About ten minutes longer than you have. We're anxious to know what you make of it."

"It changes everything," Laney says. "The way he's been successful all these years: the public relations empire, advertising, the rumors that he was pivotal in getting President Millbank elected, that he was behind the partition of Italy . . ."

"I thought that was his girlfriend," the Rooster says sullenly, "that Padanian princess—"

"You mean he's only picking winners?" Klaus demands. "You're suggesting that he's in nodal mode and simply gets behind emerging change? If that's all it is, my friend, why aren't *you* one of the richest men in the world?"

"It doesn't work that way," Laney protests. "5-SB allows the apprehension of nodal points, discontinuities in the texture of information. They indicate emerging change, but not what that change will be."

"True," agrees Klaus and purses his lips.

"What I want to know," Laney says, "what I need to know, and right now, is what Harwood is up to. He's sitting at the cusp of some unprecedented potential for change. He appears to be instrumental in it. Rei Toei is in it too, and this freelance people-eraser of Harwood's, and an out-of-work rent-a-cop . . . These people are about to change human history in some entirely new way. There hasn't been a configuration like this since 1911—"

"What happened in 1911?" the Rooster demands.

Laney sighs. "I'm still not sure. It's complicated and I haven't had the time to really look at it. Madame Curie's husband was run over by a horse-drawn wagon, in Paris, in 1906. It seems to start there. But if Harwood is the strange attractor here, the crucial piece of weirdness things need to accrete around, and he's self-aware in that role, what is it he's trying to do that has the potential to literally change *every-thing*?"

"We aren't positive," the Rooster begins, "but—"

"Nanotechnology," Klaus says. "Harwood was a major player in Sunflower Corporation. A scheme to rebuild San Francisco. Very radical restructuring, employing nanotechnology along much the lines it was employed, post-quake, in Tokyo. That didn't fly, and, very oddly indeed, it looks to us as though your man Rydell was somehow instrumental in helping it not to fly, but that can wait. My point is that Harwood has demonstrated an ongoing interest in nanotechnology, and this has manifested most recently in a collaboration between Nanofax AG of Geneva—"

"Harwood front," the Rooster says, "run through a shell corporation in Antigua—"

"Shut up," and the Rooster does. "Between Nanofax AG of Geneva and the Lucky Dragon Corporation of Singapore. Lucky Dragon is a Harwood Levine client of course."

"Nanofax?"

"Everything the name implies," says Klaus, "and considerably less."

"What's that supposed to mean?"

"Nanofax AG offers a technology that digitally reproduces objects, physically, at a distance. Within certain rather large limitations, of course. A child's doll, placed in a Lucky Dragon Nanofax unit in London, will be reproduced in the Lucky Dragon Nanofax unit in New York—"

"How?"

"With assemblers, out of whatever's available. But the system's been placed under severe legal constraints. It can't, for instance, reproduce functional hardware. And of course it can't, most particularly can't, reproduce functional nanoassemblers."

"I thought that they'd proven that didn't work anyway," Laney says.

"Oh no," says the Rooster, "they just don't want it to."

"They who?"

"Nation-states," says the Rooster. "Remember them?"

48. IN THE MOMENT

RYDELL watched this man move ahead, in front of him, and felt something complicated, something he couldn't get a handle on, but something that came through anyway, through the ache in his side, the pain that grated there if he stepped wrong. He'd always dreamed of a special kind of grace, Rydell: of just moving, moving right, without thinking of it. Alert, relaxed, there. And somehow he knew that that was what he was seeing now, what he was following: this guy who was maybe fifty, and who moved, though without seeming to think about it, in a way that kept him in every bit of available shadow. Upright in his long wool coat, hands in pockets, he just moved, and Rydell followed, in his pain and the clumsiness that induced, but also in the pain somehow of his adolescent heart, the boy in him having wanted all these years to be something like this man, whoever and whatever he was.

A killer, Rydell reminded himself, thinking of the weight lifter they'd left behind; Rydell knew that killing was not the explosive handshake exchange of movies, but a terrible dark marriage unto and perhaps (though he hoped not) even beyond the grave, as still his own dreams were sometimes visited by the shade of Kenneth Turvey, the only man he'd ever had to kill. Though he'd never doubted the need of killing Turvey, because Turvey had been demonstrating his seriousness with random shots through the door of a closet in which he'd locked his girlfriend's children. Killing anyone was a terrible and permanent thing to enter into, Rydell believed, and he also knew that violent criminals, in real life, were about as romantic as a lapful of guts. Yet here he was, doing the best he could to keep up with this gray-haired man, who'd just killed someone in a manner Rydell would've been unable to specify, but silently and without raising a sweat; who'd just killed someone the way another man might change his shirt or open a bottle of beer. And something in Rydell yearned so to be that, that, feeling it now, he blushed.

The man stopped, in shadow, looking back. "How are you?"

"Fine," Rydell said, which was almost always what he said if anyone asked him that.

"You are not 'fine.' You are injured. You may be bleeding internally."

Rydell halted in front of him, hand pressed to his burning side. "What did you do to that guy?"

You couldn't have said that the man smiled, but the creases in his cheeks seemed to deepen slightly. "I completed the movement he began when he struck you."

"You stabbed him with something," Rydell said.

"Yes. That was the most elegant conclusion, under the circumstances. His unusual center of gravity made it possible to sever the spinal cord without contacting the vertebrae themselves." This in a tone that someone might use to describe the discovery of a new but convenient bus route.

"Show me."

The man's head moved, just a fraction. Some birdlike acuity. Light winked, reflected, in the round, gold-framed glasses. He reached into the open front of his long coat and produced, with a very peculiar and offhand grace, a blade curved, upswept, chisel-tipped. What they called a tanto, Rydell knew: the short version of one of those Japanese swords. The same light that had caught in the round lenses now snagged for an instant in a hair-fine line of rainbow along the curved edge and the angled tip, and then the man reversed the movement that had produced the knife. It vanished within the coat as though a segment of tape had been run backward.

Rydell remembered being taught how you had to use something, anything, if someone was coming after you with a knife, and you were unarmed. If nothing else you were supposed to take off your jacket and roll it around your hands and wrists, to protect them. Now he imagined using the projector, in its bag, as a sort of shield, to ward off the knife he'd just seen, and the hopelessness of the idea actually struck him as funny.

"Why did you smile?" the man asked.

Rydell stopped smiling. "I don't think I could explain," he said. "Who are you?"

"I can't tell you that," the man said.

"I'm Berry Rydell," Rydell said. "You saved my ass back there."

"But not your torso, I think."

"He might've killed me."

"No," the man said, "he wouldn't have killed you. He would have rendered you helpless, taken you to a private location, and tortured you to extract information. Then he would have killed you."

"Well," Rydell said, uneasy with the matter-of-factness here, "thanks."

"You are welcome," said the man, with great gravity and not the least hint of irony.

"Well," Rydell said, "why *did* you do that, take him out?"

"Because it was necessary, to complete the movement."

"I don't get it," said Rydell.

"It was necessary," the man said. "There are a number of these men seeking you tonight. I'm uncertain of how many. They are mercenaries."

"Did you kill someone else, back there, last night? Where those patches of dried blood and Kil'Z are?"

"Yes," the man said.

"And I'm safer with you than I am with these guys you say are mercs?"

"I think so, yes," the man said, frowning, as though he took the question very seriously.

"You kill anybody else in the past forty-eight hours?"

"No," said the man, "I did not."

"Well," Rydell said, "I guess I'm with you. I'm sure not going to try to fight you."

"That is wise," the man said.

"And I don't think I could run fast enough, or very far, with this rib."

"That is true."

"So what do we do?" Rydell shrugged, instantly regretting it, his face contorting in a grimace of pain.

"We will leave the bridge," the man said, "and seek medical aid for your injury. I myself have a thorough working knowledge of anatomy, should it prove necessary."

"Unh, thanks," Rydell managed. "If I could just buy some four-inch tape and some analgesic plasters at that Lucky Dragon, I could probably make do." He looked around, wondering when he'd next see or be seen by the one with the scarf. He had a feeling the scarf was the one he'd really have to watch out for; he couldn't say why. "What if those mercs scope us leaving?"

"Don't anticipate outcome," the man said. "Await the unfolding of events. Remain in the moment."

In the moment, Rydell decided he knew for a fact his ass was lost. Just plain lost.

49. RADON SHADOW

FONTAINE finds the boy an old camping pad, left here by his children perhaps, and lays him back on this, still snoring. Removing the heavy eyephones he sees how the boy sleeps with his eyes half-open, showing the white; imagines watches ticking past, there, one after another. He covers him with an old sleeping bag whose faded flannel liner depicts mountains and bears, then takes his miso back to the counter to think.

There is a faint vibration now, though whether of the shop's flimsy fabric, the bones of the bridge, or the underlying plates of the earth he cannot tell: but small sounds come from the shelves and cabinets as tiny survivors of the past register this new motion. A lead soldier, on one shelf, topples forward with a definitive clack, and Fontaine makes a mental note to buy more museum wax, a sticky substance meant to prevent this.

Fontaine, seated on his high stool, behind the counter, sipping gingerly at his hot miso, wonders what exactly he would see, were he to follow the boy's course today via the notebook's recall function. That business with the lockboxes, and Martial getting all worked up. Where else might the boy have been? But nowhere really dangerous, Fontaine decides, if he's only chasing watches. But how was it he did that, got those lockbox lists? Fontaine puts the miso down and fishes the Jaeger-LeCoultre from his pocket. He reads the ordnance marks on its back:

G6B / 346

RA ⋀ AF

172 / 53

The 6B denoting a particular grade of movement, degree of accuracy, he knows, though the 346 is a mystery. The broad arrow, central, the Queen's mark, her property. 53 the year of issue, but 172? Could the boy somehow pry knowledge from these numbers, if the question could be put to him? Somewhere out there, Fontaine knows, every last bit of information makes its way into the stream. He puts the watch down on his Rolex pad and takes up the salty miso again. Looking down through the scratch-frosted glass countertop, he notices a recent purchase, not yet examined. A Helbros from the 1940s, styled after military watches but not an "issue" watch. Something he bought from a scavenger, down from the Oakland hills. He reaches into the counter and brings it out, a shabby thing after the G6B.

Its bezel is badly dinged, probably too badly to benefit from buffing, and the luminous on the dull black dial has gone a shade of silvery ash. He takes his loupe from his other pocket and screws it into his eye, turning the Helbros under his ten-power Cyclops gaze. The caseback has been removed, screwed back in, but left untightened. He turns it out with his fingers, to check inside for minute graven records of its repair history.

He squints through the loupe: the last repair date etched into the inside back is August 1945.

He turns it over again and studies it. The crystal is synthetic, some sort of plastic, definitely vintage and very probably original. Because, he sees, holding it at just this certain angle to the light, radiation from the original radium numerals has darkened the crystal focally, each number having in effect radiographed itself in the accidental plate of the crystal.

And somehow this, combined with the hidden date, gives Fontaine a shiver, so that he puts the caseback back into place, replaces the Helbros in the counter, checks the locks on the door, finishes his miso, and starts to ready himself for bed.

The boy, on his back, is no longer snoring, and that is a good thing.

When Fontaine lies down on his own narrow bunk, to sleep, the Smith & Wesson Kit Gun, as it is every night, is at the ready.

50. "MORE TROUBLE"

RYDELL'S father, dying of cancer, had told Rydell a story. He claimed to have gotten it from a book of famous last words, or if not famous then at least memorable.

This man was being executed in England, back in the old days, when execution was made as deliberately hard a thing as possible, and after being burned with hot irons, broken on the wheel, and various other horrific punishments, the man was shown the block, the heads-man's ax. And having been closed-mouthed and stolid throughout his various tortures, he had looked at the ax and the block and the burly headsman and made no reply at all.

But then another torturer arrived, carrying an assortment of terri-ble-looking tools, and the man was informed that he was to be disem-boweled prior to his beheading.

The man sighed. "More trouble," he said.

"IF they want me," Rydell said, wincing along beside the man with the tanto in his coat, "why don't they just grab me?"

"Because you are with me."

"Why don't they just shoot you?"

"Because we have, these men and I, the same employer. In a sense."

"He wouldn't let them shoot you?"

"That would depend," the man said.

Rydell could see that they were coming up on the nameless bar where he'd heard Buell Creedmore sing that old song. There was noise there: loud music, laughter, a crowd around the door, drinking beer and openly smoking cigarettes.

His side hurt with each step he took, and he thought of Rei Toei perched on his pillow, glowing. What, he wondered, did the projector slung over his shoulder mean to her? Was it her only means of mani-festing here, of interacting with people? Did being a hologram feel like anything? (He doubted it.) Or did the programs that generated her somehow provide some greater illusion of being there? But if you weren't real in the first place, what did you have to compare not being there *to*?

But what really bothered him, now, was that Laney, and Klaus and the Rooster too, had thought that the projector was important, really important, and now here he went, Rydell, limping willingly along beside this killer, this man who evidently worked for whoever it was was after Rydell's ass, and probably after the projector as well, and he was just going along with it. Sheep to the slaughter.

"I want to go in here a minute," Rydell said.

"Why?"

"See a friend," Rydell said.

"Is this a bid for escape?"

"I don't want to go with you."

The man regarded him from behind the thin crystal rounds of his glasses. "You are complicating things," he said.

"So kill me," Rydell said, gritting his teeth as he slung his weight around and staggered past the smokers by the door, into the warm loud beer smell and crowd energy.

Creedmore was onstage with Randy Shoats and a bass player with sideburns, and whatever they were playing reached its natural conclusion at just that point, Creedmore jumping into the air as he let out a final whoop and the music crashed down around him, the crowd roaring and stomping and clapping. Rydell had seen Creedmore's eyes flash flat and bright as a doll's in the stage light. "Hey, Buell!" Rydell shouted. "Creedmore!" He shouldered someone out of his way and kept going. He was a few feet from the stage now. "Buell!" It was just a little thing, the stage, maybe a foot high, and the crowd wasn't that thick.

Creedmore saw him. He stepped down from the stage. The singer's pearl-button cowboy shirt was open to the waist, his hollow white chest gleaming with sweat. Someone handed him a towel and he wiped his face with it, grinning, showing long yellow teeth and no gum. "Rydell," he said. "Son of a bitch. Where you been?"

"Looking for you, Buell."

The man with the knife put his hand on Rydell's shoulder. "This is unwise," he said.

"Hey, Buell," Rydell said, "get me a beer, okay?"

"You see me, Rydell? I was fuckin' Jesus' son, man. Fuckin' Hank Williams, motherfucker." Creedmore beamed, yet Rydell saw the thing that was waiting there to toggle into rage. Someone handed Creedmore two tall cans, already opened. He passed one to Rydell. Creedmore splashed cold malt liquor down his chest, rubbed himself with it. "Damn, I'm good."

"We can be too easily contained here," the man said.

"Leggo my buddy there," said Creedmore, noticing the man for the first time. "Faggot," he added, as if further taking in the man's appearance and seeming to have difficulty placing it in any more convenient category of abuse.

"Buell," Rydell said, reaching up and grabbing the man's wrist, "want you to meet a friend of mine."

"Looks like some faggot oughta be kilt with a shovel," Creedmore observed, slit-eyed and furious now, the toggle having been thrown.

"Let go of my shoulder," Rydell said to the man, quietly. "It doesn't look good."

The man let go of Rydell's shoulder.

"Sorry," Rydell said, "but I'm staying here with Buell and a hundred or so of his close personal friends." He looked at the can in his hand. Something called King Cobra. He took a sip. "You want to go, go. Otherwise, just kill me."

"Goddamn you, Creedmore," Randy Shoats said, stepping heavily down from the stage, "you fucking drug addict. You're drunk. Drunk and ripped to the tits on dancer."

Creedmore goggled up at the big guitar player, his eyes all pupil. "Jesus, Randy," he began, "you know I just needed to get a little loose—"

"Loose? Loose? Jesus. You forgot the words to 'Drop That Jerk and Come with Me'! How fucked do you have to be to do that? Fuckin' audience knew the words, man; they were singing along with you. Trying to, anyway." Shoats rammed his callused thumb into Creedmore's chest for emphasis. "I told you I don't work with diz-monkeys. You're toast, under-stand? Outta here. History."

Creedmore seemed to reach far down into the depths of his being, as if to summon some new degree of honesty, in order to face this moment of crisis. He seemed to find it. Drew himself more upright. "Fuck you," he said. "Motherfucker," he added, as Shoats, disgusted, turned and walked away.

"Buell," Rydell said, "they got a table or something reserved for you here? Someplace I could sit down?"

"Maryalice," Creedmore said, thoughts elsewhere, waving in the general direction of the back of the bar. He set off, apparently after Shoats.

Rydell ignored the man with the tanto and headed for the back of the bar, where he found Maryalice seated alone at a table. There was a hand-lettered sign, on brown corrugated cardboard, done in different colored felt pens, that said ***BUELL CREEDMORE*** & HIS LOWER COMPANIONS, each of the Os done in red as a little happy face. The table was solid, side to side, with empties, and Maryalice looked like somebody had just whacked her in the head with something that didn't leave a mark. "You A&R?" she asked Rydell, as if startled from a dream.

"I'm Berry Rydell," he said, pulling out a chair and unslinging the bag with the projector. "Met earlier. You're Maryalice."

"Yes," she smiled, as if pleased with the convenience of being so reminded, "I am. Wasn't Buell wonderful?"

Rydell sat, trying to find a way to manage it that kept the rib from killing him. "They got an outlet around here, Maryalice?" He was open-ing the duffel, pushing it down around the sides of the projector, pulling out the power cable.

"You're A&R," Maryalice said, delighted, seeing the projector, "I knew you were. Which label?"

"Plug this in there, please?" Rydell pointed to an outlet just beside her, on the scabrous wall, and passed her the plug end of the cable. She held it close to her face, blinked at it, looked around, saw the socket. Plugged it in. Turned back to Rydell, as if puzzled by what she'd just done.

The man with the tanto brought over a chair, placed it at the table, and took a seat opposite Maryalice. He did it, somehow, in a way that occupied as little of anyone else's consciousness as possible. "Now you," Maryalice said to him, with a quick glance down to check the state of her bodice, "you are pretty clearly a label head, am I correct?"

"Lapel?"

"I knew you were," Maryalice said.

Rydell heard the projector humming.

And then Rei Toei was there, standing beside their table, and Rydell knew that once again he'd seen her naked for a second, glowing, white, but now she wore an outfit identical, it seemed, to Maryalice's. "Hello, Berry Rydell," she said, then looked down and tightened the strings at the top of the black thing she wore.

"Hey," Rydell said.

"Well, suck me raw with a breast pump," Maryalice said, voice soft with amazement, as she stared at Rei Toei. "I swear to God I didn't see you standing there . . ."

The man with the tanto was looking at Rei Toei too, the light of her projection reflected in the round lenses.

"We are in a nightclub, Berry Rydell?"

"A bar," Rydell said.

"Rez liked bars," she said, looking around at the crowd. "I have the impression that people in bars, though they seem to be talking to one another, are actually talking to themselves. Is this because higher brain function has been suppressed for recreational purposes?"

"I just love your top," Maryalice said.

"I am Rei Toei."

"Maryalice," Maryalice said, extending her hand. The idoru did likewise, her hand passing through Maryalice's.

Maryalice shivered. "Had about enough, this evening," she said, as if to herself.

"I am Rei Toei." To the man with the tanto.

"Good evening."

"I know your name," she gently said to the man. "I know a great deal about you. You are a fascinating person."

He looked at her, expression unchanged. "Thank you," he said. "Mr. Rydell, is it your intention to remain here, with your friends?"

"Time being," Rydell said. "I have to phone somebody."

"As you will," the man said. He turned to survey the entrance, and just then the scarf came strolling in and saw them all, immediately.

More trouble, thought Rydell.

51. THE REASON OF LIFE

LANEY'S two favorite Tokyo bars, during the happier phase of his employment at Paragon-Asia Dataflow, had been Trouble Peach, a quiet sit-and-drink place near Shimo-kitazawa Station, and The Reason of Life, an art bar in the basement of an office building in Aoyama. The Reason of Life was an art bar, in Laney's estimation, by virtue of being decorated with huge black-and-white prints of young women photographing their own crotches with old-fashioned reflex cameras. These were such modest pictures that it took you, initially, a while to figure out what they were doing. Standing, mostly, in crowded streetscapes, with the camera on the pavement, between their feet, smiling into the photographer's lens and thumbing a manual release. They wore sweaters and plaid skirts, usually, and smiled out at you with a particularly innocent eagerness. Nobody had ever explained to Laney what this was all supposed to be about, and it wouldn't have occurred to him to ask, but he knew art when he saw it, and he was seeing it again now, courtesy of the Rooster, who somehow knew Laney liked the place in Aoyama and had decided to reproduce it, off the cuff, here in the Walled City.

In any case, Laney prefers it to the barbershop made of misaligned graphics tiles. You can just look at these girls, in cool monochrome renditions of wool and flesh and other textures of cities, and he finds that restful. It was strange though, to sit in a bar when you didn't have a body present.

"They're coy about it," the Rooster is saying, of Libia and Paco and how it may be that they've succeeded in hacking Cody Harwood's most intensely private means of communication. "They may have physically introduced an agent into Harwood Levine's communications satellite. Something small. Very small. But how could they have controlled it? And how long would it have taken, undetected, to effect a physical alteration in the hardware up there?"

"I'm sure they found a more elegant solution," Klaus says, "but the bottom line is that I don't care. Access is access. The means to access are academic. We've hacked Harwood's hotline. His red telephone."

"And you have a tendency to pat yourselves on the back," Laney says. "We know that Harwood's had 5-SB, but we don't know why, or what he's doing with nodal apprehension. You seem to be convinced it's something to do with Lucky Dragon and this half-baked Nanofax launch."

"Aren't you?" asks Klaus. "Nanofax units are going into every Lucky Dragon in the world. Right now. Literally. Most of them are fully installed, ready to go operational."

"With the faxing of the first Taiwanese teddy bear from Des Moines to Seattle? What's he hope to gain?" Laney concentrates on his favorite girl, imagining her thumb on the plunger of a hypodermic-style manual release.

"Think network," the Rooster puts in. "Function, even ostensible function, is not the way to look at this. All function, in these terms, is ostensible. Temporary. What he wants is a network in place. Then he can figure out what to do with it."

"But why does he need to have something to do with it in the first place?" Laney demands.

"Because he's between a rock and a hard place," responds Klaus. "He's the richest man in the world, possibly, and he's ahead of the curve. He's an agent of change, and massively invested in the status quo. He embodies paradoxical propositions. Too hip to live, too rich to die. Get it?"

"No," Laney says.

"We think he's like us, basically," Klaus says. "He's trying to hack reality, but he's going strictly big casino, and he'll take the rest of the species with him, however and whatever."

"You have to admire that, don't you?" says the Rooster, out of the depths of his silent faux-Bacon scream.

Laney isn't sure that you do.

He wonders if the Rooster's reiteration of The Reason of Life incorporates the tiny, six-seater bar downstairs, the darker one where you can sit beneath very large prints of the pictures the girls themselves were taking: huge abstract triangles of luminous gelatin-printed white panty.

"Can you get me that kind of look-in on Harwood's stuff anytime?"

"Until he notices you, we can."

52. MY BOYFRIEND'S BACK

CHEVETTE had had a boyfriend named Lowell, when she'd first lived on the bridge, who did dancer.

Lowell had had a friend called Codes, called that because he tumbled the codes on hot phones and notebooks, and this Saint Vitus reminded her of Codes. Codes hadn't liked her either.

Chevette hated dancer. She hated being around people when they were on it, because it made them selfish, too pleased with themselves, and nervous; suspicious, too prone to make things up in their heads, imagining everyone out to get them, everyone lying, everyone talking behind their back. And she particularly hated watching anyone actually do the stuff, rub it into their gums the way they did, all horrible, because it was just so gross. Made their lips numb, at first, so they'd drool a little, and how they always thought that was funny. But what she hated about it most was that she'd ever done it herself, and that, even though she had all these reasons to hate it, she still found herself, watching Saint Vitus vigorously massaging a good solid hit into his gums, feeling the urge to ask him for some.

She guessed that was what they meant by it being addictive. That she'd gotten just that little edge of it off the country singer sticking his tongue in her mouth (and if that was the only way to get it, she thought, she'd pass) and now the actual molecules of diz were twanging at receptor sites in her brain, saying gimme, gimme. And she'd never even been properly strung out on the stuff, not how they meant it when they said that on the street.

Carson had coordinated on a Real One sequence about the history of stimulants, so Chevette knew that dancer was somewhere out there past crack cocaine in terms of sheer gotcha. The addiction schedule was a little less merciless, in terms of frequency, but she figured she'd still just barely missed it, chipping with Lowell. Lowell who'd explain in detail and at great length how the schedule he'd worked out for using it was going to optimize his functionality in the world, but never result in one of those ugly habit deals. You just had to know how to do it, and when to do it, and most important of all, why to do it. Powerful substance like this, Lowell would explain, it wasn't there just for any casual jack-off recreational urge. It was there to allow you to do things. To empower you, he said, so that you could do things and, best of all, finish them.

Except that what Lowell had mainly wanted to do, dizzed, was have sex, and the diz made it impossible for him to finish. Which had been okay by Chevette, because otherwise he tended to finish a little on the quick side. The Real One sequence had said that dancer made it possible for men to experience something much more like the female orgasm, a sort of ongoing climax, less localized and, well, messy.

Dancer was pretty deadly stuff, in terms of getting people into bed in the first place. Strangers doing dancer together, if there was any basis for attraction at all, were inclined to decide that that was basically a fine idea, and one to be acted on right away, but only provided the other party seemed agreeable to doing it until both were pretty well dead.

And people did wind up dead around the stuff; hearts stopped, lungs forgot to breathe, crucial tiny territories of brain blew out. People murdered one another when they were crazy on the stuff, and then in cold blood just to get some more.

It was one ugly substance and no doubt about it.

"You got any more of that?" she asked Saint Vitus, who was dabbing at the spit-slick corners of his mouth with a wadded-up tissue, dots of blood dried brown on it.

Saint Vitus fixed her with his slitty glasses. "You've got to be kidding," he said.

"Yeah," said Chevette, pushing off the stool, "I am." Must've been the time of night. How could she even have thought that? She could smell his metallic breath in the sound box.

"Got it," said Tessa, pulling off the glasses. "Crowd's thinning. Chevette, I'll need you to help me get the camera platforms together."

Saint Vitus smirked. At the thought, Chevette guessed, of somebody else having to do something like work.

"You haven't seen Carson, have you?" Chevette asked, stepping to the window. The dwindling crowd, seen from above, was moving in one of those ways that there was probably a logarithm for: milling and dispersing.

"Carson?"

She spotted Buell Creedmore, just in front of the stage, talking with a big guy in a black jacket, his back to the sound booth. Then the big guitar player, the one with the squashed cowboy hat, jumped down from the stage and seemed to be giving Creedmore a hard time. Creedmore tried to say something, got shut up, then managed to say something short, and by the look on his face, not too sweet, and the guitar player turned and walked away. Chevette saw Creedmore say something to the other guy, gesturing back in her direction, and this one turned and headed that way, his face concealed, from just this angle, by a dusty swoop of black-painted cable.

"He was here before," Chevette said. "That's why I Frenched the meshback and ran out the door. Didn't you wonder?"

Tessa looked at her. "I did, actually. But I thought maybe I was just getting to know you better." She laughed. "Are you sure it was him?"

"It was him, Tessa."

"How would he know we're up here?"

"Somebody told him at the house? You talked enough, before, about your docu."

"Maybe," Tessa said, interest waning. "Help me get the platforms tethered, okay?" She handed Chevette four black nylon tethers, each one tipped with a mini-bungee and a metal clip.

"Listen," Chevette said, "I'm not up for a night at Cognitive Dissidents, okay? I don't think you are either. I just watched your friend here gum enough dancer to wire a mule."

"Chevette," Tessa said, "we're up here to document, remember? We're going interstitial."

Saint Vitus sniggered.

"I think where we're going is to sleep, Tessa. Where's the truck?"

"Where we parked it."

"How'd you get the balloons back here?"

"Elmore," Tessa said. "Has one of those caps, and an ATV to go with it."

"See if you can find him again," Chevette said, starting down the ladder. "We could use a lift back."

Chevette wasn't sure what it would actually take to get Tessa to give up on Cognitive Dissidents. Worst case, she might actually have to go there, if only to make sure Tessa was okay. Cog Diss was a rough enough place even if you didn't have your head buried in a pair of video glasses.

She went down the ladder and headed out onto the floor, where God's Little Toy was already descending, under Tessa's control. She reached up, got it tethered, and turned to signal Tessa, in the sound booth, to start bringing the others down.

And found herself looking, for however many dreamlike seconds, before he hit her, into Carson's eyes.

Hard and in the face, just like he'd done before, and she saw those same colors, like a flashback; saw herself falling back, across the big beige couch in his loft-space, blood splashing from her nose, and still not believing it, that he'd done that.

Except that here she went over into a couple of Creedmore's remaining audience, who caught her, laughing, saying "Hey. Whoa," and then Carson was on her again, grabbing a handful of Skinner's jacket—

"Hey, buddy," said one of the men who'd caught her, holding up his spread hand as if to block the second punch that Carson, his face as calm and serious as she'd seen it in the editing booth at Real One, was aiming at her. And looking into Carson's eyes she saw nothing there like hatred or anger, only some abstract and somehow almost *technical* need.

Carson tried for her, past that stranger's upraised hand, and her protector yelped as one of his fingers got bent back. It deflected the blow, though, and gave Chevette time to twist out of that grip.

She backed off two steps and shook her head, trying to clear it. Something was wrong with her eyes.

Carson came after her, that same look on his face, and in that instant she knew that she knew neither who he was nor what it was that was wrong with him.

"You just didn't get it, did you?" he said, or that was what she thought she heard him say, feeling a tear run down from her swelling eye, her head still ringing.

She took a step back. He came on.

"You just didn't get it."

And then a hand came down on his shoulder and he spun around. And went down, the man behind him having done something that Chevette hadn't seen.

And she saw that it was Rydell.

It wasn't.

It was.

Rydell in a rent-a-cop's black nylon jacket, looking at her with an expression of utter and baffled amazement.

And Chevette got it, right then and absolutely, that she was dreaming, and felt the most enormous sense of relief, because now she would wake up, surely, into a world that would make sense.

On the floor, Carson, rolling over, got to his knees, stood up, shook himself, brushed a squashed cigarette-filter from the sleeve of his jacket, and suckerpunched Rydell, who saw it coming and tried to move aside, so that Carson's fist slammed into his ribs, rather than his stomach, as intended.

And Rydell screamed, in shrill animal pain, doubled over—

And that was when the guy with the black leather car-coat, the fresh-looking black buzzcut, black scarf knotted up high around his neck, this guy Chevette had never seen before, stepped up to Carson. "Mistake," she thought she heard him say. He took something from the pocket of his black coat. Then: "You're not on the menu."

And he shot Carson, right up close, without looking down at the gun in his hand.

And it was not a loud sound, not loud at all, more like the sound of a large pneumatic nail-gun, but it was final and definitive and accompanied by a yellow-blue flash, and Chevette could never remember, exactly, seeing this, though she knew she had: Carson blown back by however many thousand foot-pounds of energy trying to find their way to kinetic rest at just that one instant in his body.

But it didn't take, in memory; it did not stick, and she would be grateful.

And grateful too, though for other reasons, that this was when Tessa, in the sound booth overhead, killed the lights.

53. (YOU KNOW I CAN'T LET YOU) SLIDE THROUGH MY HANDS

RYDELL knew that sound: a subsonic projectile through a silencer that slowed it even more, draining off the expanding gases of the ignited charge, and still the muzzle velocity would be right up there, and the impact, where it was localized . . .

He knew this through the pain in his side, which felt like a white-hot ax blade between his ribs; he knew it through his shock (he was literally in shock in a number of ways) at discovering Chevette (this version of Chevette, with really different hair, more the way he'd always wished she'd wear it). He knew it in the dark that followed the report, the dark that followed the death (he was pretty sure) of whoever the man was who'd gone after Chevette, the man he'd decked, the man who'd gotten up and, it felt like, driven Rydell's broken rib halfway through his diaphragm. He knew it, and he held on to it, for the very specific reason that it meant the scarf was a trained professional, and not just some espontaneo in a bar.

Rydell knew, in those first instants of darkness, that he had a chance: as long as the scarf was a pro, he had a chance. A drunk, a crazy, any ordinary perp, in a pitch-dark bar, that was a crapshoot. A pro would move to minimize the random factor.

Which was considerable, by the sound of it, the remaining crowd, and maybe Chevette as well, screaming and heaving and struggling to get out the door. That was bad, Rydell knew, and easily fatal; he'd been a squarebadge at concerts, and had seen bodies peeled off crowd barriers.

He stood his ground, nursing the pain in his side as best he could, and waited for the scarf to make a move.

Where was Rei Toei? She should've shown up in the dark like a movie marquee, but no.

And zooming past Rydell's shoulder, toward where he'd last seen the scarf, there she was, more comet than pixie, and casting serious light.

She circled the scarf's head twice, fast, and Rydell saw him bat at her with the gun. Just a ball of silver light, moving fast enough to leave trails on Rydell's retina. The scarf ducked, as she shot straight in at his eyes; he spun and ran to the left. Rydell watched as the light expanded slightly, to whiz like cold, pale ball lightning around the perimeter of the dark bar, people moaning and gasping, screaming as she shot past. Past the struggling knot at the door, where several lay unconscious on the floor, and still no sign of Chevette.

But then the Rei-sphere swung in and down, and Rydell spotted Chevette on her hands and knees, crawling in the direction of the door. He ran over to her as best he could, his side feeling like it was about to split; bent, grabbed her, pulled her up. She started to struggle.

"It's me," he said, feeling the complete unreality of seeing her again, here, this way, "Rydell."

"What the *fuck* are you doing here, Rydell?"

"Getting out."

The blue flash and the nail-gun *fwut* were simultaneous, but it seemed to Rydell that the flick of the slug, past his head, preceded it. In immediate reply, one tight white ball of light after another was hurled past him from behind. From the projector, he realized, and likely straight into the scarf's eyes.

He grabbed Chevette under the arm and hustled her across the floor, adrenaline flooding the pain in his side. The stream of projected light, behind him, was just enough to show him the wall to the right of the door. He hoped it was plywood, and none too thick, as he pulled the switchblade from his pocket, popped it, and drove the blade in over-hand, just at eye level. It punched through, up to the handle, and he yanked it sideways and down, hearing an odd little sizzle of parting wood fiber. He made it down to waist height, twisted it, back to the left, and three-quarters of the way up the other side before he heard the glass-like *tink* of the ceramic snapping.

"Kick. Here," he said, striking the center of his cutout with the stub of the blade. "Brace up against me. Kick!"

And she did. She could kick like a mule, Chevette. The section gave way with her second try, and he was boosting her up and through, trying not to scream at the pain. He was never sure how he made it through himself, but he did, expecting any second one of those subsonics would find him.

There were people unconscious, outside the door, and other people kneeling, trying to help them.

"This way," he said, starting to limp in the direction of the ramp and the Lucky Dragon. But she wasn't with him. He swung around, saw her headed in the opposite direction. "Chevette!"

He went after her but she didn't slow down. "Chevette!"

She turned. Her right eye swelling, bruised, swimming with tears; the left wide and gray and crazy now. As if she saw him but didn't register who it was she saw. "Rydell?"

And all this time he'd thought about her, remembered her, having her there in front of him was something completely different: her long straight nose, the line of her jaw, the way he knew her lips looked in profile.

"It's okay," he said, which was absolutely all he could think of to say.

"It's not a dream?"

"No," he said.

"They shot Carson. Somebody shot him. I saw somebody shoot him."

"Who was he? Why'd he hit you?"

"He was—" She broke off, her front teeth pressing into her lower lip. "Somebody I lived with. In LA."

"Huh," Rydell said, all he could manage around the idea that the scarf had just shot Chevette's new boyfriend.

"I mean I wasn't with him. Not now. He was following me, but, Jesus, Rydell, why'd that guy . . . Just walked up and *shot* him!"

Because he was going after me, Rydell thought. Because he wanted to wail on me and I'm supposed to be theirs. But Rydell didn't say that. "The guy with the gun," he said, instead, "he'll be looking for me. He's not alone. That means you don't want to be with me when he finds me."

"Why's he looking for you?"

"Because I've got something—" But he didn't; he'd left the projector in the bar.

"You were looking for me, back there?"

I've been looking for you since you walked out. I've been working up and down the face of the waking world, every last day, with a tiny little comb, looking for you. And each day shook out empty, never never you. And he heard in memory the sound those rocks made, punching into the polymer behind the Lucky Dragon on Sunset. Pointless, pointless. "No. I'm working. Private investigation for a man named Laney."

She didn't believe him. "Carson followed me up here. I didn't want to be with him. Now you. What is this?"

Laney says it's the end of the world. "I'm just here, Chevette. You're just here. I gotta go now—"

"Where?"

"Back in the bar. I left something. It's important."

"Don't go back there!"

"I have to."

"Rydell," she began, starting to shake, "you're . . . you're—" And looked down at her open hands, the palms dark with something. And he saw that it was blood, and knew that it would be the boyfriend's, that she'd crawled through that. She started to sob, and wiped her palms down her black jeans, trying to get it off.

"Mr. Rydell?"

The man with the tanto, carrying Rydell's duffel in the crook of his arm as though it were a baby.

"Mr. Rydell, I don't think it would be advisable for you to attempt to leave the bridge. A watch has almost certainly been posted, and they will shoot you rather than permit the possibility of your escape." The pallid glare of the fluorescents chained overhead winked in the round lenses; this lean and concise man with perfectly blank, perfectly circular absences where eyes should be. "Are you with this young woman?"

"Yes," Rydell said.

"We must start toward Oakland," the man said, handing Rydell the duffel, the solid weight of the projector. Rydell hoped he'd gotten the power cable as well. "Otherwise, they will slip past and cut us off."

Rydell turned to Chevette. "Maybe they didn't see us together. You should just go."

"I wouldn't advise that," the man said. "*I* saw you together. They likely did as well."

Chevette looked up at Rydell. "Every time you come into my life, Rydell, I wind up in . . ." She made a face.

"Shit," Rydell finished for her.

54. SOME THINGS NEVER HAPPEN

THE Gunsmith Cats alarm watch taped to the wall of Laney's box brings him home from the Walled City. It buzzes to announce the Suit's impending arrival. The Suit has no watch of his own but is relentlessly punctual, his rounds timed to the clocks of the subway, which are set in turn by radio, from an atomic clock in Nagoya.

Laney tastes blood. It is a long time since he has brushed his teeth, and they feel artificial and ill-fitting, as though in his absence they have been replaced with a stranger's. He spits into a bottle kept for this purpose and considers attempting the journey to the restroom. Importance of grooming. He feels the stubble on his cheeks, calculating the effort required to remove it. He could request that the Suit obtain an electric disposable, but really he prefers a blade. He is one of those men who has never grown a beard, not even briefly. (And now, some small voice, one always best ignored, suggests: he never will.)

He hears the old man, in the next box, say something in Japanese, and knows that the Suit has arrived. He wonders what model the old man is building now, and sees, in his mind's eye, with hallucinatory clarity, the finishing touches being put on a model of Colin Laney.

It is a "garage" kit, this Laney kit, a limited run produced for only the most serious of enthusiasts, the otaku of plastic model kits, and as such it is molded from styrene of a quite nauseous mauve. The plastic used in garage kits tends to uniformly ghastly shades, as the enthusiast-manufacturers know that no kit, assembled, will ever remain unpainted.

The Laney the old man is detailing is an earlier Laney, the Laney of his days in LA, when he worked as a quantitative analyst for *Slitscan,* a tabloid television show of quite monumental viciousness: this Laney wears Padanian designer clothing and sports a very expensive pair of sunglasses, the frames of which are even now being picked out in silver by the old man's narrowest sable, scarcely more than a single hair.

But this waking dream is broken now by the advent of the Suit's head, his hair like the molded pompadour of some archaic mannequin. Laney feels, rather than sees, the precision with which the Suit's black eyeglass frames have been most recently mended, and as the Suit crawls in, beneath the flap of melon blanket, Laney smells the rancid staleness the Suit's clothing exudes. It is strange that any odor produced by a warm body should suggest intense cold, but the Suit's somehow does.

The Suit is bringing Laney more of the blue syrup, more Regain, several large chocolate bars laden with sucrose and caffeine, and two liters of generic cola. The Suit's painted shirtfront seems faintly self-luminous, like the numerals of a diver's watch glimpsed far down in the depth of a lightless well, a sacrificial cenote perhaps, and Laney finds himself adrift for just an instant in fragments of some half-remembered Yucatan vacation.

Something is wrong, Laney thinks; something is wrong with his eyes, because now the Suit's luminous shirt glows with the light of a thousand suns, and all the rest is black, the black of old negatives. And still somehow he manages to give the Suit two more of the untraceable debit chips, and even to nod at the Suit's tense little salaryman bow, executed kneeling, amid sleeping bags and candy wrappers, and then the Suit is gone, and the glare of his shirt, surely that was just some artifact of whatever process this is that Laney is here to pursue.

LANEY drinks half of one of the bottles of cough syrup, chews and swallows a third of one of the candy bars, and washes this down with a swallow of the lukewarm cola.

When he closes his eyes, even before he puts the eyephones on, he seems to plunge into the flow of data.

Immediately he is aware of Libia and Paco, directing him. They do not bother to speak or to present, but he knows them now by a certain signature, a style of navigation. He lets them take him where they will, and of course he is not disappointed.

A lozenge opens before him.

He is looking down into what he takes to be Harwood's office, in San Francisco, at Harwood seated behind a vast dark desk littered with architectural models and stacks of printout. Harwood holding a telephone handset.

"It's an absurd launch," Hardwood says, "but then it's an insane service. It works because it's redundant, understand? It's too dumb not to work."

Laney does not hear the reply, and takes this to mean that Libia and Paco have hacked a security camera in the ceiling of Harwood's office. The audio is ambient sound, not a phone tap.

Now Harwood rolls his eyes.

"People are fascinated by the pointlessness of it. That's what they like about it. Yes, it's crazy, but it's *fun*. You want to send your nephew in Houston a toy, and you're in Paris, you buy it, take it to a Lucky Dragon, and have it re-created, from the molecules up, in a Lucky Dragon in Houston . . . What? What happens to the toy you bought in Paris? You keep it. Give it away. Eviscerate it with your teeth, you tedious, literal-minded bitch. What? No, I didn't. No, I'm sorry, Noriko, that must be an artifact of your translation program. How could you imagine I'd say that?" Harwood stares straight ahead, stunned with boredom. "Of course I want to give the interview. This is an exclusive, after all. And you were my first choice." Harwood smiles as he calms the journalist, but the smile vanishes the instant she begins to ask her next question.

"People are frightened of nanotechnology, Noriko. We know that. Even in Tokyo, seventeen-point-eight of your markedly technofetishistic populace refuses to this day to set foot in a nanotech structure. Here on the coast, I'd point to the example of Malibu, where there's been a very serious biotech accident, but one which is entirely unrelated to nanotech. It's actually being cleaned up with a combination of three smart algae, but everyone's convinced that the beaches are alive with invisible nanobots waiting to crawl up your disagreeable pussy. What? 'Unfriendly cat'? No. There's something wrong with your software, Noriko. And I do hope you're only writing this down, because we negotiated the interview on a nonrecorded basis. If any of this ever turns up in any recorded form at all, you'll not be getting another. What?

Good. I'm glad you do." Harwood yawned, silently. "One last question, then."

Harwood listens, pursing his lips.

"Because Lucky Dragon is about convenience. Lucky Dragon is about being able to purchase those things you need, really need, when you need them, twenty-four seven. But Lucky Dragon is also about fun. And people are going to have fun with these units. We've done enough research that we know that we don't really know what, exactly, Lucky Dragon customers will find to do with this technology, but that's all part of the fun." Harwood explored the recesses of his left nostril with the nail of his little finger but seemed to find nothing of interest. "Blow me," he said. " 'Inflate'? I don't think so, Noriko, but I'd have that software checked, if I were you. 'Bye." Harwood puts the phone down, stares straight ahead. It rings. He picks it up, listens. Frowns.

"Why doesn't that surprise me? Why doesn't that surprise me in the least?" He looks, to Laney, as if he's on the verge of laughing. "Well. You can try. You can certainly try. Please do. But if you can't, then he'll kill *you*. All of you. Every last one. But I shouldn't worry about that, should I? Because I've got your brochure here, and it's really a wonderful brochure, printed in Geneva, spare no expense in presentation, full-color, heavy stock, and it assures me that I've hired the best, the very best. And I really do believe that you are the best. We did shop comparatively. But I also know that he is what he is. And God help you."

Harwood hangs up.

Laney feels Libia and Paco tugging at him, urging him elsewhere.

He wishes that he could stay here, with Harwood. He wishes that he and Harwood could sit opposite one another across that desk, and share their experience of the nodal apprehension. He would love, for instance, to hear Harwood's interpretation of the node of 1911. He would like to be able to discuss the Lucky Dragon nanofacsimile launch with Harwood. He imagines himself sending a replica of the garage kit Laney—though "sending" isn't the word, here—but where, and to whom?

Libia and Paco tug him to the place where that thing is growing, and he sees that it has changed. He wonders if Harwood has looked at it recently: the shape of a new world, if any world can be said to be new. And he wonders if he will ever have the chance to speak with Harwood. He doubts it.

Some things never happen, he reminds himself.

But this one always does, says the still small voice of mortality.

Blow me, Laney tells it.

55. BRIGHT YOUNG THINGS

\LATER Fontaine would remember that when he woke, hearing the sound at his door, he thought not of his Smith & Wesson but of the Russian chain gun, plastered away beneath gypsum filler and gauze some four months earlier, out of sight and out of mind.

And he would wonder about why that was, that he'd thought of that particular ugly thing as he became conscious of something clicking urgently against the glass of the shop door.

"Fontaine!" A sort of stage whisper.

"Spare me," Fontaine said, sitting up. He rubbed his eyes and squinted at the luminous hands of a soulless black Japanese quartz alarm, a gift of sorts from Clarisse, who liked to point out that Fontaine was frequently late, particularly with the child support, in spite of own-ing such a great many old watches.

He'd gotten about an hour's sleep.

"Fontaine!" Female, yes, but not Clarisse.

Fontaine put his trousers on, slid his feet into his cold clammy shoes, and picked up the Kit Gun. "I'll say it was self-defense," he said, glancing back to see his mystery boy sprawled whale-like on the camp-ing pad, snoring again but softly.

And out through the shop, where he made out the face of Skinner's girl, though somewhat the worse for wear, really major serious shiner going there, and looking anxious indeed.

"It's me! Chevette!" Rapping on his glass with something metal.

"Don't break my damn window, girl." Fontaine had the gun out of sight, by his side, as was his habit when answering the door, and he saw now that she was not alone; two white men behind her, the one a big, brown-haired, cop-looking person, and the other reminding him of a professor of music known decades before, in Cleveland. This latter causing Fontaine a prickling of neck hair, though he couldn't have said exactly why. A very *still* man, this one.

"Chevette," he said, "I'm *sleeping*."

"We need help."

"'We' who, exactly?"

"It's Rydell," she said. "You remember?"

And Fontaine did, though vaguely: the man she'd gone down to Los Angeles with. "And?"

She started to speak, looked lost, glanced back over her shoulder.

"A friend," the one called Rydell said, none too convincingly. He was hugging a cheap-looking drawstring bag, which seemed to contain a large thermos, or perhaps one of those portable rice cookers. (Fontaine hoped that this wasn't going to be one of those pathetic episodes in which he was mistaken for a pawnbroker.)

"Let us in, Fontaine. We're in trouble."

You probably *are* trouble, by now, Fontaine decided, after whatever it was got you the black eye. He started unlocking the door, noticing how she kept glancing either way, as if expecting unwanted company. The cop-looking one, this Rydell, was doing the same. But the professor, Fontaine noted, was watching him, watching Fontaine, and it made him glad to have the Kit Gun down by his leg.

"Lock it," Chevette said, as she entered, followed by Rydell and the professor.

"I'm not sure I want to," Fontaine said. "I might want to show it to you."

"Show it to me?"

"You in the plural. Show you the door. Follow me? I was sleeping."

"Fontaine, there are men on the bridge with guns."

"There are indeed," said Fontaine, as he rubbed his thumb over the knurls atop the little double-action's hammer.

The professor closed the door.

"Hey," Fontaine said, in protest.

"Is there another exit?" the professor asked, studying the locks.

"No," Fontaine said.

The man glanced back through the shop, to the rear wall, beyond the upturned toes of Fontaine's guest. "And on the other side of this wall, there is only a sheer drop?"

"That's right," Fontaine said, somehow resenting the ease with which the man had extracted this information.

"And above? There are people living above?" The man looked up at the shop's painted plywood ceiling.

"I don't know," Fontaine admitted. "If there are, they're quiet. Never heard 'em."

This Rydell, he seemed to be having trouble walking. He made it over to the glass-topped counter and put his duffel down on it.

"You don't want to break my display there, hear?"

Rydell turned, hand pressed into his side. "Got any adhesive tape? The wide kind?"

Fontaine did have a first-aid kit, but it never had anything anyone ever needed. He had a couple of crumbling wound compresses circa about 1978 in there, and an elaborate industrial eye bandage with instructions in what looked like Finnish. "I got gaffer tape," Fontaine said.

"What's that?"

"Duct tape. You know: silver? Stick to skin okay. You want that?"

Rydell shrugged painfully out of his black nylon jacket and started fumbling one-handed with the buttons of his wrinkled blue shirt. The girl started helping him, and when she'd gotten the shirt off Fontaine saw the yellow-gray mottling of a fresh bruise, up his side. A bad one.

"You in an accident?" He'd tucked the Smith & Wesson into the side pocket of his trousers, not a safe carry ordinarily but a convenient one under the circumstances. The worn checkered walnut of the butt stuck out just enough to get a handy purchase, should he need it. He got a roll of tape out of the top drawer of an old steel filing cabinet. It made that sound when he pulled out a foot or so of it. "You want me to put this on you? I taped fighters in Chicago. In the ring, you know?"

"Please," said Rydell, wincing as he raised the arm on the bruised side.

Fontaine tore the length of tape off and studied Rydell's rib cage. "Tape's mystical, you know that?" He snapped the tape taut between his two hands, the darker, adhesive-coated side toward Rydell.

"How's that?" Rydell asked.

"'Cause it's got a dark side," Fontaine said, demonstrating, "a light side," showing the dull silver backing, "and it holds the universe together." Rydell started to yell when the strip was applied, but caught it. "Breathe," Fontaine said. "You ever deliver a baby?"

"No," Rydell managed.

"Well," said Fontaine, readying the next strip, this one longer, "you want to breathe the way they tell women to breathe when the contractions come. Here: now breathe out . . ."

It went pretty fast then, and when Fontaine was done, he saw that Rydell was able to use both hands to button his shirt.

"Good evening," he heard the professor say and, turning with the roll of tape in his hand, saw that the boy was awake and sitting up, brown eyes wide and empty, staring at the man in the gray-green overcoat. "You look well. Is this your home?"

Something moved, behind the boy's eyes; saw, retreated again.

"You two know each other?" Fontaine asked.

"We met last night," the man said, "here, on the bridge."

"Wait a minute," Fontaine said. "He get a watch off you?"

The man turned and regarded Fontaine evenly, saying nothing.

Fontaine felt a wave of guilt. "It's okay," he said. "Just keeping it for him."

"I see."

"That's quite a watch," Fontaine said. "Where'd you get it?"

"Singapore."

Fontaine looked from the smooth gaunt wolfish face of the man who very probably wasn't a music professor to the blank and unlined face of the boy, beneath its new haircut.

"I see that you have a pistol in your pocket," the man said.

"I'm just glad to see you," Fontaine said, but nobody got it.

"What is its caliber?"

"Twenty-two long rifle."

"Barrel length?"

"Four inches."

"Accurate?"

"It's not a target pistol," Fontaine said, "but for four inches of barrel, it's not too bad." This was making him very nervous, and he very badly wanted the gun in his hand, but he thought that if he touched it now, something would happen. Something would.

"Give it to me," the man said.

"Forget it," Fontaine said.

"An undetermined number of armed men are searching for Mr. Rydell tonight. They would like to capture him alive, in order to question him, but they would certainly kill him to prevent his escape. They will kill anyone they find with him. That would simply be a matter of housekeeping for them. Do you understand?"

"Who are they?"

" 'Bright young things,' " the man said.

"What?"

"They are mercenaries, in the pay of someone who regards Mr. Rydell as being in the employ of a competitor, an enemy."

Fontaine looked at him. "Why you want my gun?"

"In order to kill as many of them as I can."

"I don't know you from Adam," Fontaine said.

"No," said the man, "you don't."

"This is crazy . . ." Fontaine looked at Chevette. "You know this guy?"

"No," Chevette said.

"You. Rydell. You know this guy?"

Rydell looked from Fontaine to the man, back to Fontaine. "No," Rydell said, "I don't. But you know what?"

"What?"

"I'd give him the gun."

"Why?"

"I don't know," Rydell said, and something seemed to catch in his voice. "I just know I would."

"This is crazy," Fontaine said, repeating himself, hearing the pitch of his own voice rising. "Come on, Chevette! Why'd you come in here? You bring these people—"

" 'Cause Rydell couldn't walk fast enough," she said. "I'm sorry, Fontaine. We just needed help."

"Fuck," said Fontaine, pulling the Smith & Wesson from his pocket, its blue steel warm with his body heat. He opened the cylinder and ejected the five cartridges into his palm. Fragile bits of brass less than the thickness of a pencil, each one tipped with its copper-coated, precisely swaged and hollowed segment of lead alloy. "This is it, right? All the ammunition I've got." He passed the man the revolver, barrel pointed at the ceiling and cylinder open, then the cartridges.

"Thank you," the man said. "May I load it now?"

"Gentlemen," said Fontaine, feeling a frustration that he didn't understand, "you may start your fucking engines."

"I suggest," the man said, inserting the five cartridges, one after another, "that you lock the door after me and conceal yourselves, out of the sight lines for the door and window. If they determine you are here, they will try to kill you." He closed the cylinder, sighted down the barrel at a blank patch of wall.

"Pulls a little to the left," Fontaine said, "single-action. You want to compensate in the sight picture."

"Thank you," the man said and was gone, out the door, closing it behind him.

Fontaine looked at Rydell, whose eyes were bright with what Fontaine suddenly saw were brimming tears.

56. KOMBINAT PIECE

"MR. Fontaine," Rydell said, "you wouldn't have another gun around here, would you?"

The three of them were sitting on the floor, in a row, their backs to the wall nearest Oakland, in the back room of Fontaine's little shop. Between Rydell and Fontaine, the duffel with the projector. The kid who'd been sleeping on the floor there was sitting up in Fontaine's narrow bunk, back against the opposite wall, clicking through something on a notebook; had one of those big-ass old military displays on, made him look like a robot or something, except you could see the bottom half of his face, see he kept his mouth open while he was doing it. The lights were all off, so you could see the steady pulse of pixel-glow leaking from the helmet, from whatever it was he kept pulling up.

"I don't deal in firearms," the black man said. "Vintage watches, knives by name makers, die-cast military . . ."

Rydell thought he'd had enough to do with knives already. "I just don't like sitting here, waiting."

"Nobody does," Chevette said beside him. She was pressing a wet cloth against her eye.

Actually what bothered Rydell most about sitting was that he wasn't sure how easy it would be to get back up. His side, with the duct tape on it now, didn't hurt too badly, but he knew he'd stiffen up. He was about to ask Fontaine about the knives when Fontaine said: "Well . . ."

"Well what?" Rydell asked.

"Well," Fontaine said, "it isn't actually part of my stock, you know?"

"What isn't?"

"I've got this lawyer, he's African Union, you know? Forced out by politics."

"Yeah?"

"Yeah," Fontaine said, "but you know how it is, people come out of a situation like that, all that ethnic cleansing and shit . . ."

"Yeah?"

"Well, they like to feel they got protection, something happens."
Rydell was definitely interested.

"Trouble is," Fontaine said, "they got this overkill mentality, over there. And my lawyer, Martial, he's like that. Actually he's trying not to be, understand? Got him a therapist and everything, trying to learn to walk around without a gun and not feel he's liable to get his ass blown away by tribal enemies, right? Like this is America, here, you know?"

"I think you're still liable to get your ass blown away by tribal enemies, in America, Mr. Fontaine."

"That's true," Fontaine said, shifting his buttocks, "but Martial's got that post-traumatic thing, right?"

"You help him with these problems? You help him by holding a weapon for him, Mr. Fontaine? Something he wouldn't want to keep on his own premises?"

Fontaine looked at Rydell. Pursed his lips. Nodded.

"Where is it?"

"It's in the wall, behind us."

Rydell looked at the wall between them. "This is plywood?"

"Most of it," Fontaine said, swinging around. "See here? This part's a patch, gypsum wall filler. We built a box in here, put it in, plastered it over, painted."

"Guess someone could find it with a metal detector," Rydell said, remembering being trained how to search for stashes like this.

"I don't think it has a lot of metal in it," Fontaine said, "anyway not in the delivery system."

"Can we see it?"

"Well," said Fontaine, "once we get it out, I'm stuck with it."

"No," Rydell said, "I am."

Fontaine produced a little bone-handled pocketknife. Opened it, started digging gingerly at the wall.

"We could get a bigger knife," Rydell suggested.

"Hush," Fontaine said. As Rydell watched, the point of the knife exposed a dark ring, the size you'd wear on your finger. Fontaine pried it up and out of the hardened plaster, but it seemed to be fastened to something. "You pull this, okay?"

Rydell slid his middle finger through the ring, tugged it a little. Felt solid.

"Go on," Fontaine said. "Hard."

Plaster cracked, tore loose, as the fine steel wire attached to the ring pulled out around the patch, cutting through it like dry cheese. A rough, inch-thick rectangle coming away in Rydell's hand. Fontaine was pulling something out of the rectangular recess that had been exposed. Something wrapped in what looked like an old green shirt.

Rydell watched as Fontaine gingerly unwrapped the green cloth, exposing a squat heavy object that looked like a cross between the square waxed-paper milk cartons of Rydell's childhood and an industrial power drill. It was a uniform, dusty olive-green in color, and if it was in fact a firearm, it was the clumsiest-looking firearm Rydell had yet seen. Fontaine held it with what would've been the top of the milk carton pointed up at an angle, toward the ceiling. There was an awkward-looking pistol grip at the opposite end, and a sort of grooved, broom-handle affair about six inches in front of that.

"What is it?" Rydell asked.

"Chain gun," Fontaine said. "Disposable. Can't reload it. Caseless: this long square thing's the cartridges and the barrel in one. No moving parts to it: ignition's electrical. Two buttons here, where the trigger would be, you just point it, press 'em both the same time. It'll do that four times. Four charges."

"Why do they call it a chain gun?"

"What this is, Martial says, it's more like a directional grenade, you understand? Or sort of like a portable fragmentation mine. Main thing he told me is you don't use it in any kind of confined space, and you only use it when there's nobody in front of you you don't mind seeing get really fucked up."

"So what's the chain part?"

Fontaine reached over and tapped the fat square barrel lightly, once, with his forefinger. "In here. Thing's packed with four hundred two-foot lengths of super-fine steel chain, sharp as razor wire."

Rydell hefted the thing by its two grips, keeping his fingers away from those buttons. "And that—"

"Makes hamburger," Fontaine said.

"I heard a shot," Chevette said, lowering her wet cloth.

"I didn't hear anything," Rydell said.

"I did," Chevette said. "Just one."

"You wouldn't hear much, that little .22," Fontaine said.

"I don't think I can stand this," Chevette said.

Now Rydell thought he heard something. Just a pop. Short, sharp. But just the one. "You know," he said, "I think I'm going to take a look."

Chevette leaned in close, her one eye purple-black and swollen almost completely shut, the other gray and fierce, scared and angry all at once. "It's not a television show, Rydell. You know that? You know the difference? It's not an episode of anything. It's your life. And mine. And his," pointing to Fontaine, "and his," pointing at the kid across the room. "So why don't you just sit there?"

Rydell felt his ears start to burn, and knew that he was blushing. "I can't just sit here and wait—"

"I know," she said. "I could've told you that."

Rydell handed the chain gun back to Fontaine and got to his feet, stiff but not as bad as he'd expected. Fontaine passed him up the gun. "I need keys to unlock the front?"

"No," Fontaine said. "I didn't do the dead bolts."

Rydell stepped around the shallow section of partition that screened them from the window in the door and the display window.

Someone in the shadows opposite cut loose with something automatic, something silenced so efficiently that there was only the machine-like burr of a slide working, and the stitching sounds of bullets. Both Fontaine's windows vanished instantly, and the glass front of the counter as well.

Rydell found himself on the floor, unable to recall getting there. The gun across the street stopped abruptly, having chewed its way through a full clip.

He saw himself down in the basement range at the academy in Knoxville, ejecting a half-moon clip from the stock of a bull-pup assault rifle, pulling out another, and slapping it into place. How long it took. The number of movements, exactly, that it took.

There was a high, thin, very regular sound in his ears, and he realized that it was Chevette, crying.

And then he was up, shoving the milk-carton nose of Fontaine's lawyer's Kombinat gun over the bottom of the square hole in the door where the glass had been.

One of the two buttons, he thought, must be a safety.

And the other filled the air outside with flame, recoil close to breaking his wrist, but nobody, really nobody, was going to be reloading anything.

Not over there.

57. EYE

AND when they are cleaning up, the next day, Fontaine will find a cardboard canister of coarse Mexican salt, holed, on the floor, in the back room.

And he will pick it up, the weight wrong somehow, and pour the salt out into the palm of his hand, through the entrance hole in the side, until out falls the fully blossomed exotic hollow-point slug that had penetrated the plywood partition, then straight into this round box of salt, upon its shelf, spending its energy there as heat. But it will be cold then, like a fanged bronze kernel of popcorn, evidence of the ways in which its makers intended it to rend flesh.

And he will place it on a shelf beside a lead soldier, another survivor of the war.

But now he can only move as in a dream, and what comes to him most strongly in this silence, this tangible silence through which he feels he moves as if through glycerine, is the memory of his father, against his mother's ardent fear, taking him briefly out, into the yard behind a house in tidewater Virginia, to experience the eye of a hurricane.

And in that eye, after the storm's initial rage, nothing moves. No bird sings. Each twig of each leafless tree defined in utter stillness, yet perhaps on the very edge of perception there can be some awareness of the encircling system. Something subsonic; felt, not heard. Which will return. That is certain.

And it is like that now as he rises and moves, seeing the boy's hands frozen, trembling, above the notebook's keys, head still helmed with that old military set. And thinks for a moment the boy is injured, but he sees no blood. Frightened only.

All guns exist to be fired, he knows, and Rydell has proven this by firing Martial's, that ugly thing, Russian, vicious booty out of the Kombinat states by way of Africa, out of wars of an abiding stupidity, ethnic struggles smoldering on for centuries, like airless fires down in the heart of a dry bog. A gun for those unable to be trained to shoot.

Reek of its propellant charge in the back of his throat, harsh and chemical. A frosting of shattered glass beneath his shoes.

Rydell stands at the door, the ungainly chain gun dangling from his hand like a duelist's pistol, and now Fontaine stands beside him, looking out into the bridge's narrow covered thoroughfare as into a tableau or diorama, and opposite, there, all glitters with red. Though surely in the shadows one would find more solid, substantial evidence, bone and gristle perhaps, and that automatic gun.

"Chevette," Rydell says, not to her but as if reminding himself of her, and turns, crunching back through the glass, to find her.

Fontaine blinks at the queer red glitter over there, the smear that someone has so instantly become, and catches something moving, high up in the periphery of vision. Silver.

Flinches, but it's a balloon, a cushiony oblate of inflated Mylar, with, it looks like, little caged articulated props and a camera. This draws even with the front of his shop, halts itself with reversing props, then neatly rotates, so that the lens looks down at him.

Fontaine looks up at the thing, wondering if it has the wherewithal to hurt him, but it simply hangs there, staring, so he turns and surveys the damage to his shop. All this glass is the most evident breakage, bullet holes themselves being not so visible. Two of them, though, have punched through a round enamel Coke sign that previously would've rated an eighty percent, but now is scarcely "very good."

It is the counter that draws him, though he dreads what he will find: his watches there beneath shards of glass, like fish in a shattered aquarium. Plucking up a Gruen "Curvex" by its faux-alligator band, he finds it not to be ticking. He sighs. Clarisse has been after him for some time now, to buy a fire safe in which to place his more valuable stock at night. Had he done so, the watches would still be ticking. But this one is, the Doxa chrono with the gently corroded dial, a favorite of his which customers pass over repeatedly. He holds it to his ear, hearing the sound of a mechanism assembled years before his own birth.

But here he sees something which will make Clarisse more unhappy still: her Another One babies lie tumbled in a heap, like some tabloid photo from a nameless atrocity, their ruptured heads and torsos oozing silicone (which is either a liquid that behaves like a solid or vice versa, Fontaine can never remember which). Not one of them has survived intact, and as he bends for a closer look he hears one repeating, endlessly, an apparent single syllable, though whether in Japanese or English he cannot tell. This briefly and deeply fascinates him, and he remembers a similar feeling, as a child, when he viewed through a police line the rubble of a movie theater in Harlem; the fire that had gutted the place had stopped short of the candy counter, but everything in that counter had melted, had poured out and solidified into a frozen stream of refined sugar, smelling much better, even over the sourness of damp ashes, than this silicone does.

And hears Chevette and Rydell talking, arguing it seems, and he wishes they would stop.

He is in the eye, and he wishes simply to know it.

58. SMALL BLUE ABSENCE

THE close-up, hand-held, shows Laney this small blue absence just in from the corner of the dead man's eye, like some radical experiment with mascara. A bullet hole, entry wound, of the most modest circumference.

"You'll note the lack of powder burns," says the one holding the camera. "Done from a distance."

"Why are you showing me this?" Harwood asks, once more the disembodied voice.

The frame pulls back, revealing the dead man, blonde in a black leather jacket, reclining against some vertical surface fogged with whorls of aerosol enamel. He looks surprised and slightly cross-eyed. Pulls back farther, revealing a second body, this one in a black armored vest, facedown on worn pavement.

"One shot each. We weren't expecting him to have a gun."

"The bridge isn't noted for adherence to firearms regulations, you know."

The man with the camera reverses it, his face appearing from an odd angle, shot from the level of his waist. "I just wanted to tell you 'I told you so.' "

"If he leaves the vicinity alive, your firm will find itself in more than contractual difficulties. You signed on to take care of *anything*, remember?"

"And you agreed to listen to our suggestions."

"I listened."

"I came out here with a five-man team. Now two of them are dead, I've lost radio contact with the other three, and I've just heard what sounded like an explosion. This environment is inherently unstable: an armed anthill. These people have short fuses and no coordinating authority. We could have a riot on our hands, and once that happens, we'll have no hope at all of taking out your man, or of capturing Rydell."

"Recapturing Rydell, you should say."

"I have one last suggestion." The man raises the camera slightly, so that his face fills the screen, his black scarf blanking the bottom third of the image.

"Yes?"

"Burn it."

"Burn what?"

"The bridge. It's a tinderbox."

"But wouldn't that take time to arrange?"

"It's already arranged." The man shows the camera a small rectangle, a remote, that he holds in his other hand. "We've been planting radio-activated incendiaries. We like to cover the options."

"But aren't our two men likely to escape in the ensuing confusion? You tell me you're afraid of a riot, after all . . ."

"Nobody's getting off this thing. It'll burn from both ends, from Bryant Street to Treasure Island."

"And how are you getting off yourself?"

"That's been taken care of."

Harwood falls silent. "Well," he says, at last, "I suppose you should."

The man thumbs a button on the remote.

Laney flicks away from the lozenge, panicking, looking for Libia and Paco.

The projector is still here, still on the bridge. He still doesn't know what part it plays, but Rei Toei must have a presence in the impending cusp.

And he sees that Harwood knows that, or feels it, and is moving, has moved, to prevent it.

He pulls the eyephones from his head and gropes through the colors of darkness, searching for a phone.

59. THE BIRDS ARE ON FIRE

CHEVETTE kept looking at the holes in the plywood partition between the front and the back of Fontaine's shop, noticing how the bullets had taken out long splinters of plywood on each side of the actual holes; extending lines, in her mind, through those holes and on back through the room.

She couldn't figure how she'd missed catching one. What it had done, though, was give her the shakes; she kept shivering, and if she didn't keep her teeth together they'd actually chatter, and she had hiccups as well, and both these things embarrassed her, so she was taking it out on Rydell and feeling sorry for him at the same time, because he looked like he was in his own kind of shock.

She was vaguely aware of people coming up to the door of the shop and looking in, but then they'd see Rydell with the chain gun and go away, fast. These were bridge people, and this was how they reacted to something like this. If they hadn't seen an armed man there, they'd have asked if everyone was okay and could they help, but otherwise it was about taking care, as Skinner had liked to put it, of your own side of the street.

She felt like she'd split in half, the part of her that was ragging Rydell for getting her into this kind of crazy shit again, and the part of her that just kept looking around and wanting to say: look at this, and how come I'm alive?

But something started beeping, in Rydell's pocket, and he took out a pair of sunglasses, black frames with cheap chrome trim, and put them on. "Hello?" he said. "Laney?"

She looked over as the one who'd talked Fontaine out of his gun opened the door, glass grating beneath it, and stepped in, looking exactly the same as when he'd left, except he had a long fresh scratch down the side of his face, where blood was beading. He took the skinny little revolver out of his pocket and handed it to Fontaine, holding it sideways with his hand around the thing you put the bullets in. "Thank you," he said.

Fontaine brought the gun up beneath his nose, sniffed at it, and raised his eyebrows questioningly.

"I've adjusted the windage," the man said, whatever that meant. "No need now to compensate for the pull."

Fontaine clicked the bullet-thing out and ejected five empty brass cartridges into his palm. He looked at these, looked up at the man. "How'd you do?"

"Three," the man said.

"I think they've got one," Rydell was saying. "There's this kid here on it. You want me to try the cable? You talk to her, Laney? She told me you used to talk with her a lot . . ." Rydell looked idiotic, standing there talking to the air in front of him, one hand up to hold the ear bead in, the other letting that crazy-ass gun hang down. She wished he'd put it somewhere, back in the wall, anywhere.

"Come *on*, Rydell," she said, but then she saw that God's Little Toy was up against the ceiling in the front of the shop, watching her. "Tessa? Tessa, you hear me?"

There was a burst of squawky static, like a parrot trying to talk.

"Tessa?"

"I'm sorry," the man in the long coat said. "The men who attacked you communicate on a number of specific channels. I am employing a jammer at those frequencies." He looked at God's Little Toy. "This device's control frequencies are unaffected, but voice communication is currently impossible."

"Tessa!" Chevette waved frantically at the balloon, but it only continued to stare at her with its primary lens.

"What do you mean, burn it?" she heard Rydell say. "Now? Right now?" Rydell pulled the sunglasses off. "They're setting fire to the bridge."

"Fire?" She remembered Skinner's caution around that, how careful people were with cooking gas, matches; how a lit butt thrown down could earn you a broken nose.

But Rydell had the sunglasses on again. "I thought you said to get out? What do you mean, leave her? Damn, Laney, why don't you make some sense for once? Why—Laney? Hey?" She saw Rydell's tension as he took off the glasses. "Listen up. Everybody. We're leaving now. Laney says they're setting fire to the bridge." Rydell bent, wincing, and opened his bag, hauling this silver thing out. She saw it glint in the light from outside. Like a big steel thermos. He pulled out some coiled cables and tossed her a length. "Find a socket." He had another cable in his hand now and was standing over the boy with the old military eye-phone rig. "Hey. Kid? We have to borrow the notebook. Hear me?" The helmet came up and seemed to regard him blindly but sentiently, like the head of a giant termite. Rydell reached down and took the note-book, unhooking the lead to the helmet. Chevette saw the boy's mouth close. The notebook's screen showed the black dial of a clock. No, Chevette saw, it was an old-fashioned watch, enlarged to the size of a baby's face.

Rydell studied the two ends of the cable he held, then tried a socket on the back of the notebook. Another. It fit. Chevette had found an out-let, set crookedly into one of Fontaine's walls. She plugged the cable in and passed Rydell the other end. He was plugging the cable from the notebook into the silver canister. He plugged the power cable in beside it. She thought she heard it start to hum.

And a girl was there, pale and slim, glowing with her own light, naked for an instant between them. And then she wore Skinner's jacket, faded horsehide. Black jeans, a black sweatshirt, lug-soled runners. Everything cleaner and somehow sharper than what Chevette wore, but otherwise identical.

"I am Rei Toei," the girl said. "Berry Rydell, you must leave the bridge now. It is burning."

"You said that you knew my name," the man in the overcoat said, the long thin scratch on his face black in the light she gave off. "In the tavern."

"Konrad," the glowing girl said, "with a 'K.' "

The man's eyebrows rose, above his round gold glasses. "And how do you know that?"

"I know many things, Konrad," the girl said, and as she said it, became, for a few seconds, another girl, blonde, the irises of her blue eyes ringed with black.

The man seemed carved from some incredibly dense wood, heavy and inert, and Chevette thought for some reason of dust motes floating in sunlight in an old museum, something she'd seen once but could not remember where or when. "Lise," he said, a name as if dredged from some deep place of pain. "Yesterday. I dreamed I saw her, in Market Street."

"Many things are possible, Konrad."

Rydell had taken a pink fanny pack from his duffel and was strapping it around his waist. It had a grinning cartoon dragon screened on the front. As Chevette watched, he zipped it open and unfolded a pink bib, which he fastened around his neck. The bib said LUCKY DRAGON SECURITY in square black letters. "What's that?" Chevette asked him.

"Bulletproof," Rydell said. He turned to the glowing girl. "Laney says I should leave the projector here. But that means we leave you—"

"That is what I want," she said. "We are about to find our way to the heart of Harwood's plan. And change it. And change everything." She smiled at Rydell then, and Chevette felt a twist of jealousy.

Chevette became aware of noise approaching, the revving and whining of overtaxed electric engines. There was a crashing of metal on wood, and Fontaine sprang away from the door. A three-wheeled ATV slammed to a halt outside, Tessa straddling its seat behind a moon-faced boy who wore a black meshbacked cap, backward, and a black T-shirt. Tessa was wearing her input glasses and had a control glove on either hand. She pulled off the glasses and pushed hair back from her eyes. "Come on, Chevette."

"Get off the damn trike, honey," the round-faced boy said. "Don't have a lot of turning radius in here."

Tessa hopped off the bike and stepped into the shop, looking up at God's Little Toy. "I'm not getting any audio," she said.

The boy punched the engines mounted in the ATV's rear hubs, reversing one. The trike lurched around and back, then forward, turning so that he faced back toward San Francisco. "Come *on,* honey," he said.

"I'm picking up flames on two cameras," Tessa said. "This sucker's on fire."

"Time to go," Rydell said, putting his hand on Chevette's shoulder. "Mr. Fontaine, you get you a ride here with Chevette."

"I'm not going anywhere, son," Fontaine said.

"It's on fire, Mr. Fontaine."

"It's where I live."

"Come on, Rydell," Chevette said, grabbing him by his waistband.

Tessa had climbed back on, behind her meshbacked driver, and was putting her input glasses on. "Jesus," Tessa said, "I don't believe the angles I'm getting . . ."

Chevette tugged Rydell through the door and climbed on the back of the ATV, sort of sidesaddle, leaving room for Rydell. "Wait," Rydell said, "we can't just leave them here . . ."

" 'We'? Hey, boy, I'm not carrying you—" But the moon-faced boy saw the chain gun then and stopped.

"Go on," said Fontaine, who stood now with his arm around the shoulder of the boy who'd worn the helmet, whose eyes regarded Rydell with a sort of animal calm. "Go on. We'll be okay here."

"I'm sorry," Rydell said. "I'm sorry about your shop . . ."

"Your ass be sorry, you don't get out of here."

Chevette heard a woman start screaming, toward San Francisco. She yanked his waistband, hard. The fly button popped off his khakis. He climbed on the back of the ATV opposite her, hanging on with one hand, the chain gun in the other.

The last she saw of the glowing girl, she was saying something to the man she'd called Konrad. Then Tessa's meshback popped it and they took off toward the city. "Good-bye, Fontaine," Chevette shouted, but she doubted he ever heard her.

Remembering the night of a hill fire above the sharehouse, the birds in the brush all around the house waking in the dark, sensing it. All their voices.

And now through the plywood patchwork overhead she hears it too: the drumming of conflagration.

60. RATS KNOW

FONTAINE knows the bridge is burning when he looks out and sees a rat streak past, toward Oakland. Then another, and a third. Rats know, and the bridge rats are held to be most knowing of all, through having been hunted so thoroughly by the bridge's host of feral cats and by innumerable equally feral children armed with slingshots cobbled from aircraft aluminum and surgical tubing. These bridge slingshots are lethal not only to rats, their users favoring balls of dense damp clay, a trick held over from the Middle Ages and not to be underestimated.

Fontaine watches the rats flash past and sighs. He has a fire ax here, somewhere, salvage from a tug sank in China Basin in 2003, and an extinguisher too, but he can't imagine these will be of much use, although chopping a hole in the back wall and falling into the bay is a possibility. He wonders if there actually are sharks there, as the bridge children like to believe. He knows for a fact there are mutant fish, warped, it is said, by oxides leaching off the piers of the cable towers.

But Fontaine has survived many disasters, both municipal and marital, and there is in him that which believes, against all odds or hope, that all will simply, somehow, be well. Or that in any case there is usually not much to be done about certain things, or in any case not by him.

So, now, rather than digging through the closet, where he remembers, possibly, putting that fire ax, he picks up his push broom and begins tidying the front of the shop, sweeping as much of the glass as possible into a single drift beside the door. Glass, he reflects, sweeping, is one of those substances that takes up relatively little space until you break it. But it is also, he recalls being told, if considered over truly cosmic stretches of time, a liquid. All the glass in every pane in every window, everywhere, is in the infinitely slow process of melting, sagging, sliding down, except it would be unlikely that any one pane survive the millennia required to be reduced to a solid puddle.

While outside the rats are being joined by fleeing humans, as diverse a company of them as only the bridge can offer. He hopes that

Clarisse and the children are safe; he's tried to phone, but no answer, and there seemed little point in leaving a message, under the circumstances.

He looks back and sees Rydell's hologram girlfriend kneeling beside the bunk, talking to the boy. Beside the boy sits the professor who had borrowed the Kit Gun, and they strike Fontaine just then as a family group, unlikely perhaps but not without warmth. Fontaine has lived long enough with technological change that he really doesn't question the why or what of the girl: she is like a game program that comes out and sits in your room, he thinks, and some people would like that just fine.

Now he comes to an obstacle in his sweeping: the butchered Another One dolls in their puddle of consensual silicone. At least none of them are talking now. It looks terrible, cruel, when he pushes the broom up against them, amid shards of glass, so he leans the broom against the counter, fishes one from the glass by its limp arms. He carries the faux Japanese baby outside and stretches it on its back in front of the shop. The others follow, and he is laying out the last when a fat woman, fleeing heavily toward Treasure Island, clutching what appears to be a bedsheet-load of wet laundry, notices what he is doing and starts to scream. And screams all the way out of sight, and can still be heard as he turns back into the shop, thinking of Tourmaline, his first wife.

There is smoke in the air now, and maybe it is time to find that ax.

61. FUTUREMATIC

THAT shape that Laney sees when he looks at Harwood, at the idoru, at Rydell, and these others, has never before been a place for him, an inhabitable space. Now, driven by a new urgency (and augmented by virtually the entire population of the Walled City, working in a mode of simultaneity that very nearly approximates unison) he succeeds in actually being there, within a space defined by the emerging factors of the nodal point. It is a place where metaphor collapses, a descriptive black hole. He is no more able to describe it to himself, experiencing it, than he would be able to describe it to another.

Yet what it most nearly resembles, that place where history turns, is the Hole he has posited at the core of his being: an emptiness, as devoid of darkness as it is of light.

And Harwood, he knows immediately, though without knowing how he knows, is there.

—Harwood?

—Colin Laney. An evening for miracles. The unexpected.

—You told them to burn the bridge.

—Is there no privacy?

—You're trying to stop her, aren't you?

—I suppose I am, yes, although without knowing exactly what it is I'm attempting to stop her from doing. She's an emergent system. She doesn't know herself.

—Do you? Do you know what you want?

—I want the advent of a degree of functional nanotechnology in a world that will remain recognizably descended from the one I woke in this morning. I want my world transfigured, yet I want my place in that world to be equivalent to the one I now occupy. I want to have my cake and eat it too. I want a free lunch. And I've found the way to have it, it seems. Though you have too. And what, we have to ask ourselves, went wrong there?

—You chose it. You chose to take 5-SB. In the orphanage, we volunteered to be test subjects, but we had no idea what we were taking.

—And I chose to take 5-SB based on results collected from you, Laney. You and a girl named Jennifer Mo, who subsequently became the homicidally obsessed stalker of an astonishingly boring actor named Kevin Burke. She committed suicide while holding him hostage at a meditation retreat in Idaho.

Laney knows the story of Jennifer Mo; it has haunted him since he first read it, several years ago, as a classified government document.

—Why hasn't it gotten you, Harwood? Why hasn't it kicked in?

—Perhaps because I'm too perfectly self-obsessed to become interested in anyone else. It's been all gravy for me. The next best thing to knowing the future. Better, actually: just that little degree of free will and we're so much more happy, aren't we? And looking backward is very nearly as much fun as looking forward, though our digital soup does thin out rather rapidly, that way down the time-line. Amazing, though: that business around Curie's husband . . . Changed *everything,* and who knows? I ask you, Laney, who knows?

—We do.

—Yes, we do.

—It's changing again. Tonight.

—This morning, rather. Pacific Standard. Very early. But, yes, it is. And I'm here to see that it changes in the directions I prefer it to, and not in others.

—We're going to try to stop you.

—Of course. That's the shape of things tonight, isn't it? I couldn't expect otherwise.

Now Laney feels two things simultaneously: a coldness, physical and inescapable, rising beneath his heart, and the secret, ranked presence of the individual inhabitants of the Walled City, arrayed behind him like clay soldiers set to march forever across the floor of an emperor's tomb. Yet these will move, should Laney require them, and he senses as well the presence of Rei Toei, and he knows that the configuration is not yet complete.

—She's here, Laney. She's in the flow. You've done that, you and your friends. But it won't help now, because I'm going where you won't find me. For the duration. Till the deal is done. Your friends aren't the only ones who learned how to secede.

And with the cold rising around his heart, Laney knows that this is true, that Harwood is going now, inverting himself into an informational wormhole of the sort the Walled City exists within—

And reaches down (it seems like down, though in this place there is neither direction nor ordination), a legion reaching with him, to find—

62. LOS PROJECTOS

SILENCIO is remembering the rusting cans of fire, in the yards of los projectos, how the men stand and spit and warm their hands. Playboy and Raton he had met around such a fire, and now there is the smell of the cans in this room, and he is frightened, and even this kind one, who makes her own light and speaks to him in the language of his mother (but kind) will not keep the fear away, and he wishes only to return to the watches, to their faces and conditions and values, this universe that has discovered him, this mode of being, without which there is only the fear.

Crouching here on the black man's bed, the kind one glowing beside him, he feels the fear come very big, and the black man in the closet, throwing things out, and Silencio wants only the watches.

At the edge of his mind wait men with dog's teeth and wings, their faces blacker than the face of the black man with the watches. Their faces are the black of the drug men rub into their gums.

"Bring the projector closer," she tells the man, this one who stilled Playboy and Raton, and Silencio sees that for the time she speaks she is another, her hair smooth gold, the bones of her face another's bones. "Bring the notebook. Be very careful of the cable." And the man shifts the silver thing Silencio fears (now Silencio fears everything) closer, and brings the watch finder to the bed, still on its wire.

"Connect the eyephones. Quickly!" The man puts the wire from the hat into the watch finder and hands Silencio the hat. Inside, Silencio sees, are the pictures that fit against the eyes, and they are pictures of the watch on the screen of the finder, and Silencio feels relief, the fear moving away, back to the edge of things where the dog-toothed men are. He puts the hat over his eyes.

And is in another place, nothing up or down, but something spreading forever, wider than the yards of los projectos or any other space he has ever seen.

But the one who shines is there, and beside her another, less clear.

"This is Mister Laney," she says, in the language of Silencio's mother. "You must help him. He needs to find a watch. This watch." And she holds in her palm the watch Silencio had seen on the screen. It is a LeCoultre "Futurematic," a back-winder, black dial, with wind reserve. Silencio knows its serial number, its bid history, its number in today's auction. "Someone is taking it away, and you must follow it."

Silencio looks from the beautiful face of the Futurematic to the face of the woman.

"You must find it for him—"

And the watch is gone, and she is gone, and the other with her, leaving Silencio in that place that is only wide, and without color or shape, and Silencio thinks he might cry now.

But very far away, he feels it, the watch. He knows it, and it is there still, but only this distance, these gray fields of light. Gone again.

No. There is the system: the system of all the watches. Similarities. Differences. The words. A coding. Nothing is lost within the system, and the Futurematic rises inside as though it were lifting through clear water. It is within his grasp.

And gone again. Blankness.

No. He wants it. He enters the system again.

He crosses the gray fields, seeing only the Futurematic. Where it has gone . . .

63. FUNICULAR

RYDELL had had a certain amount of riot-control training in Knoxville and knew something, in theory anyway, about fires and natural disasters, but nothing had prepared him for the weirdness of clinging one-handed to the back of an ATV, while Elmore, the meshback Chevette's friend had somehow talked into driving, gunned it back toward Bryant Street through the bridge's upper level. Rydell had never seen a vehicle here before, aside from bicycles, and he suspected that under normal circumstances they wouldn't have been allowed to get very far.

But these were not normal circumstances, nor was this in any way a normal place. People were boiling out of the upper parts of the squatter's community like ants out of a broken nest, and what struck Rydell about it now was the quiet with which they were doing it. These were not, in some sense, civilians, but hardened survivors used to living on their own in a community of similar people. There were a few people screaming, and probably running the wrong way, or in circles, but from the moving vantage point of the bucking, pitching ATV, it was hard to tell. Rydell's impression was mainly of determination; they'd decided that the place was burning, and they'd decided they were getting out. Most people seemed to be carrying something. A few were carrying small children, more carried household goods, and Rydell had seen at least three carrying guns.

Elmore's style of getting through the crowd was straightforward; he'd gun it toward whoever was in his way, sounding an irritating little horn that Rydell suspected nobody was hearing anyway, and trust that people would get out of his way. Which they managed to do, some just barely, until the ATV's right back wheel clipped a stack of yellow plastic vegetable crates and brought that down on top of a couple of heavily tattooed characters in lederhosen and paint-splattered construction boots. Elmore had to hit the brakes then, and Rydell saw Chevette flip off; he couldn't grab her, because he had the chain gun in the hand nearest her and no way to put it down.

Blocked by the pile of empty yellow crates, Elmore whipped it into reverse, pulled back about four feet, and popped it, plowing into the crates and the men in lederhosen, who promptly went lateral, swarming over the pile of crates and grabbing Elmore, who didn't look to Rydell like fighting material. "Get off him," Chevette's girlfriend shouted, trying to keep from being pulled from the saddle with the driver. Rydell slung the chain gun up and put it in the face of one of the tattooed men. The guy blinked at it, looked Rydell in the eye, and started to go after him, but some cop reflex caused Rydell to bellow "LAPD! Get on the ground!"—which made absolutely no sense under the circumstances, but seemed to work. "This is a gun," he added, and remembered Fontaine's advice that the chain gun was anything but directional.

"You people are crazy," snapped one of the tattooed men, barechested and elaborately inked, scrambling over the yellow crates, the light catching on a round steel stud in his lower lip. His partner was right behind him.

Rydell jumped down and found Chevette struggling to extricate herself from what seemed to be a pile of squashed eggplant. As he was turning back to the ATV, he saw a woman with a crew cut and serious biceps tackle Elmore, who went over into the crates.

"Where's Tessa?"

"I don't know," said Rydell, taking Chevette's hand. "Come on." As soon as they were away from the ATV, which in any case wasn't going anywhere, Rydell began to get the idea that something was seriously wrong here. While most of the way from Fontaine's, people had been running toward Bryant, now he saw they were running back, and now you could see the fear. "I think it's burning there, by the ramp," Rydell said. You could see the smoke now, and Rydell noticed how quickly it was thickening.

"Where's Tessa?"

"Lost her."

A young girl came running, screaming, with her shirt on fire, from the direction of the city. Rydell tripped her, handed Chevette the chain gun, and bent to roll the girl over, smothering the flames. The girl just kept screaming, and then she was up and running, though Rydell saw that her shirt had been extinguished. He took the chain gun back from

Chevette. "We don't want to try that way," he said. He didn't want to think about what might be happening there, if the crowd was trying to force its way through flame. "Come on, let's try this." He tugged her through the doorway of a café, deserted, cups of coffee on the tables, music playing calmly, steam rising from a pot of soup on a hotplate behind the counter. He pulled her behind the counter, and into the tight little kitchen, but found that while there were windows, they'd been barred against thieves with elaborately welded grids of rebar. "Shit," he said, leaning to peer through the salt-crusted pane, trying to estimate the drop here, in case they could find a way.

Now it was her turn to grab him, pull him out, but she pulled him out into the path of a fresh batch of panicked bridge people, fleeing whatever was happening toward Bryant. They both went down, and Rydell saw the chain gun drop through a hole sawn in the deck to admit a bundle of sewage-tubing. He braced for an explosion when the thing hit bottom, but none came.

"Look," Chevette said, getting to her feet, pointing, "we're at the foot of Skinner's tower. Let's try to get up there."

"There's no way off that," Rydell protested, his side killing him as he got up.

"There's nothing to burn, either," she said, "once you're past the 'ponics operation."

"Smoke'll get us."

"You don't know that," she said, "but down here it'll get us for sure." She looked at him. "I'm sorry, Rydell."

"Why?"

"Because I was trying to make all this your fault."

"I sure hope it's not," he said.

"How've you been?"

Rydell grinned, in spite of everything, that she'd ask him this now. "I missed you," he said.

She hesitated. "Me too." Then she grabbed his hand again, heading for the plastic around the foot of the cable tower. It looked as though people had cut their way out. Chevette stepped through a five-foot slit. Rydell ducked to follow her. Into warm jungle air and the smell of

chemical fertilizer. But there was smoke here too, swirling under the
glare of the grow lights. Chevette started coughing. Shadows of people
fleeing raced across the translucent plastic. Chevette went to a ladder
and started climbing. Rydell groaned.

"What?" She stopped and looked down.

"Nothing," he said, starting up after her, biting his lip each time he
had to raise his arms.

In the distance he could hear sirens, a weird, rising cacophony that
blended together, wove in and out, like a concert performed by robot
wolves. He wondered if it had sounded like that in the minutes after the
Little Big One.

He really didn't know how much of this ladder he could manage. It
was metal, stuck to the wall with that super-goop they used here, and
he looked up and saw Chevette's plastic-cleated feet vanish through a
triangular opening.

And he realized he was smiling, because that really was her and
those really were her feet, and she'd said she'd missed him. The rest of
the way didn't seem so hard, but when he got up and through, sitting on
the edge for a breather, he saw that she'd started climbing up the slanted
girder, hanging on to either side of the blunt-toothed track that the little car, which he could make out up at the top, ran on.

"Jesus," Rydell said, imagining himself having to follow her.

"Stay there," she said, over her shoulder, "I'll try to bring it down for
you." Rydell watched her climb, worried about grease, but she just kept
going, and soon she was there, climbing into the car, which from here
looked like one of the waste bins out behind Lucky Dragon, but smaller.

Rydell heard an electric engine whine. With a creak, the little car,
Chevette in it, started down.

He got to his feet and the smoke caught in his lungs, his side stab-
bing him each time he coughed.

"Somebody's been up here," she said, when she reached the bottom. "The grease shows it. I was up here earlier, looking around, and
there was dust on it."

"Somebody probably lives here," Rydell said, looking around at the
dark flimsy walls that sheathed the tower twelve feet up from the plat-

form he stood on. He climbed into the car, and she pushed a button. The car groaned, creaked, and started up the girder.

The first thing Rydell wasn't prepared for, as they cleared the screening wall, was the extent of the fire. It looked as though the end by Bryant was completely aflame, huge clouds of black smoke billowing up into the night sky. Through that he could see the lights of emergency vehicles, dozens of them, it looked like, and above the creaking of the cog wheel he could still hear the concert of wailing sirens. "Jesus," he said. He looked in the other direction, toward Treasure, and that was burning too, though it didn't seem as intense, but maybe that was just distance.

"You got a flashlight?" Chevette asked.

He unzipped his Lucky Dragon fanny pack and fished out a little Lucky Dragon disposable he'd helped himself to back in LA. Chevette twisted it on and started up the ladder that led to the hole in the floor of the little tower-top cube she'd lived in when Rydell had met her. Just a square opening there, and he saw her shine the light into it. "It's open," she said, not too loud, and that made Rydell start up after her.

When he climbed through, into the single room, she was shining the light around. There was nothing here, just some garbage. There was a round hole in one wall, where Rydell remembered there had been an old stained-glass window before.

He saw the expression on her face in the glow from the flashlight. "It's really not here anymore," she said, as if she didn't quite believe herself. "I guess I thought it would still be here."

"Nobody lives here now," Rydell said, not sure why he had.

"Roof hatch is open too," Chevette said, shining the light up.

Rydell went to the old ladder bolted to the wall and started up, feeling damp splintery wood against his palms. He was starting to get the idea this might have been a very bad idea, climbing up here, because if the whole bridge were going to burn, they probably weren't going to make it. He knew the smoke was as dangerous as the fire, and he wasn't sure she understood that.

And the second thing he wasn't prepared for, as he stuck his head up through the hatch, was the barrel of a gun thrust into his ear.

His buddy with the scarf.

64. TAG

AND as Harwood recedes, and the rest of it as well, amid this spreading cold, and Laney feels, as at a very great distance, his legs spasming within their tangle of sleeping bags and candy wrappers, Rei Toci is there, and passes him this sigil, clockface, round seal, the twelve hours of day, twelve of night, black lacquer and golden numerals, and he places it on the space that Harwood occupied.

And sees it drawn in, drawn infinitely away, into that place where Harwood is going; drawn by the mechanism of inversion itself, and then it is gone.

And Laney is going too, though not with Harwood.

"Gotcha," Laney says, to the dark in his fetid box, down amid the subsonic sighing of commuter trains and the constant clatter of passing feet.

And finds himself in Florida sunlight, upon the broad concrete steps leading up to the bland entrance to a federal orphanage.

A girl named Jennifer is there, his age exactly, in a blue denim skirt and a white T-shirt, her black bangs straight and glossy, and she is walking, heel to toe, heel to toe, arms outstretched for balance, as if along a tightrope, down the very edge of the topmost step.

Balancing so seriously.

As if, were she to fall, she might fall forever.

And Laney smiles, to see her, remembering the orphanage's smells: jelly sandwiches, disinfectant, modeling clay, clean sheets . . .

And the cold is everywhere, now, somewhere, but he is home at last.

65. OPEN AIR

FONTAINE, wielding the ax now, reflects that he has lived quite a long time and yet this experience is new: to lift the heavy head above his own and bring it down against the shop's rear wall, the plywood booming. He's a little surprised at how it simply bounces off, but with his next swing he's reversed the head, so that the sharp, four-inch spike, rather than the blade, contacts the wall, and this digs most satisfyingly in, and on a third blow penetrates, and he redoubles his efforts.

"Need us some air," he says, as much to himself as to the two seated on his bunk, the gray-haired man and the boy with his head down, lost in the helmet again. To look at these two, you'd think there was no problem, that the bridge wasn't burning.

Where'd that hologram girl go?

Still, this chopping is getting somewhere, though his arms are already aching. Hole there the size of a saucer, and getting bigger.

No idea what he'll do when he's got it big enough, but he likes to keep busy.

And this is the way it always is, for Fontaine, when he knows that things are bad, very bad indeed, and very likely over. He likes to keep busy.

66. BULKLIFT

CHEVETTE climbs through the hatch in the roof of Skinner's room to find Rydell kneeling there in his Lucky Dragon security bib, but the critical factor here is the man from the bar, the one who shot Carson, who's got a gun pressed into Rydell's ear and is watching her, and smiling.

He's not much older than she is, she thinks, with his black buzz cut and his black leather coat, his scarf wrapped just so, casual but you know he takes time with it, and she wonders how it is people get this way, that they'll stick a gun in someone's ear and you know they'll use it. And why does it seem that Rydell finds people like that, or do they find him?

And behind him she can see a plume of water arcing higher than the bridge, and knows that that must be from a fireboat, because she's seen one used when a pier on the Embarcadero burned.

God, it's strange up here, now, with the night sky all smoke, the flames, lights of the city swimming and dimmed as the smoke rolls. Little glowing red worms are falling, winking out, all around her, and the smell of burning. She knows she doesn't want Rydell hurt but she isn't afraid. She just isn't now, she doesn't know why.

Something on the roof beside her and she sees that it's a glider up on its own little frame, staked to the asphalt-coated wooden roof with bright sharp spikes.

And other things piled beside it: black nylon bags, what she takes to be bedding. Like someone's ready to camp here, if they need to, and she understands the buzz-cut boy wanted to be covered, if he had to stay, to hide. And it comes to her that probably he's responsible for the burning of the bridge, and how many dead already, and he's just smiling there, like he's glad to see her, his gun in Rydell's ear.

Rydell looks sad. So sad now.

"You killed Carson," she heard herself say.

"Who?"

"Carson. In the bar."

"He was doing a pretty good job putting your lights out."

"He was an asshole," she said, "but you didn't have to kill him."

"Fortunately," he said, "it isn't about who's an asshole. If it were, our work would never be done."

"Can you fly this?" Pointing at the glider.

"Absolutely. I'm going to take this gun out of your ear now," he said to Rydell. He did. She saw Rydell's eyes move; he was looking at her. The boy with the buzz cut hit him in the head with the gun. Rydell toppled over. Lay there like a big broken doll. One of the glowing red worms fell on his stupid pink bib, burned a black mark. "I'm going to leave you here," he said. He pointed the gun at one of Rydell's legs. "Kneecap," he said.

"Don't," she said.

He smiled. "Lay down over there. By the edge. On your stomach." The gun never moved.

She did as she was told.

"Put your hands behind your head."

She did.

"Stay that way."

She could watch him out of the corner of her eye, moving toward the glider. The black fabric of its simple triangular wing was catching a breeze now, thrumming with it.

She saw him duck under the kite-like wing and come up within the carbon-fiber framework extending beneath it. There was a control-bar there; she'd seen people fly these on Real One.

He still had the gun in his hand but it wasn't pointed at Rydell.

She could smell the asphalt caked on the roof. She remembered spreading it with Skinner on a hot windless day, how they heated the hard bucket of tar with a propane-ring.

The world Skinner had helped build was burning now, and she and Rydell might burn now with it, but the boy with the buzz cut was ready to fly.

"Can you make it to the Embarcadero with that?"

"Easily," he said. She saw him shove the gun into the pocket of his black coat and grip the bar with both hands, lifting the glider. The breeze caught at it. He walked into the wind, reminding her somehow of a crow walking, one of those big ravens she'd grown up seeing, in Oregon. He was within a few feet of the edge now, the side of Skinner's room that faced China Creek. "You and your friend here caused me a great deal of trouble," he said, "but you're either going to burn to death or asphyxiate now, so I suppose we're even." He looked out, stepped forward.

And Chevette, without having made any conscious decision at all, found herself on her feet, moving, drawing the knife Skinner had left for her. And ripping it down, as he stepped from the edge, through the black fabric, a three-foor slash, from near the center and straight out through the trailing edge.

He never made a sound, then, as he went fluttering down, faster, spinning like a leaf, until he struck something and was gone.

She realized that she was standing at the very edge, her toes out over empty air, and she took a step back. She looked at the knife in her hand, at the pattern locked there by the beaten links of motorcycle chain. Then she tossed it over, turned, and went to kneel beside Rydell. His head was bleeding, from somewhere above the hairline. His eyes were open, but he seemed to be having trouble focusing.

"Where is he?" Rydell asked.

"Don't move your head," she said. "He's gone."

The breeze shifted, bringing them smoke so thick the city vanished. They both started to cough.

"What's that sound?" Rydell managed, trying to crane his neck around.

She thought it must be the sound of the fire, but it resolved into a steady drumming, and she looked out to see, just level with her, it seemed, the block-wide impossible brow of a greasy-gray bulklifter, OMAHA TRANSFER painted across it in letters thirty feet high. "Jesus Christ," she said, as the thing was upon them, its smooth, impossibly vast girth so close she might touch it.

And then it jettisoned its cargo, close to two million gallons of pure glacial water destined for the towns south of Los Angeles, and she could only cling to Rydell and keep her mouth shut against the weight and the surge of it, and then she was somewhere else, and drifting, and it seemed so long, so long since she'd slept.

67. SILVER CASTLE

IN the gray fields Silencio finds a silver castle, an empty place and somehow new. There are no people here, only empty hallways, and he wonders why someone would build such a thing.

The system of the watches leads him deeper, deep within, each hallway like the last, and he is tired of this, but the Futurematic is there still, and he will find it.

And when he does, at last, in a very small room at the root of the silver world, he discovers that he is not alone.

There is a man, and the man looks at Silencio and does not believe Silencio is there, and the man's eyes fill with a fear that Silencio feels must mirror his own fear, and Silencio wishes to tell the man he has only come here to find the watch, because it is part of the system of hands and faces and applied numerals, and Silencio means no harm, but the man's eyes are like the eyes of those to whom Raton shows the knife, and someone coughs behind Silencio. And turning, Silencio sees a terrible man, whose head is a cloud of blood, and whose mouth is open in a red-toothed scream, and the mouth does not move when this man says, "Hello, Harwood."

But now somehow he is with the bright one again.

She tells Silencio to remove the hat, and he does, inside it the pictures of the castle, fading, and the room is filled with smoke, and out through the broken door is more smoke, and the black man, the gray branches of his hair hanging limp now, has cut a hole in the wall with his ax. Not a big hole but he puts his head and shoulders out through it now, and Silencio sees him jerk as if something strikes him. And he draws back inside, eyes wide, and wet, wet, running with water, and water is falling past the hole and the gray hair sticks in its tangles to the man's face, and now more water comes down, into the tunnel like a street, beyond the door, so much water.

And the man in the long coat is standing there, hands in his pockets, and he watches the water come down, and Silencio sees the lines in this man's cheeks deepen. Then this man nods to Silencio, and to the black man, and goes out through the broken door.

Silencio wonders if it is wet in the silver castle too.

68. THE ABSOLUTE AT LARGE

BOOMZILLA in the Lucky Dragon, back in there for what he knows is the first time they work this Lucky Dragon Nanofax, not a game but how you copy solid shit from one store to another. Not sure he gets that but there's free candy and big drinks for the kids, of which he is opting to be very definitely one, right now, but it's gone sideways with the bridge burning, and those motherfucker bulklifters come drop a fuckload of water on it, got about a hundred fire trucks and everything here, police, tactical squads, helicopters up in the air, so Lucky Dragon can't do the special thing for the first time they use the Lucky Dragon Nanofax, manager's going lateral, walks the aisle talking to himself. But the store's doing business big-time, home office won't let him close, and Boomzilla's started eating candy bars free because the securities are watching the smoke still rise off the wet black garbage, all that's left this end, so you can see the real bridge there, the old part, black too, hanging out in the air like something's bones.

And finally the manager comes and reads from a notebook, ladies and gentlemen, this momentous occasion, jaw jaw, and now they are placing the first object in the unit in our Singapore branch (Boomzilla sees on TV, out on the pylon, it's a gold statue of the Lucky Dragon himself, smiling) and it will now be reproduced, at a molecular level, in every branch of our chain throughout the world.

Checker and two securities, they clap. Boomzilla sucks on the ice in the bottom of his big drink. Waits.

Lucky Dragon Nanofax has a hatch on the front Boomzilla could fit through, he wanted to, and he wonders would that make more Boomzillas other places and could he trust those motherfuckers? If he could, he'd have a tight posse but he doesn't trust anybody, why should they?

Light over the hatch turns green, and the hatch slides up and out crawls, unfolds sort of, this butt-naked girl, black hair, maybe Chinese, Japanese, something, she's long and thin, not much titties on her the way Boomzilla likes but she's smiling, and everybody, the manager, checker, securities, they jaw-hang, eyes popped: girl straightening up, still smiling, and walks fast to the front of the store, past the security counter, and Boomzilla sees her reach up and open the door, just right on out, and it'll take more than a naked Japanese girl get anybody's attention out there, in the middle of this disaster shit.

But the crazy thing is, and he really doesn't get this, standing looking out through the doors at the video pylon, so that he has to go outside and fire up his last Russian Marlboro to think about it, after, is that when he sees her walk past the screens there, he sees her on every last screen, walking out of every Lucky Dragon in the world, wearing that same smile.

Boomzilla still thinking about this when his Marlboro's done, but thinks it's time for a Lucky Dragon Muff-Lette microwave, he thinks of that as his businessman's breakfast, and he's got the money but when he gets back in they got no Muff-Lette, fucking firemen ate them all.

"Fuck that," he tells them. "Why don't you fax me one from fucking Paris?"

So security throws his ass out.

69. EVERYTHING TAKES FOREVER

RYDELL wakes to pain, in what has been the nearest approximation of heaven he's known, this miraculously dry, brand-new, extremely high-tech sleeping bag, curled beside Chevette, his ribs on fire, and lies there listening to the helicopters swarming like dragonflies, wondering if there's maybe something bad for you in the stuff that holds duct tape on.

They'd found this bag, hermetically sealed in its stuff sack, in the wake of the flood, snagged on one of the spikes that held the scarf's hang-glider rack to the roof. And no more welcome find there ever was, to get out of wet clothes and into dry warmth, the bag's bottom water- and probably bullet-proof as well, a very expensive piece of ordnance. And lie there watching two more bulklifters come, huge, slow-moving cargo drones diverted from their courses, it will turn out, according to a plan arrived at several years before by a team of NoCal contingency planners, to dump still more water, extinguishing the fire at the Treasure end and damping down the central span as well. And each one, depleted and limp, starting to rise immediately, free of ballast, in a sort of awkward elephantine ballet.

And held each other, up there, into the dawn, sea breeze carrying away the smell of burning.

Now Rydell lies awake, looking at Chevette's bare shoulder, and thinking nothing much at all although breakfast does begin to come to mind after a while, though he can wait.

"Chevette?" Voice from some tinny little speaker. He looks up to see a silver Mylar balloon straining on a tether, camera eye peering at them.

Chevette stirs. "Tessa?"

"Are you okay?"

"Yeah," she says, voice sleepy. "What about you?"

"It's a feature," the voice from the balloon says. "Action. Big budget. I've got footage you won't believe."

"What do you mean it's a feature?"

"I'm signed. They flew up this morning. What are you doing up there?"

"Trying to sleep," Chevette says and rolls over, pulling the bag over her head.

Rydell lies watching the balloon bob on its tether, until finally he sees it withdrawn.

He sits up and rubs his face. Rolls out of the bag, and stands, stiffly, a naked man with a big patch of silver duct tape across his ribs, wondering how many TV screens he's making, right now. He hobbles over to the hatch and climbs down into darkness, where he relieves himself against a wall.

"Rydell?"

Rydell starts, getting his ankle wet.

It's Creedmore, sitting on the floor, knees up, wet-look head between his hands. "Rydell," Creedmore says, "you got anything to drink?"

"What are you doing up here, Buell?"

"Got in that greenhouse thing down there. Thought there'd be water there. Then I figured my ass would boil like a fucking catfish, so I climbed up here. Sons of bitches."

"Who?"

"I'm fucked," Creedmore says, ignoring the question. "Randy's canceled my contract and the goddamn bridge has burned down. Some debut, huh? Jesus."

"You could write a song about it, I guess."

Creedmore looks up at him with utter despair. He swallows. When he speaks, there is no trace of accent: "Are you really from Tennessee?"

"Sure," Rydell says.

"I wish to fuck I was," Creedmore says, his voice small, but loud in the hollow of this empty wooden box, sunlight falling through the square hole above, lighting a section of two-by-fours laid long way up to make a solid floor.

"Where you from, Buell?" Rydell asks.

"Son of a bitch," Creedmore says, the accent returning, "New Jersey."

And then he starts to cry.

Rydell climbs back up and stands on the ladder with just his head out, looking toward San Francisco. Whatever Laney was on about, that end of the world thing, everything changing, it looked like it hadn't happened.

Rydell looks over at the black mound of sleeping bag and reads it as containing that which he most desires, desires to cherish, and the wind shifts, catching his hair, and when he climbs the rest of the way, back up into sunlight, he still hears Creedmore weeping in the room below.

70. COURTESY CALL

IN the cab to Transamerica he closes his eyes, seeing the watch he gave the boy, where time arcs in one direction only across a black face, interior time gone rudderless now, unmoored by a stranger's reconstruction of Lise's face. The hands of the watch trace a radium orbit, moments back-to-back. He senses some spiral of unleashed possibility in the morning, though not for him.

The bridge, behind him now, perhaps forever, is a medium of transport become a destination: salt air, scavenged neon, the sliding cries of gulls. He has glimpsed the edges of a life there that he feels is somehow ancient and eternal. Apparent disorder arranged in some deeper, some unthinkable fashion.

Perhaps he has been too long in the pay and the company of those who order the wider world. Those whose mills grind increasingly fine, toward some unimaginable omega-point of pure information, some prodigy perpetually on the brink of arrival. Which he senses somehow will never now arrive, or not in the form his career's employers have imagined.

In the atrium he describes the purpose of his visit as a courtesy call. He is disarmed, searched, cuffed, and taken, per Harwood's orders, by his seven captors, into an elevator.

And as its doors close he feels grateful that they are excited, and inexperienced, and have cuffed his hands in front, rather than behind his back.

By the time the express elevator reaches Harwood's office floor, he will be alone.

He touches the buckle of his belt, and thinks of the simple yet perfectly efficient tool concealed between the layers of fine Italian calf.

And exists in the moment.

71. YAMAZAKI

YAMAZAKI, grim and nervous, descends into the early morning rush hour accompanied by a very large Australian, shaven-headed, with one mutilated ear.

"You knew he was here?" the large man asks.

"He desired secrecy," Yamazaki says. "I am sorry."

Yamazaki leads the Australian to the cardboard city and points out Laney's carton and its entrance.

"This one?"

Yamazaki nods.

The Australian produces a knife that telescopes silently at the touch of a button, both its edges serrated. He slits the top from Laney's carton, lifting it like the lid of a box of cereal, and Yamazaki sees the stickers of Cody Harwood that he glimpsed once before.

The Australian, much taller than Yamazaki, stands staring down into the carton. Yamazaki himself is not yet ready to look.

"What was he running from?" the Australian asks.

Yamazaki looks up at the man's small, fiercely intelligent eyes, set in a face of the most abiding brutality. "Toward," Yamazaki says. "He ran toward something."

A train arrives in the depths of the system, shunting a wall of stale warm air toward the surface streets and a new day.

72. FONTAINE

FONTAINE comes back from the blackened ribs toward Bryant with a jug of water and two Red Cross sandwiches. It's strange out there, very much the post-disaster scenario and not to his liking. Media vehicles outnumber emergency, though there are plenty of those. The body count is remarkably low, he gathers, and puts this down to the nature of bridge folk, their seriousness in survival and a certain belief in unorganized cooperation. Probably, he thinks, he'll never know what any of this was about, in terms of causality, though he's sure he's been witness to something.

He hopes Chevette and her boyfriend have made it through, but somehow he assumes they have, and the professor has gone, off about whatever business a man of his sort pursues, and that is business best not known about. Martial will have to be told that his chain gun is gone, but that's just as well. (Opposite his shop, someone has sprayed a great deal of that stuff called Kil'Z, lest the smear that the chain gun left there prove seropositive in any troublesome way.)

As he comes up to the shop he hears the sound of someone sweeping broken glass, and sees that it is the boy, flatfooted in his big white shoes, and sees that the kid's done quite a good job of it, really, down to rearranging things on the surviving shelves. That silver piece of hardware, like an oversized cocktail shaker, enjoys pride of place, up behind the glassless frame of Fontaine's counter, between lead soldiers and a pair of trench-art vases beaten from the Kaiser's cannon casings.

"Where'd she go?" Fontaine asks, looking up at this.

The boy stops sweeping, sighs, leans on his broom, says nothing.

"Gone, huh?"

The boy nods.

"Sandwiches," Fontaine says, handing one to the boy. "We're going to be roughing it out here, for a while." He looks up at the silver canister again. Somehow he knows it no longer contains her, whoever, whatever she was. It has become as much history, no more, no less than the crude yet wistfully dainty vases pounded out of shell casings in some French trench. That is the mystery of things.

"Fonten."

He turns, sees Clarisse there with a shopping bag in her arms. "Clarisse."

Something troubled there, in her sea-green eyes, some worry or concern. "You okay, then?"

"Yes," he says.

"I thought you dead, Fonten."

"No."

"I brought you food."

"The kids okay?"

"Scared," she says. "They with Tourmaline."

"I'd be scared too, then."

A smile twitches the corner of her mouth. She comes forward, shifting the bag aside. Her lips brush his.

"Thank you," he says, taking the heavy bag, from which fine smells arise. "Thank you, Clarisse."

He sees tears in the corners of her eyes. "Bastard," she says, "where's my dolls?"

"I'm sorry," he says, as gravely as he can manage, "but they were victims of the terrible fire."

And then they both start to laugh.

73. SILENCIO

"WHERE did you find it?"

"Treasure Island," the boy lies, passing the watch, a solid brown wafer of corrosion, across the glass countertop.

Silencio peers through his loupe at the damp biscuit of metal. He scores the rust with a diamond scribe. "Stainless," he admits, knowing the boy will know that that is good, though not good as gold. Worth the price of a meal.

"I want to see you fix it," the boy says.

Silencio twists the loupe from his eye and looks at the boy, as if noticing him for the first time.

"I want to see you fix it." The boy points down, indicating the watches arrayed beneath the glass.

"The bed," Silencio says. "You were here with Sandro, when we restored that Vacheron."

Silencio brings the restoration bed from the rear of the shop, a square cushion, ten inches on a side. He places it on the counter and the boy bends close, to see the velvety green surface made up of millions of manipulators.

Silencio places the watch on the bed. They watch as it rises smoothly on edge, as if of its own accord, and then seems to sink, impossibly, as if through the shallow bed and the glass beneath. Vanishing like a coin set into soft mud . . .

Silencio looks at the watch on his wrist, a military Jaeger-LeCoultre, RAAF. "Nine minutes," he said. "There's coffee."

"I want to watch," the boy says.

"Nothing to see."

Within the bed, the rusted disk of the watch is being read and disassembled. Molecules are moving. In nine minutes it will rise again, bright and perfect as the day it first left its factory in Switzerland.

"I want to watch," the boy says.

Silencio understands. He goes to get the coffee.

THANKS

TO everyone who waited for this one with even greater patience than usual, particularly my publishers, as personally and wonderfully represented by Susan Allison and Tony Lacey.

To Deb and Graeme and Claire, with love, for putting up with far more than the ordinary basement-dwelling.

To Julia Witwer, for being this text's first reader and more.

The following are special friends of this book: Gordon Begg, Judith Beale, Jessica Eastman, Karl Taro Greenfeld, Mark Halyk, Richard Kadrey, Kevin Kelly, Lueza Jean Lamb, Roger Trilling, Jack Womack. Thank you all.

And to the post-cyberpunk contingent in Mexico City, who, though I declined their thoughtful offer of the definitive alternative tour, encouraged me, with their warm enthusiasm, through the writing of a crucial chapter in the Hotel Camino Real.

MAY 10, 1999

VANCOUVER, B.C.